Not What He Ordered

Taylor County Brides

Book One

Laurean Brooks

Scrivenings
PRESS
Quench your thirst for story.
www.ScriveningsPress.com

©2021 Laurean Brooks

Published by Scrivenings Press LLC
15 Lucky Lane
Morrilton, Arkansas 72110
https://ScriveningsPress.com

Printed in the United States of America

Paperback ISBN 978-1-64917-121-4

eBook ISBN 978-1-64917-122-1

Cover by Diane Turpin, www.dianeturpindesigns.com

(Note: This book was previously published in 2017 by Mantle Rock Publishing LLC and was re-published as is when Scrivenings Press acquired the publishing rights in 2021.)

Acknowledgments

Thank you to Pam Watts Harris and Kathy Cretsinger for a wonderful job editing.

Thank you to Diane Turpin for creating a gorgeous cover.

I would also like to acknowledge Dennis Miller, the gracious gentleman who recently retired from the main library in Abilene, Texas, for sending pages of research with interesting historical tidbits to add to and enrich this story.

Chapter One

Denton, Texas
Late September 1883

Carrie Franklin had never set foot inside a saloon. Mama would tan her hide if she could see her now. But Mama was in heaven, and her brother Blake was inside that sinful place drinking and gambling away his wages. The same as he'd done the past two months. She'd warned her brother she would leave if he didn't quit his riotous living. And this was the last straw.

Carrie's sharp-toed shoes clopped against the boardwalk, making hollow sounds. Coal-oil street lights dispelled the darkness, lighting her steps. Just as she'd thought, Blake's horse was tethered to the hitching post alongside two others. How should she approach him?

Standing before the swinging doors, she wiped sweaty palms down the sides of her skirt. Loud piano music and raucous laughter reached her ears and disturbed the otherwise peaceful town. Carrie hiked her shoulders and drew in what might be her last breath of fresh air for a while.

As she stepped up to the bat-wing doors, they flew open, and a giant of a man staggered out. Jim Counce, known as "Big Jim," stumbled across the boardwalk. Carrie clapped a hand to her chest and jumped out of the way, or he would have flattened her.

The drunk man grabbed at air and fell against a support post. Gripping it, he raised his head. His glassy gaze raked her. Carrie's heart pounded when he graced her with a toothless grin.

As she whirled to push through the swinging doors to a safer place inside, his large hand clamped onto her arm, and he dragged her toward him. Rank body odor and stale whiskey stung her nostrils. She coughed and held her breath.

"Well, well, purty lady, did you come by to see Big Jim?"

Carrie struggled to free herself. "Take your grimy hands off me or I'll—"

He threw his head back and laughed. "You'll what . . . scream? Nobody'd hear ya."

She inhaled, then regretted it. Her stomach lurched. If she didn't get free soon, she'd throw up. Recalling her mother's saying, "You will catch more flies with honey than with vinegar," Carrie brandished Big Jim with a smile. Patting his arm with her free hand, she spoke in a sugary voice. "Nice to see you, Mr. Counce, but I have to go. My brother's in there. I need to see him."

Big Jim sneered. "That Franklin kid's your brother?" His grip on her arm tightened. "Well, don't you worry your purty little head none. Your brother's havin' hisself a good time, buyin' drinks for ever'body. They're settin' up for a game of poker."

How dare he! Blake had promised Carrie he wouldn't squander his wages this month.

Big Jim bent and brushed his mouth against her ear. His hot breath burned her earlobe. "If you'll just relax, Big Jim will show you an even better time."

She wrenched to free herself, but his vise-like grip tightened. "Please . . . you're hurting me."

"Sorry, but quit tryin' to git away." He graced her with a gap-toothed grin. "I like a little spunk in my women. Makes for a good time." He shook his head. "Don't like prudes. Cain't have no fun with one. A purty gal like you wouldn't be a prude, would ya?"

Carrie eyed him without replying.

He fingered a lock of her hair near her shoulder. "Treat Big Jim nice and he'll show you a night you'll not likely forget."

He traced her jawline with a callused thumb. "Smooth as silk. Mmm, Mmm, you sure are a cute little thang. How about a little kiss for a lonely ol' man?"

Carrie flung his hand from her face. She'd never been mauled by a man and didn't aim for this to be the first time.

The drunk dragged her closer. "You're a feisty one. What's wrong, Big Jim ain't good enough fer ya?" His hairy arm snaked around her waist, yanking her closer, and smashing her face into his sweaty shirt. If she quit struggling, would he loosen his grip? Carrie paused to catch her breath and to plan her next move.

Big Jim mistook her pause for surrender. "That's more like it, gal. Just relax and give Big Jim that kiss he's been wantin'." He slackened his hold and lowered his head. The coarse stubble of his beard stung as it grazed Carrie's cheek.

Anger and adrenaline raced through her. She pushed against him, raised her foot, and kicked him in the shin.

"Ow-w-w!" He let go and hopped around on one foot, cursing under his breath. "You little wench! You'll pay!"

The menacing gleam in his eye told Carrie it was now or never. Before he could grab her again, she shoved him. The big oaf stumbled backward to the edge of the boardwalk, flailing his arms as he hit the ground with a thud.

Carrie clenched onto the support post, a hand pressed to her pounding heart. Big Jim lay spread-eagle, flat on his back in the dusty street beneath a dim street light. A rock lay beneath his head. He was not moving.

What had she done? Was he unconscious or . . . ? No! She would not consider it. But what if he never came to? The sheriff would come after her. She would go to prison or . . . even hang. No, they didn't hang women, did they?

If Big Jim recovered, she wasn't any better off. He had a reputation for getting revenge, no matter how minor the offense.

Last spring Big Jim's neighbor, Mr. Clancy, came by his place to borrow his mule. Since Big Jim was nowhere to be found, the neighbor took the mule without asking. When Big Jim found Mr. Clancy plowing with his mule, he tied the old man up behind his horse and dragged him across the field while he pleaded for mercy.

It took Mr. Clancy a month to recover, and the law found no fault with Jim Counce. The sheriff stated that Mr. Clancy's taking the mule without Big Jim's consent was the same as stealing.

Who would believe Carrie if she tried to explain she was defending herself? It would be her word against Big Jim's. And the townspeople would want to know what a nice young lady was doing outside the saloon. She could hear the gossip now.

Carrie's gaze darted from the drunken man lying in the street to the saloon doors, then to the darkened buildings across the street. The town was peaceful except for those renegades inside the saloon. The bat-wing doors opened. A tall, slim cowboy stepped through.

Carrie hiked her skirt and ran down the boardwalk as he yelled after her, "Miss! Miss! Why are you in such an all-fired hurry?"

Gasping for breath, she ducked down the alley and behind the saloon where her horse waited. Carrie swung up into the saddle, turned her pinto toward home, and dug in her knees.

If Big Jim was in a drunken stupor, he would likely sleep until noon. If he was . . . not breathing . . . No, she still wouldn't think about that.

The next train out of Denton would pull in around four a.m., and she planned to be on it. Carrie had time to pack and get out of town before her brother came dragging in around mid-morning, his usual routine.

Could the cowboy identify her as she fled? The streetlight was dim, and she had covered her face as she ran. But if he found Big Jim lying in the dust and reported it to the sheriff, the law would be looking for the person who hurt him.

She remembered the sheriff's office had been dark. He'd probably gone home for the night. That should buy her a little more time.

~

CARRIE GALLOPED INTO THE YARD. The old, white frame house stood like a beacon, its paint peeling, the porch and roof in need of repair. Since Ma and Pa had been gone, there had been no money for repairs.

She slid off the horse and led him to the water trough before piling up some hay in another trough. She stroked his silky mane and groaned. "I've gotten myself into an awful mess, and I don't know but one way out."

Within the next hour, Carrie had changed into suitable traveling clothes and stuffed three dresses and other necessary items into a large valise. She dropped it near the front door. With her bag packed and closed, Carrie shuffled through a drawer for writing paper and pen. She couldn't disappear without letting her brother know something. If tonight was like other Friday nights, Blake would spend it at the saloon and stumble in tomorrow morning to sleep it off. She sank down in the rocker, a pen in hand, her weary body begging for a nap. But lying down would only wrinkle her dress.

She dipped the pen in ink and began her letter.

Blake, you promised you would stop gambling and drinking. I can't live this way any longer. I've bailed you out of jail for the last time. You are on your own.

By the time you read this, I will be gone."

She stopped short of confessing she'd seen his horse tied outside the saloon. It was best no one knew she had been in town. Not even Blake.

Carrie ended the note with, "*You will find the pinto tied near the trough outside the depot. I'll write and let you know something later, when I'm settled in. Take care of yourself."*

She signed her name and propped the note against the sugar

bowl. She couldn't imagine how her brother would make it without her, but it was time he learned to fend for himself.

As the Grandfather clock clanged eleven times, Carrie made herself comfortable in the old rocker and closed her eyes. She awoke at three-thirty, picked up her burdensome valise, and lugged it to the barn. After balancing it on the horse, Carrie climbed up in the saddle and nudged the pinto into a fast trot. She worried the sheriff might be waiting for her at the depot, but she would have to take her chances. A single tear trickled down her cheek.

Lord, please help me out of this mess.

She had only been trying to keep her promise to her mother. If someone other than the lone cowboy had been lurking in the shadows across the street, he might have gotten a good look at her face as she hovered over Big Jim's still body under the streetlight. Even if no one recognized her, a pinto horse was easy to identify.

Carrie was in plenty of trouble, but she would not waste time mulling over it. She had a train to catch. She prayed her meager savings would take her far away. Her job as a seamstress didn't pay much, but she had secretly tucked away a small sum. Otherwise, she and Blake would have gone hungry. Hopefully the money would take her far from Denton. Somewhere no one would think to look for her.

A HANDFUL of people milled about inside the train station. Several stood in the ticket line. Carrie walked to the back. The couple in front of her bought tickets for Cisco. Carrie strained her ears to hear the price. She had enough money to take her farther than she'd thought. Farther from the sheriff in Denton.

When she reached the ticket window, she asked the ticket master, "Sir, can you recommend any towns farther west than Cisco?"

He grunted before he answered. "Abilene is a thriving town.

People are heading there by the droves. All kinds of businesses have popped up since the railroad came through last year."

"How much is the fare?" She might find a job in Abilene. If not, in a town nearby.

He stated the price. Not as much as she'd guessed. Carrie laid the money on the counter. "I'll take a ticket to Abilene, please."

She tucked the change and her ticket in her reticule, then found a vacant bench and sat down for a fifteen-minute wait.

"Excuse me. Do you mind if I sit here?"

Lost in her thoughts, the feminine voice startled Carrie. She glanced up into wide, brown eyes. She judged the attractive brunette woman to be near her age. "No, of course not." Carrie slid over to make room.

"Thank you." After the young woman sat down and arranged her skirt, she extended a gloved hand. "I'm Molly Taylor. I took the train from Arkansas yesterday and spent the night in town with my aunt. Are you from here? You might know her. Rose Johnson?"

Carrie coughed. Molly was her employer's niece? Of all the people to cross her path. Careful not to say too much, Carrie introduced herself and added, "Yes, I know your aunt. Mrs. Johnson runs the most fashionable dressmaker's shop in the county. Of course, we should give her talented seamstresses their share of the credit." Carrie could almost hear her mother cautioning her about boasting.

She hated to leave Mrs. Johnson without giving notice, but the incident with Big Jim made the choice for her. Reporting to the sheriff that the drunk had harassed her would profit nothing since he, like everyone else, trembled at the sight of Jim Counce.

Her traveling companion smiled. "Top-notch fashions, I might add. As stylish as any Paris creation I've seen. And you are right in saying Aunt Rose could not do it without a few talented seamstresses." Molly shifted to face her. "Then you're from here?"

Carrie decided she could trust Molly with a little information since it was unlikely she'd see her again. "Yes, I am."

As she and Molly talked, two men walked in and stood near the door. One man was tall and wiry, the other short and stocky. The tall one might be the cowboy who stepped out of the saloon last night as she fled. Carried ducked her head and looked up, straining to hear their conversation. To her relief, Molly was preoccupied with shuffling through her purse.

The tall man shook his head. "Did you hear what happened to Big Jim?"

Carrie's heart raced as she strained to hear more.

The short man replied. "Nope, I ain't. What happened to the big oaf?"

The tall man grinned. "Ol' Jim got what was comin' to him last night. And the funny part was, it was a woman who done him in. I saw her runnin' away when I stepped outside the saloon."

The short man slapped his knee. "A woman? Well, if that ain't the funniest thing."

Carrie's breath caught. She kept her head down. This was the man who had seen her fleeing. "Done him in?" Did that mean Big Jim was . . . ? *Oh, no!* The sheriff was looking for a woman. Was he on his way to her house at this moment? She was a fugitive! Carrie shifted her body to gaze down the track. Where was that train? Couldn't it arrive early just once?

Unaware of her inner turmoil, Molly chattered away about her visit with her aunt. Carrie nodded occasionally while trying to hear more of the men's conversation. Too late. The topic had changed to the dry weather.

At that moment, a voice boomed over the speaker, "West-bound train arrives in five minutes! Passengers, gather your luggage and report to loading ramp."

Working herself into a frenzy was pointless. Carrie exhaled slowly and rose. The two ladies picked up their bags and merged into the line with the other departing passengers.

When they were settled in their seats, Carrie's companion announced, "You'll think I've lost my mind, but I want you to know I'm a mail-order bride on my way to meet my future husband."

Shock must have registered on Carrie's face because the young woman blushed. "It's not exactly for the reasons you may think. Since the war, there's been a shortage of men all over the South. In my state of Arkansas more than others. It was either answer an ad for a mail order bride or wind up a spinster. I don't want my brother or parents to feel obligated to support me. As scarce as jobs are for women, I think this was my best choice."

Carrie whispered, "Aren't you afraid this man won't turn out to be who he's claimed to be?"

"Not at all. Slim Hanks and I have exchanged more than a dozen letters over the past eight months. I think if the man walked up to me right now, I'd know him. I'm already half in love with Slim, just through our correspondence."

The mail-order bride idea intrigued Carrie, if it did sound risky. "I've heard about the shortage of women out west. And because men left their homes to join the Gold Rush, I believe there's a shortage of marriageable men in places like California. But the west is wild and untamed. It would be dangerous for ladies. Especially young ones."

"True. But the shortage isn't as far west as you may think. Baird, Texas is where I'm headed. Just past the central part of Texas."

"I'd still be skeptical." Carrie envied Molly in a way. She was young and had a destination, plus someone waiting for her. A man who promised to provide her with a secure future.

Molly sighed. "Speaking of skeptical, my friend Katy was supposed to join me on this trip as a mail order bride. She and I planned this together. It was even her idea. She corresponded with a rancher named Josh Kramer who lives south of Abilene in a town called Buffalo Gap. They exchanged letters for seven months. Then yesterday, Katy came to see me in tears. Her face was broken out in hives. She always breaks out when she's upset. Katy said she couldn't go through with her part of the plan."

"What reason did Katy give for breaking the agreement?" Carrie wanted to hear details. Marrying someone you had never met sounded scary but intriguing at the same time.

"Josh Kramer seems to be a secretive person, introverted at best. He didn't reveal much about himself in his letters. Katy thought he might be hiding something. He wrote about his ranch and the weather, but left out all the personal information about his family and himself, even after she asked again and again. Mr. Kramer did mention his Aunt Em, who lives with him."

"I would be suspicious too. I can't fault Katy for changing her mind."

How could a woman know what awaited her when she answered one of those ads? The man could be an outlaw. Was Josh Kramer's picture plastered on Wanted posters all over Texas? Carrie could imagine him as a brooding cowboy with beady, close-set eyes and a sneering mouth with a handlebar mustache above it.

"Where did you say Katy was to meet this man?"

"The Abilene stop. Mr. Kramer lives nearer Buffalo Gap, but the train doesn't run through there."

"Abilene is where I'm headed," Carrie commented.

Molly squealed. "What a wonderful coincidence. I have a favor to ask of you. I mean, if you don't mind. I've worried myself sick about how to get word to Mr. Kramer that Katy backed out. He will be waiting for her at the Abilene depot." Molly shifted to face Carrie. "Will you give him a message?"

Carrie scrunched up her face. "I . . . I'm not comfortable approaching strangers, but I hate to think the man will be left waiting and never know what happened."

"Please, Carrie," Molly begged. "I would tell him myself, but I get off in Baird and it's one stop before Abilene. Someone needs to tell Mr. Kramer that Katy Davis couldn't go through with the agreement. As you said, it would be awful if he never knew why she didn't show up. He will probably be heartbroken enough when you tell him."

Carrie doubted it. If Mr. Kramer was secretive about revealing personal information to Katy, he probably wasn't that interested in her. "I suppose I could. How will I know who he is?"

"Josh Kramer is in his mid-twenties, tall with dark hair and brown eyes. He'll have a red bandana tied around his neck."

"A red bandana?" Carrie swallowed hard. "That sounds like a bandit!"

Molly giggled. "That's funny. It's not what you think. He and Katy needed a simple way to identify one another."

"How was he supposed to recognize Katy?"

Molly's gaze raked Carrie. "You won't believe this. Katy planned to be wearing a light blue jacket over a dark skirt, similar to the one you're wearing. And Katy is also blonde and petite." Molly winked. "She is twenty-two. You could easily pass for her."

"Twenty-two? That's my age." Carrie flicked a speck of soot from the sleeve of her jacket and fingered the neckline. "I made this outfit."

"Really? It's very pretty, and fashionable. Katy makes her own clothes too. I'm terrible at sewing. I've never liked it. My talent is cooking. I hope that makes up for my lack in the sewing department." She giggled and added, "I wonder if Slim chose me over the other ladies for my cooking skills. I told him I could make the best soup beans and cornbread that he will ever put in his mouth. Three other ladies answered the ad, but he chose me."

"You could be right." Carrie would miss Molly's bubbly personality. The young woman had kept her mind off ensuing problems.

JUST AFTER SEVEN-THIRTY, the brakes on the Texas and Pacific squealed. As the train slowed, the conductor yelled, "Next stop, Baird! Departing passengers, gather your baggage and prepare to exit."

Carrie's vivacious companion gave her a quick hug before she rose. "Well, this is where I get off. Nice talking to you."

"You, too, Molly. I hope we run into each other again."

"I would like that. And it's possible. Baird and Abilene are only a few miles apart." She pulled a piece of note paper from her reticule and wrote something. "Here's my address if you want to stay in touch." Carrie tucked the paper in her reticule. "Don't forget to tell Josh Kramer about . . ."

"Katy . . . Davis?"

"Yes, Katy Davis."

"I won't forget." It was all she could think of. Strangers made her nervous, men the most. But she'd promised to deliver the message, and she would. "I . . . don't know my address yet, but I'd like us to keep in touch."

"So would I. You could tell me how Mr. Kramer took the news. Well, I'd better get in line."

Molly picked up her bags and merged with the other departing passengers. She turned to wave one last time. Carrie waved back and closed her eyes to relax for what she thought was a minute but must have been several.

"Next stop Abilene!" The brakes squealed in reply. "Prepare to disembark."

Carrie picked up her valise and melded into the long line of passengers. It must be true that Abilene was a booming town.

Inside the depot, a throng of people bustled about, some buying tickets, others searching for the ones who were supposed to meet them.

She scanned the station for a tall, dark-haired man fitting the description of the mysterious Josh Kramer. Two middle-aged men wandered about scanning the faces of passengers inside the depot. One man was short and stout, the other paunchy. Neither wore a red bandana around his neck. This was taking longer than Carrie had thought. She should be searching for a job and a place to sleep tonight. The description Molly gave her of Mr. Kramer did not fit any of these men. What if he had backed out of the agreement too?

After twenty minutes of studying every man who walked through the door, Carrie set her luggage on the floor near a bench and sat down. If the man showed up, finding him would be easier after the crowd thinned. Meanwhile, she had to plan her next move. After she relayed her message to Josh Kramer, she would visit the shops across the street to inquire whether they were hiring. She was tempted to leave now, but she'd made a promise to Molly and meant to keep it.

"Excuse me." A smooth baritone voice above her tickled her ears.

Carrie gazed up into dark, flashing eyes that seemed to pierce through to her soul. The tall cowboy wore a black Stetson over coal-black hair with curls that caressed his ears. His strong jaw suggested determination and tenacity. A little lower, a red bandana circled his tanned neck. Molly had failed to mention that Josh Kramer was handsome. But she couldn't have known. Only a braggart would expound on his looks in a letter.

"Are you the woman I'm looking for?"

Carrie's heart raced. *If only I were.* When she tried to speak, her mouth went dry and her tongue stuck in place as if it were glued. "I . . . I—" was all she could manage.

The cowboy shuffled his large booted feet which gleamed with fresh black polish. "Well, what are you waiting for? A ranch doesn't run itself. It's a ten-mile ride. We'd better get going."

Her tongue came unglued. "Mr. Kramer, I'm not—." It was all she could get out before he

pointed to the valise at her feet.

"Where are your other bags? Is this all the luggage you brought?" His hooded gaze paralyzed her tongue again. Carrie could only nod as he bent, snatched up her valise, and tramped outside.

She jumped to her feet and hurried after him, catching up as he set her bag in his buckboard. "But, Mister Kramer, I'm not—."

"Are you ready to go, Miss Davis? I have a long day ahead of me."

"Mr. Kramer, I need to tell you something."

He threw up his hands. "Whatever it is can wait until we get to the ranch. I'm a busy man. I have a ranch to run and Aunt Em needs help with the canning. She's been at it since daybreak. She's the only reason I insisted she place the ad."

Miss Davis? He really did believe she was his mail-order bride. "Your aunt needs help with canning?" Katy was supposed to become his bride, not a servant.

"That's right. The last of the garden is coming in, carrots and tomatoes." His brow creased as he studied her. "You do know how to can?"

"Yes, but—." Why did he persist in asking questions about her abilities?

"Our growing season is longer in west Texas than what you're use to in Arkansas. Aunt Em likes to work in the cool of the day. She works too hard, wears herself out. That's the reason I insisted she place an ad for help around the house."

Help around the house? But, Molly had told her that Katy Davis had answered an ad for mail-order bride. Could this cowboy have duped her into expecting matrimony when all he really wanted was a woman to become a servant to him, and to his aunt? Not that she, Carrie Franklin, minded hard work. It was . . . well, the principle of the thing.

Chapter Two

Take it easy, Carrie admonished herself, releasing a breath. Why should she be upset at this cowboy? She wasn't the woman who had been tricked. Katy Davis should have been the recipient of whatever game he was playing. But Miss Davis had sensed something was awry, then backed out.

Carrie had to make him listen, if he would let her talk. "Mr. Kramer—"

"Call me Josh."

Before she could say another word, he wrapped his large hands around her waist, tossed her up in the air, and planted her backside on the buckboard seat. "Let's head to the ranch. Time's a wasting."

He walked around to the other side while she arranged her skirt in a ladylike manner and climbed up on the seat.

Carrie reached across and gripped his arm. "Josh, you should know something."

"What?"

She held his gaze, determined not to flinch. "I did not come here looking for a husband."

His dark eyebrows drew together as he released the brake on the wagon. Instead of looking at her, he stared straight ahead. "Good, then we have that much in common. The last thing I want is a troublesome woman chasing after me. I wondered if my aunt might have . . . Forget it." He shook the reins. "Giddyup!"

The wagon lurched forward as the chestnut horses took off at a gallop, kicking up dust. Carrie fought to keep her balance. She fanned at the dust and grit, and coughed. Her head spun, trying to fit the pieces of this strange puzzle together.

How had she ended up beside this handsome cowboy, headed to his ranch? Her intentions were innocent. She was to relay a message to this man to explain Katy Davis's absence.

Nothing made sense. Josh Kramer proclaimed he did not want a wife. Then why did he advertise for one? Molly stated that Katy Davis answered an ad for a mail-order bride. None of it made sense. And his aunt needed house help? What did that mean?

How could she make Josh listen?

She was not Katy Davis. If only she'd worn the green dress instead of the light blue jacket over a dark skirt. Was his remark about "a troublesome woman" aimed at her? Not fair. He had no right to pronounce judgment on her when he didn't even know her. She had a good mind to grab her valise and jump out of the wagon. She would if the horses weren't moving at a fast trot.

How much money did she have left if she did decide to bail? Carrie felt inside her purse and fingered the four remaining coins in the bottom. Four quarters to her name. Carrie didn't have enough to pay for a hotel room. Not the one in Abilene, for sure.

Calm down. Think this through.

She could argue with this cowboy until she turned blue in the face, or she could ride along to his ranch and spend the night. At least she would have a roof over her head. She and Mr. Kramer would not be alone. Both he and Molly had mentioned his aunt. Mr. Kramer said she needed help with canning. Besides, Josh Kramer owed her something. He had thwarted her plans. She might have found a job at a shop in Abilene if he hadn't deposited her like a sack of horse feed onto his buckboard. What kind of man treated a lady like that?

Carrie's best option was to let Josh assume she was Katy Davis, just for tonight. She would help his aunt catch up on canning and get a good night's sleep in a soft bed at the Kramer ranch. In the morning, she would borrow the buckboard to return to Abilene. By this time tomorrow, surely she would have a job.

Returning to Denton was not an option. Everyone in town, including the sheriff, quaked at the sight of Big Jim Counce. Even if she had money for the return ticket, the brute would be waiting for her—if he was able. Carrie shuddered. The next time she might get the worst end of the deal.

If he wasn't alive . . . she would not consider that.

Josh studied her from beneath hooded lids. "Are you all right, Miss Davis?"

"I'm fine, thank you." She squirmed in her seat as he returned his gaze to the road.

Tonight she would have food in her stomach and a roof over her head. It was the best plan she could come up with. Too late to argue anyway. They were well on their way.

Determined to make the best of the situation, Carrie smoothed her skirt and forced herself to relax. Maybe this cowboy's aunt would supply the missing pieces to the mail order bride quandary. One thing was certain; she had no intention of assuming the place of Katy Davis as Josh Kramer's wife. This sullen cowboy was definitely not her cup of tea.

Though not yet midday, the sun blasted down. Perspiration beaded Carrie's brow. She pulled a handkerchief from her reticule and pushed up her hat brim to wipe it away. A few minutes later, they passed beneath the entrance to the Kramer ranch.

Josh reined in the horses near a sprawling log house with a large porch. He hopped down, reached in the wagon for Carrie's valise, and set it on the porch. Before she could rise, Josh's hands spanned her waist. He swung her down and set her on the porch beside her luggage.

Pushing his Stetson up on his forehead, he yelled, "Aunt Em! Your help has arrived."

The screen door swung open. A short, plump woman with salt

and pepper hair hurried out onto the porch, her face flushed and damp. Carrie guessed her to be in her early sixties. The woman dried her face with the hem of her apron and smiled. The lines around her soft brown eyes crinkled when she looked at Carrie. She instantly relaxed with the sweet, grandmotherly woman.

Josh nodded toward her. "This is my aunt, Miss Davis. Aunt Em, meet Katy Davis."

Aunt Em patted her hair. A few tendrils had escaped the salt and pepper bun on top of her head and hung loose and wet about her ears.

"I must look a sight. Been standin' over that hot stove all mornin'. You children come on in out of this scorchin' heat and cool off."

She turned to Josh. "You need to rest a spell before you head back out to the pasture. I just drew a fresh bucket of cool water from the cistern. It won't stay cool long."

She patted Carrie's arm and lamented, "Autumn arrived last week accordin' to the calendar, but you can't tell it here in this part of Texas. Our summers ain't for the fainthearted. I'm sure it's hotter here than what you're used to in Arkansas."

Since Carrie had never been there, she searched her mind for a non-committal reply. "At least the heat will soon be over."

"Cooler weather won't get here for at least another month. We've still got plenty of carrots and tomatoes in the garden." Aunt Em opened the screen door and gestured for Carrie to precede her. "I can't promise it's comfortable inside with all the heat from the cannin'. Sometimes I step over to the window to get a breath of fresh air."

Josh stepped inside and set Carrie's valise on the floor. He bent to kiss his aunt's cheek. "I'll take that cool glass of water, then I have to leave. We have a couple of sick cows. Looks like mange. The veterinarian is meeting Luke and me in the north pasture in thirty minutes."

Josh's aunt filled two glasses with water from a dipper in a wooden bucket. She handed one to Carrie, the other to Josh.

Mason jars and canning lids covered the kitchen table. Half the jars were filled with tomatoes, the other half carrots. Two crates of empty jars-waited on the floor near the stove. A serrated knife and a pile of peelings lay on the work counter.

Josh gulped the water down and plunked his glass on the table. "Gotta go." He adjusted his Stetson on the way out. The screen door popped shut behind him.

At the sound of disappearing hoof beats, Aunt Em patted Carrie's arm. "Let me show you to your room."

Carrie picked up her valise and followed. Rose-sprigged wallpaper gave the room a dainty appeal. The dark furniture contrasted with the creamy Chenille bedspread with a large rose embroidered in its center. A pink and cream braided rug lay on the hardwood floor beside the bed.

Carrie smiled. "This is pretty. It looks like a real lady's room."

"That's because it belonged to Josh's mother. Claire feminized it after Josh's pa died." Aunt Em paused to clear her throat. "I need to say somethin', dear, but I don't know how to go about it. I have to say it now, though, so things don't get out of hand."

She knows I'm not Katy Davis. But how? "I . . . I can explain." Carrie's heart thumped against her ribcage.

The older woman raised a hand. "No, I'm the one who needs to explain. Please, hear me out. I have a confession to make and it's not an easy one." She wrung her hands and fingered the wet tendrils at her temple. "I placed the mail-order bride ad in the papers. Not my nephew."

Carrie pressed a hand to her throat. What was she saying? "You placed the ad? But why—?"

Aunt Em propped her hands on her hips. "Because it's high time Josh settled down with a good little wife. The problem is, he and I don't see eye to eye on what's best for him. I took the place of his ma after she left. I try to look out for his best interests."

Aunt Em resumed wringing her hands. "Josh claims he's not the least bit interested in matrimony. I told him he's not met the right woman. But knowing how stubborn he can be, I took it on myself to find him the right wife. I answered letters from three young ladies from three different states. After reading yours, I figured you'd be the best fit. You and Josh both come from rural areas, and though yours was a farming area, it's not that different from a ranch. I'm guess you can milk a cow, raise a garden, and tend to livestock. It takes a hardy gal to live in these parts.

"Josh wants nothing to do with women, because he doesn't trust them. 'They're either deceivers or gold diggers.' His words, not mine. He stayed angry a long time at his ma for marrying again after his pa died. Said she'd betrayed his pa's memory. But the woman who really burned Josh was Leah. That was last fall. It's time he got over her."

Aunt Em gave Carrie a sheepish look. "But that's not for me to talk about. If or when Josh wants to tell you about Miss Leah, he can. I've already said too much. I just wanted you to know why you may get the silent treatment."

She said "Miss Leah" like the name left a bad taste in her mouth. Carrie didn't know whether to be relieved or shocked at this revelation. "Miss . . . Mrs . . . ?"

"Emma Roberts, but call me Aunt Em. I was married fourteen years, but I've been widowed twenty-eight. Hal and I were not blessed with children of our own. He died in '55 and I lived alone for a year. Then my younger brother, Josh's father, asked me to move in and help Claire when she found out she was expectin'. When Josh was two weeks old, I started to leave. But Claire asked me to stay, to consider this my home. She said she couldn't run the house without my help. The new baby took so much of her time and energy." Aunt Em shrugged. "I stayed and have become a fixture here, you might say."

"I'm sure you were a big help to her."

"Yes. Claire was . . . still is . . . the social butterfly. She enjoys hosting parties and decorating the house for Christmas and other occasions, but she's not big on housekeeping. That's where I came in. Running a house seems to be my God-given talent."

"Aunt Em," Carrie interjected. "If—."

"May I call you Katy?" The older woman's smile warmed Carrie's heart. "We've finally met after all those months of exchangin' letters. I feel as if I already know you."

Should she divulge her secret or keep quiet? She decided to keep quiet. "If Josh doesn't know about the ad for the mail order bride, why does he think I'm here?" Carrie wanted to be sure she'd heard Josh correctly.

Aunt Em blushed. "I told a little white lie. He's insisted for the past two summers that I get help around the house. Says I'm not a spring chicken anymore." She hesitated. "Anyway, I placed an ad in several papers. He thinks the ad was for domestic help. Don't get me wrong. It's true what he said about me getting on up in years, but that's not why I placed it."

Aha! Josh's aunt had not been honest either. Carrie felt a little better knowing she wasn't alone in this deception. The way she figured it, both she and Aunt Em would have the devil to pay when he discovered the truth.

"I'd like to see Josh married and settled with two or three young 'uns before I leave this world." Her gaze raked Carrie before she winked. "After meeting you, I think you'll do just fine."

Her? Marry Josh Kramer and have . . . children? Carrie's breath caught in her throat. Since her parents' death, she had not planned past the next day. Her job, along with keeping house for herself and Blake, had been exhausting. Trying to watch out for her brother drained her more.

Did Aunt Em expect her to persuade Josh to marry her? Impossible! If she ever did consider marriage, the man wouldn't be a stranger. Or one who disliked her. Josh had made no bones about the way he felt.

If she had persisted and told him who she really was before they left the depot, she wouldn't be in this jam. Josh thought she was his aunt's domestic help, whereas Josh's aunt expected her to become his bride. Carrie closed her eyes to mentally untangle the web of deceit that had ensnared her.

Josh's aunt deserved the truth. She opened her mouth to confess. "I need to tell you—."

Aunt Em rushed on. "Katy, promise me you won't mention any of this to Josh. I'll be in hot water if he knows I tricked him. That boy has a temper."

That did it. How could she confess to her part in the deceit when Josh's aunt was also mixed up in it? Both she and Aunt Em stood to lose something. Carrie was more concerned about the repercussions Aunt Em might face.

She huffed out a breath. "I won't tell him what you did."

"About your letters, I apologize for the muddled replies. You must've thought Josh was a strange man, not answering the simplest questions, but I thought it best you met him first. I figured after you got to know him, the questions would answer themselves.

"My nephew is a good boy. Never gave his parents or me a minute's trouble." She winked." He could be a might mischievous. But enough of that. I've talked too much already. I imagine you're plum tuckered out after your long trip. Why don't you lie down and rest a spell?"

"I'm not the least bit tired. Do you need help with the canning? I used to help my mother."

Aunt Em winked. "I won't turn down any offer of help. Your mama started you young in the kitchen, didn't she? You were only seven when she died."

"Seven . . . teen," Carrie blurted before she thought. She and Blake lost their parents five years ago, when their buggy flipped over a mile from home. No one knew exactly how it happened, but a passerby found the missing wheel several yards down the road in a ditch.

Aunt Em frowned. "I could've sworn you wrote 'seven' in one of your letters."

Carrie's heart pounded. She couldn't reveal the truth now. Besides her own guilt, she didn't have the heart to disappoint this sweet woman. She had felt an instant kinship with Josh's aunt. She might even learn to like Josh if he'd give her half a chance. Instead of replying to Aunt Em's remark, Carrie announced, "I'm ready to tackle the canning, if you are."

"Then let's be at it." The older woman led the way to the kitchen and pulled out a checkered apron. "Here, put this on. We wouldn't want to ruin your pretty dress." She handed Carrie a long knife. "I've finished the tomatoes. You peel and slice the carrots while I sterilize these jars."

By mid-afternoon, quart jars of carrots packed into steaming jars lined the kitchen floor. Carrie laid her knife on the table. A mountain of peelings lay in a box beneath the table as proof she had put in a decent day's work. Blotting her face with the hem of her apron, she said, "I'm out of carrots."

Aunt Em wiped the moisture from her face with the back of her hand. "So you are. Glory be! That's all of them. Let me have the last ones you peeled in your bowl. I'll candy them for supper. It should suffice. Josh should be in around sundown. You never know the exact time."

"I'll help with supper. Just tell me what to do." Although her brother rarely complained, cooking was not one of Carrie's talents. If she weren't leaving tomorrow, she could learn a few tips from Aunt Em. The older woman had been kind and patient with her.

If only she didn't have to leave. Aunt Em made her feel as if she belonged with her and Josh. Carrie sighed. Why allow herself to dream an impossible dream? When she found a job in town, she would move into a boarding house and get out of their lives.

"That's sweet of you to offer to help." Aunt Em nodded toward the ripe tomatoes on the window sill. "You can slice those while I warm up the beef roast. If Josh doesn't show up by sundown, we'll go ahead and eat without him."

An hour later, the kitchen was filled with the delicious aroma of beef roast, candied carrots simmering on the stove, and pan-fried cornbread. Hoof beats sounded outside. Carrie watched through the window as Josh slid off his black stallion and led it into the barn. She paused a few seconds to admire his broad shoulders and tapered waistline and grabbed a handful of silverware.

Josh clomped into the kitchen and began soaping his hands. "What's for supper?"

Aunt Em rolled her eyes toward Carrie. "This boy has a hollow leg."

Josh bent and kissed her cheek. "I can't help it if I'm a growing boy."

"Ha! I'd believe that if you were eighteen. But you're twenty-six now. On your way to thirty."

He groaned. "Please . . . don't remind me I'm getting old. Are we ready to eat?"

Aunt Em set the succulent roast in the center of the table. "Be patient. Let Katy set the silverware out."

Katy? Carrie's conscience pricked. She hated to deceive these nice folks, but telling the truth meant disappointing them plus losing credibility. Their opinion of her mattered, although she'd only known them a few hours.

Besides, if she told them the truth tonight, they might throw her out. And where could she go? No, it was better to keep quiet and rest her weary body in a comfortable bed. Tomorrow would be soon enough to leave the Kramer Ranch.

Aunt Em scooped lima beans into a serving bowl and picked up the plate of cornbread. She set them next to the candied carrots and the roast encircled by celery, onions, and potatoes. Carrie made room for the tomatoes, then stepped back to admire the array of colorful vegetables against the checkered tablecloth.

"The table looks pretty." She hadn't eaten a meal like this since Mama and Papa died. She missed the delicious food, but most of all she missed the family conversations they'd had around the table.

"It's how the food tastes that counts," Josh commented.

Aunt Em groaned. "See. I told you eatin' was foremost on his mind."

"He's probably ravenous from putting in a hard day's work."

"Yep. Well, what are we waiting for? Let's eat."

Carrie waited for Josh and his aunt to pull out their chairs, then did likewise. When they were seated, Carrie picked up her fork and waited for Aunt Em to take the first bite. When the older woman made no move, Carrie laid her fork down. Why were they staring at her?

Aunt Em sighed. "Josh, will you say the blessing, please?" She extended one hand to Carrie and the other to Josh, gesturing for them to also join hands across the table.

Carrie's face flamed. She should have known to expect them to say grace. She and her brother had stopped after their parents died. Soon after they passed, she asked Blake to stand in for Papa and bless the food. He ridiculed her, so she never asked him again.

Carrie felt Josh's gaze on her and looked up. What had he read on her face? His hand was stretched toward her, palm up. She placed hers in the large callused one and trembled. Josh's rough fingers wrapped around hers, exuding warmth, tenderness, and a sense of belonging. How could one glean so much from a touch?

She closed her eyes and waited. Josh cleared his throat. "Lord, we thank you for the bounty you've provided, for the hands which prepared it and for rain in due season. We appreciate the number of calves you added to our herd this spring. We know all good gifts come from You. For that we give You the praise. Amen."

When Carrie opened her eyes, Josh offered the bowl of carrots to her. "Thank you." She dished out a portion and passed it to Aunt Em.

Josh's aunt passed him the cornbread. He sighed. It had been a long day, what with going to town to pick up Miss Davis and coming back to doctor cattle.

"How are those sick cows farin'?"

Aunt Em had read his mind. He took a slice and passed the plate to Katy. "Doc says they'll be fine."

"What's ailin' them?"

"Mange, but I think we caught it in time. Only infected three head."

Obviously unfamiliar with the disease, Katy asked, "How did the doc know it was mange?"

Josh grinned. "Crusty spots on the base of the tail and inside the flanks. He scraped the spots to take a sample. He'd brought a small microscope along, even let me look through it. Fascinating, those vicious little mites being magnified to the size of monsters."

Aunt Em scooped a piece of pie out for herself. "Did he bring anything to treat it with?"

"Yes, a large bottle of ointment. We doused it on the affected areas, wearing gloves. We'll keep those three head quarantined until the signs are gone."

Josh chanced a glance at Katy's squeamish face. Mange and its treatment must not be one of her favorite meal topics. He'd better change the discussion to something more palatable.

Aunt Em wiped her mouth. "I'm glad y'all caught it before it infected the whole herd."

"Me too. But, we may want to change the subject." His gaze slid from Katy's pinched face to his aunt's glowing one. "Our guest has turned pale. Miss Davis, you will have to excuse our unsavory mealtime topics. We forget our manners. It's not often that we entertain guests."

Aunt Em patted Katy's hand. "She's more than a guest. I hope she'll be with us a long while. I'm sorry, dear. I shouldn't have brought up the diseased cattle. You do look a bit peaked. Would you like something to settle your stomach? Maybe bicarbonate of soda?"

She took a deep breath. "No, I'm fine."

Josh noticed her color had not returned. Time to change directions, delve into her background. From his experience, most women liked to talk about themselves. Katy Davis was different. She didn't give out information unless prodded. Was she hiding something? She certainly acted like it. Most women couldn't be trusted. He'd learned that the hard way.

"Remind me what you did for a living."

"I . . ." She focused her gaze on Aunt Em.

"Katy worked in her uncle's mercantile."

"And what did that entail?"

Katy shrugged. "The usual things a clerk does." Her eyelids fluttered as she looked down at her glass.

"You know what working in a store entails." Aunt Em huffed. "She stocked shelves and waited on customers, added up their bills."

Josh folded his arms across his chest. Aunt Em had expertly thrown a cog in his wheel of questions. As long as she provided the answers, Katy didn't have to. Something was going on, and he didn't like the smell of it. He would bide his time. The truth always surfaced, given time.

They finished supper with talk of the weather and fluctuating beef prices. Josh nodded at the ladies. "I would like to excuse myself." He rose and filled the large pot with water, setting it on the stove. He had performed this same ritual every night since he was twelve.

Josh sat back down to sip his water and watch Katy bustling about the kitchen. She appeared to float from the counter to the table and back, clearing dirty dishes. Why would a pretty, young woman give up a job in her uncle's store in Hope, Arkansas, to answer an ad for domestic help in distant Buffalo Gap?

The clues didn't add up. Josh prided himself on being a good judge of character. Katy could not hold eye contact with him for more than two seconds. That might be to his advantage. If he gazed into those gorgeous cat eyes very long, he might lose his head.

Josh recalled how light Katy felt when he'd lifted her from the buckboard. *Whoa* . . . He mentally shook himself. He should not be dwelling on that.

Katy avoided his questions, but something else bothered him.

Why had Aunt Em placed an ad in newspapers when she could have hired a local woman? And why would a woman like Katy travel four hundred miles on a lurching, noisy train to take a domestic job?

He rubbed his chin in thought. What had she said when he'd climbed up on the buckboard beside her? Ah-hh . . . yes. *"I did not come here looking for a husband."*

Why would she blurt those words unless it was her backhanded way of saying she did expect matrimony? Women could be fickle. They often said opposite of what they meant. He had learned that from Leah Jackson, the girl with hair the color of ripe chestnuts and honey-colored eyes that had mesmerized him. A good reason to be wary of females.

Shortly before Leah came along, Josh's pa died. His mother proclaimed she would never marry again, but a year later she changed her mind. She met a charmer who had booked a suite at the fancy hotel in Abilene. Mark Callahan worked at the top of the cattle industry. He hailed from California and wore a fancy suit, stayed in town six weeks, and courted Josh's mother day and night. He even managed to get invited to dinner at the Kramer ranch a few times. The charmer took his mother to dinner many times and attended church with them. At the end of his prolonged stay, he proposed to her, married her, and swept her off to Sacramento.

The last thing Josh wanted was to give his mother away at the wedding. Especially to that man. It galled him to even attend the ceremony. But Aunt Em could be persuasive, so he made it through the ritual. Since his mother moved away, Josh ran the ranch with the help of three regular hands. It took a while, but he finally acknowledged that his mother's new husband might not be so bad after all. When Mark and his mother came for their first visit, Josh admitted, though only to himself, that he might be wrong. What he once felt was disloyalty to his father now warmed his heart. His mother's new husband treated her like a lady, and he'd never seen her happier.

Why was he thinking about his mother's new marriage and

Leah's treachery when he should be trying to solve the present mystery? Katy had nothing in common with Leah and his mother. Unless solving it proved his theory that women could not be trusted. He had been wrong about his mother, but Leah was a different story. Would Katy prove to be another Leah?

And why was he comparing her to Leah? Leah was the woman he had loved. Katy was only hired help.

Josh pulled his attention back to Katy, who stood beside his aunt washing dishes. There was bound to be more to her story. She could have found a position closer to home.

His gaze followed Katy from the table to the dishpan then back to the table to gather more dishes. If Miss Davis thought she could get her claws in him, she'd better think again. Running the ranch was enough responsibility without the bonds of matrimony. He would avoid her as much as possible, ensure they weren't alone for any length of time.

Josh reared back, balancing his chair on two legs. He crossed his arms, eying her. "What part of Arkansas are you from?" An undetectable emotion flickered in her eyes before her gaze flitted to Aunt Em.

Aunt Em flung a dishtowel across her shoulder and answered for her. "The southern part. Katy's from Hope, Arkansas."

Why did Katy keep allowing Aunt Em to answer for her? It made him wonder if his aunt was hiding something. If they both were hiding something.

CARRIE LET HER SHOULDERS RELAX. Aunt Em had saved her hide again. She didn't know why Josh's aunt kept speaking up for her. Was it to cover her own misdeed? How long before she blurted out something that gave her away? Carrie could kick herself for not asking Molly more questions about Katy Davis. But she didn't know she would be posing as the woman.

Josh directed his gaze at her "What is Hope's population?"

"I don't know, but it's a fair-sized town." Carrie's lips quivered. She'd almost let slip she'd worked as a seamstress, then remembered Katy worked in her uncle's mercantile.

Carrie bit her lip under Josh's hooded gaze. His questions, laced with suspicion, made her queasy. To divert his attention, she grabbed the dishcloth and swished it across the table. He must have realized she wanted him to move because he rose and tramped outside.

She whooshed out a long breath. Tomorrow the sham would be over. She would find a job. Any job. Except one at the local saloon. She had a nice soprano voice she reserved for working around the house. She would not use it to entertain a bunch of wild, drunken men.

Josh marched in with an armload of kindling and dropped it in the box behind the stove. Carrie passed a dripping plate to Aunt Em but directed her question at Josh. "Do you mind if I borrow the buckboard in the morning?"

His poker expression told her nothing. He glanced at his aunt as if waiting for her answer. Aunt Em's mouth opened, then closed. She flung the dishtowel onto her shoulder. "Well, I don't see any reason you can't ride into town with Josh in the morning. He's goin' into Abilene to pick up feed and to get supplies for me at the mercantile."

"But I—." Carrie needed to go alone, but arguing would raise Josh's suspicions. His gaze followed her everywhere, a sign he suspected something. She had no choice. While he bought supplies, she could look for a job. She'd planned to take the buckboard to Buffalo Gap, but Abilene was a booming town. One of the dress shops should be hiring.

Guilt washed through her belly, wrenching her gut. She had to find work. Forcing a weak smile she replied, "That will be fine."

If Josh discovered she had duped him, facing Big Jim might be the easier alternative.

Chapter Three

Tomorrow, Carrie hoped to have the prospect of a job. Then her conscience could rest easy. Deception did not sit well with her. It had been a long day, and the hot kitchen didn't help matters. Sweat beaded on the back of her neck and on her forehead as she dried a plate. She had plaited her long hair and let the braid hang down her back.

When the last dish had been put away, Aunt Em wiped her brow. "Everything's done in here. What do y'all say we go out and sit a spell on the porch. A cool breeze is blowin' in from the west."

Josh piped up. "I have to water the horses."

Aunt Em sent him a reproving look. "Katy's already filled the water trough."

Josh had made it clear he didn't relish her company, but Carrie didn't care. "Count me in. I can't wait to get some fresh air." Perspiration still dripped down the back of her neck from several hours of canning.

The ladies walked out to the porch. Josh picked up a cane-back chair and followed, placing it several feet from the ladies. He plopped down in it and gazed off into the distance.

Aunt Em made herself comfortable in the porch swing. "Now, doesn't this feel good?"

Carrie sat beside her and lifted her braid off her neck to feel the cooler air. "Yes. It's refreshing after the heat in the kitchen."

Josh unfastened a button near the top of his shirt and stretched his lanky legs out in front of him. Carrie pulled her gaze from him to the paddock where the horses swished their tails.

His aunt wasted no time starting a conversation. Patting Carrie's hand, she announced, "Josh, this gal has proved her worth in the kitchen. Katy here is no stranger to hard work. In these parts, a man needs to consider that when lookin' for a mate. If he's got any smarts about him."

Carrie's face burned and not from the heat. She picked imaginary lint off her bodice and glanced up at Josh.

The crease between his brows proved he didn't share his aunt's opinion. He brushed the remark aside with, "Then you should be happy. A hard worker is what you wanted."

Carrie raised her chin. "I was raised on hard work, and Aunt Em is easy to work with."

"Thank you, dear. After that long trip, I figured you'd be plum tuckered out, but you've held up well. Even watered the livestock and gathered the eggs."

Josh folded his arms across his chest and closed his eyes, letting his aunt know he wanted no further discussion on the topic. She could remedy that. Carrie rose and yawned. "I'm tired. I think I'll call it a night. What time should I get up to help with breakfast?"

Aunt Em sighed. "I get up at daybreak to get breakfast started. Can you milk a cow?"

"Of course. I've milked one since I was small."

"Good. You can milk Gert now. She should be in the barn waitin'. She'll be in the same spot in the mornin'. Josh, take Katy out there and introduce her to our Guernsey gal. Gert don't take much to strangers. You'll want to familiarize yourself with her before you try to milk her."

Josh disappeared inside the house and reappeared swinging the milk pail by its handle. "I'm ready."

Katy followed him to the barn where he lit a lantern. The

brown and white spotted cow spied Josh and walked into a stall. He patted her shank, pulled up the milking stool, and plunked down on it. "Gert knows me, so let me start the milking, then I'll turn it over to you."

Katy watched over his shoulder. When the pail was half full, she said, "Let me finish."

The unfamiliar voice startled the cow. Gert turned her head and spied Katy and let out an ear-splitting bellow. Her tail slapped Josh on the side of his face, knocking him and the stool backward.

Josh jumped up, spitting and sputtering. "You old bag of bones! I ought to—." He must have remembered he was in the presence of a lady since he cut his sentence short. Katy covered her mouth to smother a giggle, but her quaking body gave her away.

Josh wiped his wet face on his shirtsleeve. "You think it's funny, do you?"

She cleared her throat. "If you could have seen your face when . . . well, never mind."

He waved toward the stool. "All right. It's your turn, little lady. Good luck."

Katy bit her bottom lip and took her place on the stool. Miraculously, the bucket was still upright. She took the stool but before she started to milk, she spoke to Gert in a gentle voice. "Gert, I promise not to hurt you. You be still now, and we will be fine."

The cow did not move until Katy had filled the pail. Josh scratched his head. "How did you do that? Gert is cantankerous with me, worse with strangers. But you seem to have a way with her."

Katy shrugged. "It's in the tone of voice and your touch. Animals can sense those things."

JOSH TURNED over in bed and yanked at the sheet wrapped around his ankles. Why couldn't he sleep? He was exhausted yet wide awake.

That bothersome woman! She was the cause. He didn't trust Katy Davis any farther than he could throw her. What lay behind the sweet, innocent façade and those alluring cat eyes? Most men would be lured in. Not him. No, siree. He didn't know what kind of game she was playing, but his eyes were wide open. She hadn't fooled him for one second.

On the other hand, Aunt Em didn't suspect a thing. Which wasn't like her. He could not believe his aunt's gullibility. She was usually a good judge of character, but she'd obviously been taken by Katy's charm and sweet disposition.

He hadn't had a chance to warn his aunt. It wasn't so much what Katy said, but how she reacted—even stammered—over his questions that sent up a red flag.

For one thing, she had faltered when he'd asked what part of Arkansas she hailed from. Should he chalk it up to nervousness? He'd been told that his size and the looks he gave people sometimes intimidated them. Others claimed his hooded eyes made them nervous.

According to the Good Book, he was supposed to give Katy the benefit of the doubt. His aunt had stressed that plenty of times. Whatever the young woman was up to, Aunt Em had taken a liking to her. And to be fair, Katy had worked hard today. No telling how many quarts of carrots and tomatoes the ladies had canned.

Wait. Was that part of her plan? Butter up Aunt Em and get in his good graces, then make her move. But for what? That was the question. Would she try to coerce him into matrimony?

His aunt regularly implied he should settle down with a good woman. Josh didn't see that happening any time soon. He was gun-shy when it came to females. He'd considered marriage once and had come out scathed in the process.

"Never again."

His aunt' voice drifted across the hall. "Josh, were you talkin' to me?"

I said that aloud? "Just mumbling to myself." He'd swear at age sixty-two Aunt Em's hearing was still as sharp as that of a young blue-tick hound.

"You'd best be gettin' some shuteye. Mornin' will be here before you know it."

He adored his aunt. She'd been more like a mother to him than his real one. "Good night, Aunt Em."

"Good night, hon. Sleep tight."

Josh rolled over on his back, clasped his hands behind his head, and stared at the ceiling. Katy Davis insisted on going into town in the morning. She'd asked to borrow the buckboard, meaning she had planned to go alone.

Why? Was she sending a telegram to someone? He could see the telegram now. *All going as planned. Easy pickings at Kramer Ranch.*

Wait just a doggone minute! Josh sat straight up in bed and stroked his chin. Katy planned to meet someone in town. Probably a man. That had to be it.

He hadn't considered she might not be alone in her scheme. Was a man involved with her in conspiring to take the Kramer ranch? Well, he'd throw a cog in her wheel. Miss Davis would not get out of his sight for one minute. He would stay vigilant. He was too wise to fall for her tricks. She would not get a thing over on him. Flipping over to his side, he punched his pillow. His mind at ease, Josh soon fell asleep.

CARRIE CLEARED dishes from the table while Aunt Em poured steaming water from a kettle into the dish pan. "I hope you slept well."

"The bed was comfortable, thank you." She couldn't fault it for keeping her awake. Her conscience was the culprit. She had tossed and turned until the wee hours. She should have tried harder to tell Josh who she really was at the train station, before he swooped her away.

Now the safest option was the coward's way. Find a job in town, first, then tell Josh and his aunt she wasn't cut out for ranch living. All right, that would be another fib. Fibbing was wrong, but so was deception. How could she get out of this dilemma without hurting someone? Why hadn't she thought of this beforehand? Someone would get hurt. More than one.

Carrie stacked the dirty plates beside the dishpan. Less than twenty-four hours after arriving, the Kramer house felt like home. She wished she could stay, but Josh would eventually discover the truth, and she was not equipped to face his fury. She sensed a seething volcano beneath his cool veneer.

I wish Mama was here. She'd tell me what to do. Mama would first give her a strong admonishment for getting involved in the deception.

Then she would say, "Carrie, always be yourself. Never pretend to be someone you aren't. Deception will get you into trouble. According to the Good Book, it's no different from lying."

Aunt Em plunged a plate beneath the sudsy water, rinsed it, and handed it to her. "Looks like another hot day in Texas."

"Yes, ma'am." Carrie took the plate and wiped it.

"Anything in particular you need from town? If we have it here, you're welcome to it."

"No, but thank you anyway. There's something I need to attend to in town." The woman was so sweet, Carrie wanted to hug her. But that would make it more difficult to follow through with her plan.

"Well, if you don't mind my sayin' so, you don't seem too happy about goin'."

Carrie dried a spoon, keeping her eyes on it. "It's a . . . personal matter."

"All right. I won't pry. You two have a good time and don't feel a need to hurry back."

Was Aunt Em trying her hand at matchmaking? Good luck. Josh wanted nothing to do with her.

Josh's voice boomed through the screen door. "Horses are hitched and raring to go."

Carrie tied on her bonnet, patted Aunt Em's arm, and hurried out to join him.

After a silent hour-long ride, they entered the busiest part of Abilene. Dust kicked up as wagons rolled by and cowboys galloped past. Carrie scanned the businesses on either side of the street. Two saloons, a grocery store, a mercantile and a general store. The feed mill was just ahead.

She turned to Josh and asked, "Do you know where I can find a fashionable dress shop?" She preferred to work in a shop that carried the latest fashions like Rose Taylor's shop where she'd been employed.

FASHIONABLE DRESS SHOP? Josh had not considered Katy might be the highfalutin type, but he could be wrong. Well, she could have lofty ambitions as long as they didn't include him.

Josh reined in the horses at the feed mill. "I know of one. Wait here. I'll just be a few minutes."

She nodded but fidgeted with her fingers, as if she wanted to scramble off the buckboard and strike out on her own. He would not let that happen.

Josh helped the proprietor stack feed sacks onto the wagon, all the while keeping his eye on Katy. The town bustled with people, but it usually did on Saturday. Katy kept her seat, although she twisted this way and that to watch people cross the street and enter establishments.

Was she looking for someone? His jaw clenched. She would not meet with anyone without him present.

He paid the feed bill and climbed up beside her. "Aunt Em has a favorite dress shop up the street. I think there's another shop across the street." He had a distinct feeling these shops would not meet Katy's standards.

The dress Katy wore was stylish enough, although the material wasn't the best quality. It appeared to be fashioned from the muslin blend his aunt wore. Aunt Em used it to make dresses she wore around the house. For Sunday-go-to-meeting dresses, she used a better-quality fabric. He didn't recall the name of it.

Carrie pointed up ahead to the right. "That looks like the kind of dress shop I'm looking for. Pull in there, please."

Carina's Fashions? Josh had heard about the place. The shop carried top-of-the-line ladies' clothing and the merchandise was priced accordingly. If Katy could afford expensive dresses, why did she need a domestic job? He'd like to know her reasoning.

"Whoa!" He tugged on the reins. Katy laid a hand on his arm. Her emerald green eyes captured him. They could melt a man's heart if the man allowed it. He would not.

"Mr. Kramer, I'm sure you have other more pressing matters. If you will give me the directions to the mercantile, you can be on your way, and I'll meet you there in say . . . forty minutes."

On no, you don't. She was a slippery one, this Katy Davis, but she wouldn't get away from him

"Nothing too pressing. I think I'll join you." Her jaw dropped, but she said nothing. He could only guess what was running through her mind.

She managed a weak smile and flitted her lashes. "I would prefer to do this alone, if you don't mind."

I'll bet you would. "I do mind. I've been curious about this shop since it opened two years ago." Josh hopped down, walked around to her side of the wagon, and planted his booted feet in the dusty street."

Katy cleared her throat. "You will be uncomfortable in a ladies' boutique."

"I've never been in one, but it doesn't scare me in the least. Let's go." Josh grasped her tiny waist and swung her to the ground. He couldn't help noticing his fingers almost met around her middle. Taking her by the arm, he urged her up the steps and into the shop.

Josh reclined against the counter and watched Katy flit about, pulling dresses from racks, stroking the assorted fabrics and studying them, like she was a clothing inspector. Sometimes she held a dress up against her and studied her reflection in the free-standing mirror.

He yawned from boredom. Why did women take so long shopping? When he bought a suit of clothes, he traipsed into the store, asked the clerk for his size, then paid for it and left. It was that simple.

A middle-aged clerk with flame-colored hair pranced over to Katy. The woman wore a sleek, purple dress with a sheen to it. The dress was in a style he'd never seen. Katy looked up at her.

The woman pulled a shiny green dress from the rack and held it up against Katy. "May I assist you in selecting one of these lovely creations? This emerald green complements your complexion and eyes, plus its lines will flatter your shapely figure. Would you like to model it for your gentleman? This one is too large, but I'm sure we have your size in stock."

Katy blushed and shook her head. "No, thank you. I'm just looking."

The woman looked down her nose at Katy. "Then I will leave you to look." She pranced away in a huff.

Josh swaggered over to the rack where the clerk had replaced the dress. He picked up the price tag dangling from the sleeve and whistled under his breath. "You mean, you aren't buying this? Whew! I could buy a month's supply of feed for the price."

Katy scowled at him, whirled and tramped toward the exit. Josh followed her out. She stopped at the edge of the boardwalk and turned to face him. Her narrowed eyes and arms folded across her midsection warned him he'd carried his jesting too far.

Ignoring her irritation, he asked, "Where do you want to go now?"

She swung around, putting her back to him. Her words sounded forced. "Wherever *you* want to go."

Josh squelched a smile. Katy was a sassy little thing. "The only stop I have left is the mercantile."

"Then, by all means, let's go." She traipsed down the steps to the buckboard. Before he could assist her, she was seated. He walked around the wagon and hopped up, taking hold of the reins while she meticulously arranged her skirt. He clucked to the horses and off they went.

At Gossum's Mercantile, Josh set the basket on the counter and gave Aunt Em's order to the proprietor's wife. The old woman's gaze traveled from him to Katy. He stifled a groan. Agatha Gossum was known for starting rumors, even embellishing them.

"Who is the young lady?" she whispered when Katy had disappeared down an aisle.

"Someone I hired to help Aunt Em around the house."

"I see. She's not from these parts, is she?"

"No." When Josh didn't provide more information, she flitted about to fill the order.

Josh scanned the store and saw Katy in the far corner fingering a bolt of shiny, pink fabric. She unwound a length and stroked the material, caressing it between her fingers. The longing in her eyes tore at his heart.

He walked over to peruse the rose material sprinkled with tiny blue flowers. "It's pretty."

Katy shrugged and rewound the fabric around the bolt. Without a word, she headed down the canned goods aisle, probably avoiding him. Josh didn't understand it, but he wanted her to have a dress made from that fabric. Maybe he felt a smidgen of guilt for humiliating her at that stylish dress shop up the street.

Aunt Em had a treadle sewing machine. Katy could stitch herself a dress in her spare time. Even if she had ulterior motives for coming to the ranch, she deserved something.

He walked to the front and gestured for Mrs. Gossum to follow him to the fabric and notions corner. Tugging off his hat, he scratched his head. "How many yards does it take to make a lady's dress?"

Mrs. Gossum worked her mouth in thought. "Well, it depends

on the size of the woman and how full she wants the skirt. For your aunt, six yards is plenty."

He thumbed toward the aisle where he'd last seen Katy and whispered, "What about for the young lady who came in with me?"

The old lady's thin eyebrows rose. Her eyes glinted, and a smile tugged at her lips. "Ah, I see. Is she your . . . intended?"

Heat seared Josh's face. He must look a sight blushing, being a grown man. "No, of course not. I told you, I hired her to help Aunt Em with household chores." He cleared his throat and pointed to the bolt of fabric Katy had mooned over. "Cut off enough yardage to make her a dress, and I'll pay for it. I can deduct it from her first paycheck." He wouldn't, but stating it should silence the old biddie.

Mrs. Gossum pulled her lips into a smirk. "Oh. I see."

Josh didn't believe her for a second. The minute he was gone, she would start spreading the gossip all over town that Josh Kramer was headed to the altar.

Mrs. Gossum unwound the bolt. "Four and a half yards should be sufficient. She won't need nearly as much as your aunt."

He nodded. "Measure off enough to make the dress with some to spare." You never knew when a woman might make a miss-lick with the scissors. Or Katy might want to make a drawstring purse, a belt, or a ribbon to tie in her hair with the leftovers.

Mrs. Gossum measured the material and made a clean cut. She laid the scissors aside and flitted her lashes. "She will also need thread and possibly blue lace to accessorize the dress."

He threw up a hand. "Get whatever she might need, and I'll pay for it."

The clerk selected two spools of pink thread, unrolled one across the material, and eyed it. "Hmm." She repeated the procedure with the other thread, a lighter shade. She tapped the darker spool. "I believe this one is the better match."

Josh whooshed out a breath. Mrs. Gossum's method seemed to be a lot of ado about nothing. What did it matter if the thread was a shade off? Wouldn't the stitches be hidden? He wished the clerk would just wrap the fabric before Katy reappeared. He wanted to surprise her later.

After Mrs. Gossum dropped the thread and lace in a small bag, she wrapped the fabric in brown paper. Above her protests, Josh insisted she place the wrapped parcel in the basket first and arrange the grocery items on top.

"But these items will wrinkle the pretty fabric," she argued. Relenting she added, "But as they say, the customer is always right." She handed him the sack with the thread and lace. "I hope your—the young lady—enjoys her new dress."

Josh stuffed the sack in his pocket, flashing her a toothy smile. "I'm sure she will."

"So am I. You make a lovely couple, if you don't mind my saying so."

He did, but out of respect for his elders, Josh put up no argument. What good would it do? Mrs. Gossum would think what she wanted, regardless. Then she'd spread it all over town.

Josh walked up one aisle and down the other. Where was Katy? The bell above the door tinkled. He looked toward the front in time to see her retreating back through the window.

He headed to the front to pick up his basket. Mrs. Gossum cut her eyes toward the door. "Mr. Kramer, your young lady just left."

His young lady? *I don't think so.* "Thank you. Have a wonderful day." He hefted the basket onto his shoulder and stepped out on the boardwalk. Katy was already in the buckboard.

He set the basket behind her in the wagon and climbed aboard, grunting as he picked up the reins. Turning to her, he grinned. "Mrs. Gossum said you and I make a lovely couple."

Katy squared her chin and focused on the road. "Oh, really?"

Josh swallowed hard. He didn't blame Katy for being upset. He'd dogged her from store to store. But was she trying to tell him that a rancher was beneath her standards? Did she think Mrs. Gossum's pairing them was silly? Regardless of what she thought, a woman who worked as domestic help shouldn't set her sights too high, even if she was pretty.

A dull pain stabbed at his heart. Why did her rejection bother him? Because his pride had been hurt? That had to be it. He couldn't possibly have feelings for Katy Davis.

He still couldn't figure her out. What did she stand to gain by answering his aunt's ad? Why would a pretty young woman take the train all the way from Arkansas to west Texas to obtain a domestic job?

Katy said she wasn't looking for a husband. Maybe that was true. What if she was looking for a rich man? Josh wasn't rich by any means, but the ranch was a large spread, and it provided him and his aunt with a decent living.

Josh clucked to the horses, and they fell into an easy canter. The clues didn't add up. What or who was Katy looking for in town? She had done everything within her power to get rid of him when they reached that fancy dress shop.

But he'd outsmarted her. She hadn't fooled him. The woman was up to something, and he would get to the bottom of it.

If Katy Davis had her sights set on the Kramer ranch, she'd better think again.

Chapter Four

Would the return trip to the ranch never end? Katy faced forward, her back straight and her lips set in a firm, thin line. Silence ensued. Josh glanced up when a red-tailed hawk screeched, emitting the only sound besides the clop-clop of the horses' hooves.

Katy was upset because he had interfered with her plans. He suspected matrimony was her intent. Why or how she planned to snare him, he didn't know. But he'd fight to protect his own and what rightly belonged to him. That meant Aunt Em and the ranch.

And he'd see that Katy kept her end of the bargain with his aunt. He'd paid her train fare from Arkansas to Abilene to help Aunt Em with household chores. No one would take advantage of his sweet aunt. Not even this young lady with the angelic face and hair the color of corn silk.

How could a woman who looked the picture of innocence have a devious heart?

Yet if Katy was after marriage, why hadn't she already made a play for him? She'd barely looked his way, much less batted those long lashes at him. He might not be the handsomest cowboy in town, but she could do a lot worse, considering the ones he'd seen.

Another thing puzzled Josh. Katy shopped in two stores and

walked out with no purchases. Could it be he had detained her from sending a telegram to some man she was in cahoots with?

Halfway back to the ranch, he broke the silence. "What do think of Abilene so far?"

Katy shrugged. "It's a bustling town from what I can tell. Plenty of places to shop."

That was a good start. At least she was speaking to him again. "I noticed you didn't buy anything. Couldn't find what you wanted?"

She averted her gaze, exhaled a long breath. "I need to watch my spending until . . ."

Until what? If Josh didn't suspect she was a schemer, he might feel sorry for her. He readjusted his hat. "When you get paid at the end of the month, you'll have a little spending money."

She turned to face him, her eyes flashing. "Mr. Kramer, I couldn't!"

"Josh," he corrected her. "'You couldn't what?"

"I couldn't accept payment for helping your aunt. You've already given me a roof over my head, a comfortable bed, and three square meals. That is more than enough."

Incredible. Katy almost had him believing in her innocence. Almost. "Nevertheless, you will be paid for your work. Did Aunt Em discuss a salary with you?"

CARRIE SHIFTED IN HER SEAT. Josh eyed her, waiting for an answer. Katy Davis and his aunt had likely discussed a salary in their correspondence, but Aunt Em had not mentioned it since she'd arrived. What should she say?

Carrie forced herself to appear calm under his gaze. "I'll leave that up to you and your aunt. Like I said, room and board are more than enough payment."

Josh frowned. What was he thinking? Had she said something

that aroused his suspicions? She wiped clammy hands down the sides of her skirt.

"Like I said, you will be paid the wages Aunt Em agreed to."

If Josh hadn't followed her inside the dress shop, she might have gotten a job there. With luck, she'd have found a good boarding house and moved out of Josh Kramer's place this afternoon. But that was not to be. The tall, handsome cowboy stayed on her heels. He hadn't given her a chance to talk privately with anyone, much less the proprietor.

Josh was trailing her. And she didn't like it. Did he think she was a thief, that she would steal a fancy dress from Carina's shop? Or that she would pocket an item or two from Gossum's mercantile? The shimmery pink fabric sprinkled with baby blue flowers had caught her eye, but it would have to wait.

Why didn't he just come out and accuse her? He'd stuck to her like a tick to a dog. When he wasn't breathing down her neck, he was no more than a holler away.

Carrie decided to give him a dose of his own medicine. "You insisted on following me to the dress shop. I noticed you didn't buy anything either. The only time you looked at the merchandise was when you swooned over the price tag on the emerald silk dress."

He'd kept his eye on her and still watched her. She squirmed under his dark gaze like a jackrabbit caught in the sights of a rifle. It was as if he could read her thoughts.

"No, I didn't buy anything." He clapped a hand to his face, arched his back, and spoke in a high falsetto voice. "Carina didn't have a single dress in her store that flattered my figure."

Carrie giggled in spite of herself. Still, she sobered enough to ask, "Why did you come inside? I'm sure it wasn't because you enjoy my company."

He studied her and asked his own question. "Miss Davis, why did you really come here?"

Carrie swallowed around the lump in her throat. "I thought

you knew. Wasn't it your idea to hire domestic help?" She'd learned a few evasive tricks from dealing with her brother.

He shook his head. "Yes, but something isn't right. I can't quite put my finger on it."

Had she said something to arouse Josh's suspicions? Carrie turned her head, averting her gaze to the yellow wildflowers growing in a field on her side of the road. She'd already seen blue ones, orange ones, and now yellow ones resembling daisies.

Time to change the subject. "Aren't the wildflowers pretty?"

If Josh knew the whole truth, two people would be upset with her. Josh and his aunt. Aunt Em also shared in the blame, and Carrie was determined to not get her in hot water.

"Yes, they are. Now, back on topic." Josh popped his hat off and tugged it back down low on his forehead. "Something has puzzled me since we left the depot yesterday. Your first words after I set you on the buckboard were, 'Mr. Kramer, I am not looking for a husband.' Why did you say that?" His searing gaze demanded the truth.

"Because I'm not." That was simple enough. Now, if only she could make him believe her.

"If you thought I might become . . . attracted to you, then you flatter yourself, Miss Davis."

Josh's cynical tone hurt as much as his words. She bit her tongue to keep from lashing out, *Well, you aren't the most handsome man in these parts yourself.*

That could be a lie. He might very well be if attitude didn't count. With a ten in looks and a zero in attitude, he'd still flunk with a five average. She stifled a grin and cleared her throat. "I didn't consider what you were thinking."

He narrowed his eyes, focused them on her face. "Let's get something straight right now."

Carrie held his gaze, forcing herself not to blink. He was waiting for her to prod him with another question. "And what would that be?"

"You made a bargain with my aunt and with me. It's as binding as a contract, to my way of thinking. I expect you to keep your end of it. At least for a year. I think that's fair enough to ask."

Josh's words rendered Carrie speechless. She wanted to yell, "Katy Davis made that deal! Not me!"

Her plan to find a job in town just got thwarted. She was stuck in this deception whether she liked it or not. But she would like to know she had a means of support in case Josh discovered she wasn't the woman who replied to his aunt's ad. Because if that happened, he would toss her out, along with her valise. Maybe she'd better let sleeping dogs lie for now and settle into life at his ranch.

Or she could tell him the truth now, but where would she go? She could not return to Denton. Jim Counce would be waiting to get his revenge. And the sheriff could be looking for her. She didn't even know if Big Jim was alive. What if his neck had broken or he'd cracked his skull when she'd shoved him off the boardwalk? Even if she wanted to go back, she didn't have the train fare.

"Miss Davis, did you hear me?"

He insisted she call him "Josh," yet he persisted in calling her "Miss Davis." She supposed she should be thankful for that much civility. "Yes, I heard you."

"Then do you agree that committing to one year is fair?"

"It sounds fair." What choice did she have with only a few coins to rub together? She would settle into ranch living, make the best of the situation until he uncovered the truth. No one around here knew her. She should be safe.

After thirty more minutes of pressing silence, they pulled into the yard. Josh reined in the team near the porch to let her out before he drove them into the barn.

Carrie found Aunt Em at the stove stirring something that smelled delicious. The older woman wiped her brow without turning to face her. "What do you think of Abilene?"

"It's a booming place. Lots of businesses."

"Did you accomplish what you went for?"

"No." Carrie dropped her handbag on the table. She did not

want to be reminded of the way Josh had shadowed her. She scanned the kitchen. "What can I do to help?"

Aunt Em waved her stirring spoon. "You can peel those tomatoes and set the table."

AFTER JOSH WATERED THE HORSES, he picked up a brush and began to stroke one of them. Was he too hard on Katy? His conscience twinged, and he regretted the harsh tone and words he'd used. Could he have pegged her wrong by accusing her of looking for a husband? Was it possible she'd said it to keep him from getting notions about her? He had let his bad experience with another woman—namely Leah—warp his view of the fair sex in general.

The Good Book said, in so many words, to give others the benefit of the doubt. It didn't require him to be Katy's best friend, but he could show her his good side. Then she would believe that he could be polite and gracious. She'd get nothing more, or she'd get the notion he had a romantic interest in her.

Yes, he would do it. And he would continue the polite treatment until or unless she gave him good reason to suspect her of something underhanded.

Josh glanced at the box still in the wagon. The fabric he'd bought for Katy lay beneath Aunt Em's grocery items. Following his harsh words, now would not be a good time to present it to her.

Heat crept up his neck, burning his face. What had he been thinking when he bought that fabric?

He walked to the buckboard and slid the wrapped package out from beneath the groceries. Where could he hide it until he mustered enough courage to give it to her? He mentally scanned the barn for a place where neither Katy nor his aunt would find it.

His grandmother's old trunk was pushed in one corner in the loft. Katy wouldn't be likely to climb up there. Aunt Em hadn't been in the loft since rheumatism struck her joints a decade ago. And it wasn't likely Katy had any reason to snoop around up there either.

Josh climbed the ladder and tramped through the loose hay to the old trunk. Its rusty hinges creaked when he lifted the lid. He laid the fabric in the bottom part and dropped the thread and package of lace into a small compartment above before closing the lid. No one would find the fabric, and when the timing was right, he would give it to Katy.

He could drop a few hints, find out when her birthday was. If it was within the next few months, he'd have a good excuse to give her a present without her getting other ideas. The material would be from him and Aunt Em. Katy would be none the wiser, and his pride would be spared.

Smiling at his brilliant idea, Josh descended the ladder, picked up the basket of groceries, and strode toward the house. The food was on the table when he entered the kitchen. He set the basket on the counter and lifted the water pot to the stove.

Picking up the soap, he started washing his hands. "Luke and I are going to check fence lines this afternoon. We're missing five head of cattle. My guess is a post is laid over somewhere. We'll round up the strays, herd them back in, and mend the fence. I don't know how late I'll be. I'll eat and head out."

Aunt Em clucked her tongue. "You need to slow down young'un. Eatin' too fast can sour the food in your stomach."

On the way to the table Josh stopped and kissed his aunt's cheek. "It can't be helped. A ranch doesn't run itself."

He sat down at the table, muttered a quick blessing, and gobbled down his food. Katy and Aunt Em were talking about some chore yet to be done, but he paid little attention. Five minutes later, he rose and tugged on his hat. When he'd adjusted it on his head, he nodded at Aunt Em and Katy. "See you ladies tonight."

The screen door slapped shut behind him.

CARRIE WATCHED through the window as Josh mounted his horse. Was he really in that big of a hurry? If he'd had so much to do around the ranch, why hadn't he let her drive herself into town? She could hitch horses to a wagon without help from him or anyone. And she certainly hadn't needed him tagging along to every store.

Aunt Em turned to Carrie. "When we get these dishes washed, I want you to help me do some fall cleaning. I've put it off far too long. Josh doesn't have the time, and I have trouble with my back. If you'll help me roll up the rug in the living room, I'd like to hang it on the clothesline and beat the daylights out of it. When the dust is beat out of that one, we can beat the smaller ones."

The ladies rolled up the area rug and dragged it out the back door. It took several attempts to throw the cumbersome thing over the clothesline. When they finally did, both Carrie and Aunt Em were out of breath.

Carrie placed her hand over her heart and gasped, "Aunt Em . . . why . . . don't you let . . . me beat this rug . . . and the others? You mentioned . . . you needed to sort beans . . . and get them on the stove."

Aunt Em panted. "Well . . . considerin' there's only . . . one broom, I'll . . . take you up . . . on your offer." She limped toward the house, rubbing her lower back.

With every smack of the broom, dust fogged. Carrie coughed and fanned it away. She paused to get her breath and to let the dust settle. Beating rugs was a big chore, but she'd done it plenty of times. Most of the time, alone. Blake was usually off gallivanting.

She should blame him for her predicament. If her brother hadn't broken his promise, she wouldn't have gone to town that night. Today, right about now, she would be making a dress on her sewing machine at Rose Johnson's Dressmaker's shop.

Carrie whacked the rug. Rugs worked well to take out frustrations. "Take that, Blake Franklin!"

Raising the broom again, she said, "Mr. Kramer, you have no idea what I've been through. You weren't there. Take that and smoke it in your pipe, Josh Kramer."

She swatted the rug with such force, the clothesline swung back and forth. She waited until it stilled and struck the rug again. "You know nothing about me. You have a wonderful aunt who cares for you. She keeps your house and cooks for you. You've never had to scratch for every penny or had to raise a rebellious younger brother. And you still have a mother. I don't have either a mother or a father."

Tears stung her eyes. She swung the broom a third time. "You have no right to make me feel like . . . like I'm nothing. I'm as good as you are, even if I don't own any worldly possessions."

Carrie paused. "One more thing I'd like to get straight. I didn't ask to come to your ranch. If you'd given me half a chance to explain instead of tossing me on your buckboard . . ."

She whacked the rug again and grabbed her aching wrist. "Ow!" She dropped the broom. The last wisp of dust had already been beaten from it anyway.

Trudging toward the back steps, she became short of breath. Had she lost her mind? What had come over her? She could no longer keep the anger bottled.

The Good Book said to forgive others if you wanted God's forgiveness. Carrie closed her eyes. "Lord, I'm trying, but sometimes I get so angry! I'm mad at my brother, mad at Mama and Papa for leaving Blake and me alone. And now I'm mad at Josh Kramer."

If only she'd inherited her mama's calm disposition. But she'd taken after Papa, who was quick to get riled. She folded her arms across her lap and laid her head across her knees, weeping until her tears were spent. Then she sat up and wiped away the last vestiges.

She must look a sight. What would Aunt Em think if she saw her red-rimmed eyes? And what if she had witnessed her fit? She twisted, peered through the screen door. A shadow flitted across it.

No longer angry with Josh or her brother, Carrie exhaled.

Whether she'd truly forgiven them, she couldn't say. She might just be too exhausted to get upset.

How had her life gotten out of control? If only she hadn't gone to the saloon and scuffled with Big Jim, she wouldn't be hiding out somewhere far from home.

Could the law track her to Buffalo Gap? If Big Jim hadn't recovered, the sheriff might have sent a posse to search for her.

She would check for her picture on the wanted posters the next time she went to town. Carrie shuddered at the mental image of her sketched picture tacked to the post office wall.

Chapter Five

J osh tramped into the kitchen just before sundown. Katy flitted from the cupboard to the table and back, setting glasses and silverware at each place. Light on her feet, her fluid movements were similar to a waltz. He'd bet she was a graceful dancer.

He mentally kicked himself for the harsh words he'd spoken earlier. She must think him a brute. He would prove to her he could be a gentleman.

Stepping behind Aunt Em's chair, Josh pulled it out, and bowed with a flourish. "Have a seat, Aunt Em." When she was seated, he scooted her up to the table.

"Why, thank you, sweetie. You're such a gentleman." She patted his hand, beaming up at him.

Katy set the bowl of tomatoes on the table in a vacant spot. Josh hurried around to take his place behind her chair. She gave him a dubious look, twisting her lips to one side.

He gestured with his hand. "May I seat you, Miss Davis?"

She hesitated. "I-I can seat myself, but thank you."

"Oh, come on, Katy," Aunt Em coaxed. "Let Josh play the part of a gentleman."

She relented, and Josh pulled the chair back and waited until she was seated. When he slid her up to the table, a lock of her golden hair brushed against his hand. He'd never dreamed hair could feel so silky. He fought the urge to caress the strands between his fingers.

After Josh asked the blessing, Aunt Em passed him the peas. "Did you two enjoy your trip into town? Where all did you go?"

Josh scooped out some peas. "We made a stop at the feed mill, a dress shop, and the mercantile. Then we headed home."

Aunt Em clucked her tongue. "Exactly what you'd expect a man to say. Katy, let's hear your version."

She shrugged. "There isn't much else to tell."

A furrow formed on his aunt's brow. "Neither of you has much to say tonight. Which dress shop did you visit, Katy?"

Katy shifted in her chair, probably recalling the ordeal she'd gone through trying to lose him.

"I think it was called Carina's Fashions."

"Whew! Only well-to-do ladies shop there. It carries fancy dresses from what I've heard, but they come with a hefty price tag."

Katy ducked her chin. then looked up. "I didn't go there to buy. I like to check out the latest fashions. You see, I enjoy making my own clothes. I browse the nice shops to get ideas of the latest styles."

So that was why she insisted on going to Carina's. Maybe Katy wasn't ambitious after all. It still didn't explain why she'd tried to lose him.

Aunt Em laid down her fork. "That's wonderful. I didn't know you had a talent for sewing. You never mentioned it in your letters. Would you be willing to make a dress or two for me? I have a sewing machine in my bedroom." She shook her head. "I'm fair at sewing but I don't enjoy it."

Katy's green eyes sparkled, and she bubbled with excitement. "You have a sewing machine? I'd love to make you a dress. Do you have any fabric?"

"No, but the first chance we get, we will ride into town and I'll buy some. I'll get you enough fabric for a dress too. It'll be your pay for makin' mine."

Katy touched her arm. "There's no need for that. You've already done enough. I haven't earned my keep as it is."

"Nonsense. You slaved over those cannin' jars in a hot kitchen, all afternoon. Besides, young ladies ought to have pretty clothes."

Katy's face beamed. "We can choose the fabric together. When do you think we can go?"

Aunt Em sighed. "Probably not this comin' week. We'll be cannin' peppers and airin' out the bedding."

That's just great. If the ladies rode into town, Katy might buy the same fabric he'd bought for her. The way Josh saw it, he had two choices. Give Katy the fabric before she went to town or tag along with the women. And no way was he doing that. A groan escaped his throat.

Aunt Em squinted at him. "What's wrong with you, boy? Are we boring you?"

Josh rolled his eyes. "You ladies and your fashion talk. A man goes into a store. He asks for a shirt and a pair of pants in his sizes. The clerk takes the items off the shelf, wraps them, and hands him the package. It's that simple. He's ready to go about his business. He pays no mind to whether the clothes are in style. As long as they are comfortable, he's as happy as a lark."

"You can't begin to grasp the workings of a woman's mind, young man. No use tryin' to."

Josh slid his gaze to Katy. "Yep, it's all a mystery to me."

"We wouldn't want to send Josh to the mercantile to pick out our fabric," his aunt teased. "He'd likely come back with burlap."

Josh screwed up his face. "What's wrong with burlap? It's perfectly durable. And you could cinch the waist with grass string to give it shape. I have some in the barn if you want it."

Katy giggled. He liked the musical trill to her voice.

Aunt Em piped in. "Can you imagine how burlap would chafe our arms and legs? We'd have to use horse salve on the raw spots."

Katy had taken a sip of her drink. She covered her mouth to

stop it from spewing out. She managed to swallow it, then broke into a giggling fit. It was contagious. Aunt Em started to cackle, and before Josh knew it, he had joined them.

Aunt Em and Katy continued discussing fabric, patterns, lace, and buttons throughout supper. Josh grinned at their barely contained excitement. His aunt looked happier than he'd seen her in a long time. Her glowing face made him feel warm inside.

He reluctantly admitted that Katy was the one responsible for the cheerful atmosphere.

WHEN THE MEAL WAS OVER, Josh set the heavy water pot on the stove. "I'll go chop some firewood. The pile is getting low."

"You go right ahead, hon. Katy and I will do the dishes."

While Carrie stacked the dirty plates, Aunt Em said, "Sweetie, tomorrow is Sunday. I don't know what you're accustomed, but we go to church."

Carrie sighed. "We almost never missed while our parents were alive, but I haven't been to church since . . ." *Mama died.*

She bit her tongue. Aunt Em was so easy to talk to that Carrie was tempted to spill the beans. But she was playing a role. If she said too much, Josh would demand she pack her things and leave. The more she revealed, the more chance that it would happen.

Katy Davis's mother died when she was seven, while Carrie's mother was killed in an accident five years ago. Why couldn't she keep the story straight?

Picking up the dishrag, Aunt Em slanted her gaze sideways. "You said 'our parents.' You never mentioned a brother or sister in your letters. I got the impression you were an only child."

The woman didn't miss a thing. Since Carrie had already said more than she'd meant to, it wouldn't hurt to tell Josh's aunt a few of her worries. "I have a brother two years younger. I've tried to look out for him like I promised Mama I would. But he's nineteen now and has been rebellious since he turned fifteen. He never stays home and he mixes with a rough crowd."

"'Bad company corrupts good character.' I'll pray for your brother."

"Thank you."

"A lot of young men go through a wild stage. Josh never was inclined to join the wrong crowd. He's more of a homebody. Took that after his pa."

"You were lucky."

"No, we were blessed. Both Josh's father and mother were strong in the faith. They trained him in the admonition of the Lord. Plus, we prayed for him to make the right choices. I still do."

Carrie dried the last piece of silverware and handed it to Aunt Em. The screen door slammed behind Josh. He clomped across the floor and dropped an armload of wood in the box beside the stove. Brushing the debris from his shirt, he said, "That should keep you for a while."

A dark curl spiraled across his glistening forehead. Carrie fought the impulse to push it back in place. Flushed cheeks made his dark eyes look darker. Carrie couldn't pull her gaze away. My, he was handsome!

He held her gaze. "Miss Davis, may I have a glass of water, please?"

"Of course." Carrie's hand shook as she reached into the cupboard for a glass and tilted the dipper to fill it. "It should be cool."

He gulped down half of it before pausing for a breath. Then he upended the glass and drained it.

"You were thirsty. Want me to fill it again?"

He extended the glass "Yes, please."

Their fingers touched, sending ripples of warmth up her arm. The gleam in Josh's eyes told her he'd felt it too.

Aunt Em grunted. "Katy, we have a good selection of books in the study, if you like to read."

"Thank you. I do enjoy a good book. Do you have any classics?"

"Right this way." Josh motioned for her to follow him.

Books lined the floor-to-ceiling shelves on either side of the stone fireplace. Carrie scanned the titles, searching for a mystery.

He gestured with his hand. "You're welcome to take as many as you wish. Help yourself."

Carrie's gaze fell on a title. She pulled it from a shelf above. "*The Law and The Lady*. I've heard this is an intriguing detective story."

Josh's brow furrowed. "What's it about?"

"A man accused of killing his first wife."

"Did he do it?"

"I don't know. His second wife tries to prove his innocence. My friend Sophie read it. I wouldn't let her tell me the ending because it spoils the story for me."

Carrie walked from the study to the kitchen where Aunt Em was removing her apron. "May I be excused? I am a bit tired. I'd like to retire to my room to read."

Aunt Em smiled. "Of course you may, dear."

A WAVE of disappointment washed over Josh as Katy lit the lantern in her bedroom and closed the door behind her. He'd hoped she would join them on the porch. Not that he was interested in her. He just needed to learn what made her tick. A man ought not to take chances with a stranger in his home.

"Josh." Aunt Em snapped her fingers near his nose.

He blinked. "Yes?"

She propped her hands on her ample hips. "I called your name twice. Where was your mind?"

He glanced toward Katy's bedroom. Where had his mind been?

"I asked if you wanted to sit on the porch for a spell, where it's cool."

"I suppose." He'd started to mention it after supper. Without Katy, the idea had lost its appeal.

"Well, don't sound so excited."

Josh followed his aunt to the porch. A loose board creaked beneath his feet as he sank down in the swing beside her. He would remedy the noisy board when he got a slow day.

His aunt wasted no time speaking. "Did you find where the cattle were gettin' out?"

"Uh-huh. Two posts were laid over on the fence line where our ranch borders the Donovans'. The posts showed no rot, so we reset them. That should hold for a while." He sighed. "We rounded up the strays. They hadn't gotten far."

"Good. I'm glad you found them."

They were silent for a moment, enjoying a light breeze and gazing up at the clear, starlit sky. Katydids and tree frogs turned the humid September night into a cacophonous orchestra.

Aunt Em exhaled. "I saw somethin' this afternoon that about broke my heart."

"What?" Whatever it was, Katy had to be involved. And it probably wasn't good.

"I felt so sorry for Katy. We dragged the living room rug outside and hung it on the clothesline."

Josh glowered. "I told you I'd get Luke to help me do that when we got a slow day. I don't want you hurting yourself."

"Katy and I made it fine. She offered to beat the rug, so I handed her the broom and went back inside. As I was puttin' the beans on to cook, I heard a loud holler. I walked to the window and saw her beatin' the daylights out of the rug. She was yellin' at it like it was somebody who'd hurt her and she was gettin' revenge."

Somebody like me? He didn't think his barely-disguised insults had hurt her that much. "Could you hear what she was saying?"

"The only words I could make out were, 'You have no idea what I've been through!' When she didn't come back inside soon afterward, I looked out the back door. Wouldn't you know it? The poor little girl was sittin' on the back stoop, her head in her lap and bawlin' her eyes out.

"Something's bothering her and it breaks my heart 'cause I

can't help her. I don't want to pry, but I wish I knew who or what hurt Katy to the point she had a nervous breakdown."

Guilt weighed heavy on Josh's heart. He was partly responsible for Katy's emotional state. Not knowing how vulnerable she was, he'd as good as called her a gold digger.

He hadn't considered her feelings or taken the time to get to know her. Instead, he'd jumped the gun and passed judgment without any solid evidence. Common sense should have told him she wasn't a schemer. She neither looked nor acted the part.

Still, Katy seemed to be hiding something. She offered no information about herself unless asked.

After their trip to town, he had decided to give her the benefit of the doubt. If he had treated her with more kindness when she first arrived, this might not have happened. And she might have revealed more about herself. Aunt Em always said, "You draw more flies with honey than vinegar." Why not take the lid off the honey jar and see what transpired?

Josh stood. "I'm going to turn in for the night. Sleep well." He bent to kiss his aunt's cheek. "Are you coming inside?"

"No, I'll sit out here in the peace and quiet for a spell. Good night. And don't forget, tomorrow is Sunday."

"How could I?" He rubbed his midsection. "That means flap-jacks for breakfast. Yum!"

She shook her head. "Boy, all you think about is eatin'."

Josh winked. "Is there anything better?"

Aunt Em swatted at his arm, but he dodged. Chuckling, Josh ducked inside the house. Would Katy go to church with them? If he pulled up with her on the buckboard, folks would try to tie them together.

Well, he would set them straight first, before the whispering started.

"CARE FOR ANOTHER FLAPJACK?" Aunt Em offered the plate to Carrie.

"No, thank you. I couldn't eat another bite. I've already had two. I'm not sure I can finish this third one. But they are delicious."

"I'll take it." Josh extended his plate, and Aunt Em forked Carrie's leftover flapjack onto it.

"Why am I not surprised? How many does this make?"

"Only my fifth. I'm a growing boy."

"I've heard that excuse before. Coming from a twenty-six-year-old, it don't hold water."

Carrie rose. "Are you through with your plate, Aunt Em?"

When she nodded, Carrie stacked it on top of hers and took the dishes to the sink.

"Just let 'em soak, hon. We'll wash them after church. Right now we need to be gettin' dressed. It's a fairly long drive."

"Yes, ma'am." Carrie poured hot water over the dishes, refilled the kettle, and set it on the back burner.

Josh slid his chair back. "Aunt Em, do you have an extra bar of that French-milled soap? I think I'll go down to the creek and wash."

Aunt Em rose. "In your bedroom. I laid a bar on your dresser."

"I'll excuse myself to get dressed too." Carrie hurried to her room. She poured the warm water into the pretty washbowl and dunked the washcloth. Aunt Em had given her a special bar of French-milled soap also. When she rubbed the washcloth across it, a lavender scent filled the air.

Late yesterday afternoon Carrie asked about bathing, and Aunt Em pointed her to a winding creek that ran a short distance behind the house. She'd taken the soap and a towel along and enjoyed a refreshing dip. The water had been cool as it washed away the Texas dust.

The back door slammed, breaking into her reverie. Someone was whistling outside her window. She pulled the curtain aside to take a peek and smiled. Josh skipped along toward the creek, juggling a bar of soap as he whistled, *Nothing But The Blood Of Jesus.*

She giggled. He'd been a different person this morning. Why had he started being nice to her? Had he decided she was not a conniving woman after all?

If only she deserved his respect. Guilt dampened her spirits. How would this change affect their relationship? Keeping her heart closed was easier when Josh acted cool and aloof. Now she would have to work to protect it. She couldn't afford to fall for him when she was here under false pretenses.

She pulled on a sea green dress with a scalloped neckline. Sprinkled with tiny white flowers, the bodice fit snugly. The shimmering skirt flowed gracefully from the bustle to her ankles, swishing as she moved. Carrie gathered her hair at the nape of her neck with a strip of fabric she'd made from the leftover dress material.

JOSH HELPED his aunt climb onto the buckboard. She slid to the middle, leaving room for Carrie at the other end. When Aunt Em was settled, he turned to Carrie. "That's a pretty dress."

Her face grew hot. "Thank you." Carrie took it as approval when Josh's eyes sparkled as he lifted her to the buckboard. She still felt the warmth from his hands after they left her waist. She inhaled and tried to redirect her thoughts.

Aunt Em fingered Carrie's dress sleeve. "I agree. Your dress is very pretty. Did you make it?"

"Yes. I make all my dresses." She touched her hair tie. "I made this from the scraps."

"Pretty. The matching tie adds a touch of class."

Josh climbed aboard. "You ladies ready to head out?"

When his aunt nodded, he clicked to the horses and shook the reins. As they rolled along, Aunt Em described people Carrie might see at church. One was Nancy Grady. "I'll introduce you to her. You'll like her. Nancy has a sweet disposition. You two are around the same age and size. Her hair is darker than yours. The Grady ranch is only three miles west. Maybe I'll invite Nancy over for supper soon. I know you'll want to make new friends. They keep life from gettin' dull."

Josh groaned. "Katy might prefer to select her own friends."

Aunt Em raised her chin and sniffed. "I'm only trying to help." Turning to Carrie she said, "Josh calls me a busybody because I like to see to it folks are happy. Making folks happy makes me happy."

Josh flapped the reins. "Some folks might be happier left alone."

His aunt huffed. "That's what you always say."

Apparently this was an ongoing discussion between aunt and nephew. The best thing Carrie could do was stay quiet and let them work it out.

She hadn't had the time or energy to make friends back home. Taking over her mother's duties and working at the dress shop while keeping her brother out of trouble had drained Carrie. To change the subject, she gestured at the wildflowers growing along the road. "Aren't they beautiful?"

"They most certainly are," Aunt Em agreed and added, "And they had a little help. They didn't get there on their own. The Lord may have made the seed, but sunshine and rain made them flourish."

Carrie looked at Josh. While Aunt Em built a defense for herself, he had drifted off into a world of his own, ignoring every implication. She guessed from listening to their banter that Aunt Em was a practiced matchmaker, whether for friendship or romance. The letters to Katy Davis were proof.

Aunt Em's heart was in the right place, making it hard to find fault with her. She had embraced Carrie with open arms the moment they met. For the first time since her parents' death, Carrie felt safe and protected, like a part of a family. If only it were true.

Aunt Em had used trickery in her letters to Katy to make the young woman believe she would meet her prospective husband at the train depot in Abilene. At the same time, she'd told Josh the ad was for live-in domestic help.

If Carrie wasn't caught in this conglomerated stew, she'd find her situation laughable.

It hadn't been easy raising a brother born with a wild streak. Papa and Mama worried about Blake, even when he was a child. Blake liked to take risks and never backed down from a dare. One evening while Carrie sat on the porch swing with her mother, her mother was unusually quiet. After a moment, she laid a hand on Carrie's arm. "Will you make me a promise?"

"Of course, Mama. What is it?" She couldn't have guessed her mother's next words.

"If something ever happens to your Pa and me, will you raise Blake and keep him out of trouble? I fear he's headed down a destructive path although we've spent hours on our knees praying for him. The boy's got a good heart. It's his wild streak that worries me."

That was five years ago. A few months later, their parents died. Had Carrie let her mother down by running away? She'd reached her wit's end. She'd tried to stop Blake from drinking, gambling, and associating with saloon girls. Oh, how she'd tried!

But, Blake wouldn't listen. He came and went as he pleased and did whatever he pleased, regardless of her attempts to stop him. When Blake was younger, he'd argue, "You aren't my mama. I don't have to mind you." After he turned sixteen, he would laugh, and say, "Carrie, I'm grown now. Don't tell me what to do."

ONE BUCKBOARD and two buggies were parked in the shade of oaks and elms in the churchyard when Josh reined in the horses in front of the church. He let Carrie and Aunt Em out, then pulled the team under a mesquite tree where two men stood.

Carrie's gaze took in the white clapboard church with a bell in the steeple until Aunt Em ushered her up the steps. "Come on inside. There are some folks I want you to meet."

Three ladies huddled in the vestibule. One older woman with close-set eyes and a beak nose reminded Carrie of the hawk that tried to attack their chicks.

She raked Carrie with a cool gaze. A second lady looked to be in her mid-forties with dark hair and a warm smile. The third woman was a young brunette about Carrie's age. Her features and build were similar to the middle-aged woman. She guessed her to be the older woman's daughter.

The hawkish woman smiled at Carrie. "Well, who have we here, Em? Is this your niece Jennifer?"

Aunt Em pushed Carrie forward. "No. Almenia, this is Katy Davis. She is staying with us to help me around the house. Lord knows I need it, what with the garden comin' in."

Almenia nodded with raised eyebrows. "I understand. Then she's no kin of your'n?"

"That's correct. Katy hails from southern Arkansas. She arrived Friday on the morning train." Aunt Em touched Carrie's arm. "Meet Mrs. Almenia Bailey. She and her husband own a spread a few miles north of town."

"It's nice to meet you, Mrs. Bailey." Carrie offered her hand. The old woman gripped it with a cold, clammy one.

The old woman nodded. "Likewise. I hope you enjoy your stay. How long will you be with the Kramers?"

Carrie looked to Aunt Em for a reply. "We don't know. It depends on how things go."

Mrs. Bailey cut her eyes at Carrie, but before she commented, the older brunette woman piped in. "Katy, I would like you to meet my daughter, Nancy. We're the Grady's. We live two miles west of the McKinleys."

Nancy offered Carrie her hand in friendship. "Good to meet you. Maybe we could get together. We are neighbors, you know."

"I'd like that."

Nancy was petite like Carrie, a couple of years younger, with soft brown eyes and a genuine smile. Why hadn't Josh staked his claim on her? Maybe he had. She wouldn't put it past Aunt Em to try her hand at matching-making these two.

A tinge of something akin to jealousy gnawed at Carrie's insides. She dismissed it as silly. She was not looking for a husband. She had no romantic interest in Josh, nor he in her. On the surface, he appeared pleasant. But she wasn't fooled by his outward change. He only tolerated her out of respect for his aunt. Carrie sensed animosity brewing below the surface. She dreaded the day he discovered she was not the woman his aunt ordered.

A dozen women with children of all ages pranced through the door. The menfolk followed. Josh traipsed in behind them, a short, plump man at his side. They stopped in front of Carrie.

"Reverend Grissom, this is Katy Davis from Arkansas."

Carrie smiled. "Pleased to meet you." A wave of guilt washed over her. It was one thing, to pull the wool over Josh and his aunt's eyes, but deceiving a man of the cloth . . It had to be sacrilegious.

A large, husky man motioned to Josh and the reverend. As they walked away, Nancy patted her arm. "Before I forget it, Katy, there's a barn dance Saturday night at the Coopers' place. Everyone is invited. My brother is taking me. Maybe you could get Josh to take you." She turned to Aunt Em. "Don't worry, no alcohol is allowed."

Josh escort her? That would be the day. Carrie shook her head. "I don't know."

"At the Coopers' you say?" Aunt Em interjected. When Nancy nodded, she continued, "I'll make sure Josh escorts her. Young people need to socialize. It don't hurt to enjoy yourselves and meet new people."

Carrie would love to go. She'd been too exhausted for social events since her parents' fatal accident. Nancy had included Josh in the invitation, and his aunt had volunteered him to escort her. But she figured he would balk.

"Speaking of my brother," Nancy pointed to the gangly, young man entering the church, "that's Ben now." She motioned him over and pulled him forward. "Katy, this is Ben Grady, my brother. Ben, this is Katy Davis from Arkansas. She is staying with the Kramers."

Ben's blue eyes crinkled when he smiled. Carrie judged him to be a year or two older than his sister. "Nice to meet you, Ben."

He gripped her hand and squeezed it, smiling into her eyes. "The feeling is mutual, Miss Davis."

Nancy squeezed her brother's arm. "I was telling Katy about the barn dance at the Coopers'. I suggested Josh might escort her."

Ben winked. "Cowhands work long hours. We can stop by and pick you up Saturday evening."

Ben made "cowhand" sound like a slur. Was there bad blood between him and Josh? "I wouldn't want to put you out, Ben. Isn't the Kramer ranch out of your way?"

His friendly smile put her at ease. "Not at all. And it would be my pleasure, Miss Davis."

Carrie glanced across his shoulder and found Josh glowering at her. She wracked her brain, but could think of nothing she had done to earn that look.

His ill mood put a damper on her spirits. How much longer could she allow this sham to continue? If she could think of a feasible way out, she'd take it.

Carrie's conscience taunted her. *Would you? Don't you enjoy living at the Kramer ranch?"*

Life was a trifle easier since Josh's attitude toward her had softened. But Carrie wasn't fooled. She would reap his wrath when he learned of her deception.

She followed Aunt Em up the aisle and into a pew. Josh slid in beside her, taking the aisle seat. For some reason, his proximity made it difficult to breathe. She crossed her legs and tried to focus on the reverend.

After the service opened with prayer, Reverend Grissom instructed them to open their hymnals. Mrs. Grady, the organist, played with expertise as the congregation sang *Faith of Our Fathers.*

Josh's smooth baritone resonated, blending with Carrie's sweet soprano and Aunt Em's resounding alto.

Josh still acted strange. She couldn't put her finger on when it happened. The first she'd noticed him sulking was while she was talking to Ben. Had he slipped back into his former treatment of her? What had she done to trigger his bad mood?

Chapter Six

J osh sat down and placed his hymnal in the holder, determined to keep his focus on worship and the message. He didn't have chains on Katy. Why should he care if Ben Grady laid the charm on while talking to her?

In his defense, Katy was his responsibility while she was under his roof. That meant protecting her. And the gleam he'd caught in Ben's eye had spoken volumes about his intentions. The man had recently broken off his engagement to Felicity Simpson. Why, he didn't know. Neither did he care. That was Ben's personal business. But the welfare of Katy Davis was his business. Ben was likely on the prowl. He should warn Katy to be on her guard around him. She might become his next target.

As much as he tried to concentrate on Reverend Grissom's words, after the service ended he only remembered one verse.

Proverbs 3:29. Devise not evil against thy neighbor, seeing he dwelleth securely by thee.

Was that what he was doing by entertaining ill thoughts against Ben Grady? He and Ben had grown up together, gone to the same school. Ben was a couple of years his junior, closer to Katy's age.

Why did that not set well? At twenty-six, Josh wasn't old. He still had plenty of time to find a girl and settle down. He just hadn't been looking. Not since conniving Leah.

Oh, Aunt Em had tried to fix him up with two or three. But he'd balked. Nancy Grady was one of them. She was fine for somebody else, just not him. As neighbors and attending the same church, he'd known her as a kid. And though Nancy was only a couple of years younger than Katy, Josh still saw her as a freckle-faced ten-year-old with flying pigtails. She was like family to him.

He wouldn't say anything to Katy about Ben. After hearing the reverend read that scripture, it didn't seem right. She was savvy enough to see through his charm. Josh didn't see any real danger in the guy, he was just conceited. And what Ben and Katy did was none of his business.

His gut wrenched at the thought. Well, he'd better try to remember a few more tidbits from the sermon. Aunt Em would drill him on the way home.

As soon as they pulled out of the churchyard, Aunt Em cleared her throat. "What did you two think the reverend was trying to say in his sermon?"

Katy looked at him as if she expected him to answer first. He'd rather his aunt didn't know how his mind had wandered. If he let Katy answer, it would keep him out of hot water. "You go ahead, Katy. What did you think the reverend was getting at?"

"Well, it seemed his main message was be a good neighbor. If your neighbor asks for something, you let him have it. Don't wait for a more convenient time."

Let him have it? Josh liked the idea if it applied to Ben. But not in the way Katy mentioned.

Aunt Em eyed him with suspicion. "What do you say, Josh?"

"Katy took the words right out of my mouth." It was the best he could come up with. He'd hardly heard a word while fuming about something over which he had no control. Ben's intentions toward Katy. He turned to his aunt. "What message did you get from the sermon?"

She flipped her Bible open in her lap and slapped the page. "Verse 30 jumped out at me. *'Strive not with a man without cause, if he hath done thee no harm.'* If we'd all abide by those words, we'd have fewer problems with our neighbors and everybody else."

The verse smacked Josh between the eyes. He wanted to warn Katy about Ben, but were his motives purely in her best interest?

That was the big question. Josh would not let himself dwell on the truthful answer. Could be his reasons were tainted with selfishness or something worse.

TWO WEEKS FLEW by while Carrie settled into a routine at the Kramer ranch. The garden had passed its peak. Soon the growing season would end. Carrie helped Aunt Em can peppers, tomatoes, and cucumbers. She also took over feeding the chickens, milking the cow, and gathering eggs.

Wednesday morning after Josh left to attend to the herd, Carrie hung out the wash in the backyard. While she pinned Josh's work pants to the line, a cackling hen alerted her. The chicken house stood in plain view, but the racket came from the front yard. It was up to her to track down the egg. Sometimes a hen had an independent streak and liked to make her nest in an out-of-the-way place.

Carrie left the laundry basket and walked around the house. The cackling came from inside the barn. The door was cracked open. The sweet scent of hay assaulted Carrie as she slipped inside and followed the noise to the loft. She climbed the ladder and peered over at the piles of hay. A red hen stood in one corner, flapping her wings and clucking to announce her great feat. She'd lain a large, brown egg in the soft hay. Carrie stepped up into the loft and flapped her apron to shoo the hen. The hen flew down from the loft and waddled through the open barn door.

Carrie picked up the warm egg and tucked it in her apron

pocket. She turned to back down the ladder when she spied an old trunk tucked in a far corner of the loft against the wall. Should she peek inside? No, this trunk did not belong to her.

Trunks conjured up images of saucy pirates wearing eye patches, ships flying a mast of skull and crossbones, and rare treasures. Exciting adventure stories Carrie had feasted on as a child.

Curiosity won. A peek inside couldn't hurt. Carrie tramped through the hay and knelt in front of the trunk. She unlatched it and raised the lid. The scent of floral sachet assailed her nostrils. A cameo broach and locket lay in the top compartment alongside pieces from a set of china. She ran her fingers over the pretty broach. But what she found wrapped in brown paper in the bottom of the trunk made her clap a hand to her mouth.

Carrie picked up the pink fabric, looked at it, and held it against her. The same fabric she'd swooned over at the mercantile. Had Josh bought it for her? He was the only one who knew she wanted it. Then why had he hidden it? Wait. She was being silly. How could she get such an idea? He'd bought it for his aunt.

"What are you doing up here?"

Carrie flinched and jerked around. Josh stood at the top of the ladder, peering at her, his dark eyes demanding an answer. It must be noon and he'd come in to eat. Well, she'd messed up again, fallen out of his good graces once more.

Heat crept up her neck, burning her cheeks. She owed him an explanation, but nothing came to mind that seemed appropriate.

"I—I came up here to get this." Carrie pulled the egg from her apron pocket.

"Oh? And what made you decide to climb up here to look for an egg?"

Was that sarcasm in his voice? He was acting like she'd trespassed. "I'm sorry. I didn't know the barn loft was off limits. I was behind the house when I heard a hen cackling. Since the noise wasn't coming from the chicken house, I followed it and ended up in the barn. Then I realized she was up here. So . . ."

Her face must be two shades pinker than the material she clutched. She felt like a kid caught with both hands in the cookie jar.

She replaced the fabric in the trunk, careful to smooth out any creases and closed the lid. Josh must have liked the material and bought it for Aunt Em. But what reason did he have to hide it from her?

Josh chewed his bottom lip and shrugged. "You can keep it. It's yours. I was going to give it to you for your birthday. After I found out when it was."

"It's in May."

"Oh. That's not for a long time." He pushed his hat brim up and scratched his head. "Anyway, go ahead and get it out. You might find time to make a dress for the dance before Saturday night."

Carrie squealed. "Thank you! Then you're going?"

Josh shook his head. "Probably not. Aren't Ben and Nancy coming by for you?"

Carrie clenched her jaw. "I didn't say I'd go with them."

"Oh. Well, you should consider it." Before she could reply, he hopped off the ladder and tramped toward the house.

She stamped her foot. "You make me so mad, Josh Kramer! You do something nice, then you go and say something that ruins everything." The screen door slapped to. He hadn't heard a word of her ranting.

That was just fine. She would go to the dance with Ben and Nancy. That did not mean she was going as Ben's date. She pulled the fabric from the trunk and shook it out. With the canning and other chores, she'd have to put in late hours to get the dress finished in time. If Aunt Em would let her move the treadle machine into her bedroom, she'd work on it after dark. Sewing by lantern light would allow her more time to finish it.

~

AUNT EM EXCLAIMED over the fabric, smoothing it with her hand. "It's very pretty and has a nice sheen. I hope I can find a blue print in this same material."

Carrie let her assume she had purchased the material for herself. If she knew Josh had given it to her, she would read too much into his act of charity. It took little to fuel Aunt Em's romantic notions when it came to her and Josh. She had her sights on getting them hitched.

But why had Josh bought the material? Did he feel sorry for her when he'd seen her fawning over it? That was the only feasible explanation.

FRIDAY NIGHT after the women finished the supper dishes, Josh walked in with an armload of wood. Aunt Em turned around and wiped her hands on her apron. "Y'all want to sit out on the porch for a spell? It's cooler than usual tonight."

Josh dropped the wood in the box by the stove. "I need to repair a harness."

Carrie dried her hands on the dishtowel. "If you don't mind, I'd like to work on my dress." She had run the treadle machine every spare moment this week.

Aunt Em sighed. "Then I'll sit out there by myself. How's the dress comin' along?"

"I need to set the sleeves and add buttons. I stitched the button holes last night. Other than that, all it needs is adding the lace and hemming it."

"Well, I declare! You work fast, young lady. Do you mind if I see what you've done so far?"

"Not at all." Carrie led her to her bedroom where the sewing machine sat in one corner. The dress lay neatly folded in a basket. She shook it out and held it up for Aunt Em's appraisal.

The older woman's eyes widened. "That's beautiful. I can't wait until you start on mine."

Carrie laughed. "Neither can I. I can't think of anything I'd rather do than sew."

～

Two hours later Carrie ran the needle through the hem to make the last stitch. She tied a knot in the thread and snipped it. The dress was finished. All she needed to do was iron it tomorrow. Carrie folded the dress on top of the sewing basket.

Footsteps sounded on the porch. Was Josh just getting in from working on the harness? She walked into the living room and held the lantern up to check the mantle clock. Half past nine. Aunt Em had retired at eight. She'd been stitching three hours.

The front door opened, and Josh walked through it. "You want a cool glass of water?"

"Sure. My throat is parched." Carrie stepped aside to allow Josh to retrieve the bucket from the kitchen. She watched through the window as he lowered the bucket into the cistern. The full moon cast silvery beams across the barn and corral and cast an ethereal light on Josh. She pulled her gaze away and walked to the kitchen. As she set two glasses on the counter, the screen door popped.

Josh set the bucket down and dipped water into both glasses. Handing one to her, he asked meekly, "You want to sit out on the porch where it's cool?"

He was in a strange mood. Meek was not a word she would use to describe Josh Kramer. "I won't argue." Outside, he gestured for her to sit in the swing first. She did, and to her surprise, he plunked down beside her.

They sipped on their water, listening to a cacophony of tree frogs and katydids. Carrie drew in a deep breath and caught a whiff of honeysuckles. "Mm, mm."

Josh was watching her. "They smell sweet, don't they? That's one reason I wanted to sit out here." He twisted his mouth up as if what he was about to say wouldn't come easy. "Katy, I want to apologize for the way I've treated you."

"I understand. I was a stranger who came into your house. You didn't know what to expect."

"True, but that was no excuse for my rudeness. You deserved better."

No, I don't.

If he knew what she'd done . . . Josh's apology surfaced the guilt Carrie tried to ignore. If she was Katy Davis, she would graciously accept his apology and let bygones be bygones. But she had deceived both Josh and his aunt. She deserved worse than his rude behavior.

She closed her eyes to shut out his dark, sorrowful ones. *Lord, I'm in a mess of my own making. Show me the best way out of this predicament. I don't want anyone to get hurt, most of all Josh.*

He patted her arm. "You must be exhausted. You've been working late every night on your dress."

She smiled at him. "No, I'm not tired. When I'm creating a new outfit, it invigorates me."

He returned to his former train of thought. "You know, none of this is your fault. I've carried a grudge of sorts against women for some time."

"Did a woman hurt you?" She wished the words hadn't spilled out of her mouth, but since they had, she wanted to know.

Josh looked away. "Yeah. Two, really. My mother met a man and moved away to Sacramento two years after my father died. I argued it was too soon for her to be courting again. Looking back, I don't think I'd have approved of their marriage if it had been five years since my father died. Mother marrying any man seemed like treason to his memory."

"Now you accept her decision?"

"Yes. I want Mother to be happy. I didn't trust the man for a long time. He was flamboyant, brought her flowers, candy, and gifts every day. He courted and married her in six weeks. Mother loved it, but I was afraid he'd end up breaking her heart. I was wrong. It's been three years and she's still happy as can be. She and Conrad take the train at Christmas and spend two weeks with us."

"I'm glad it turned out well for you and for your mother. When problems come up within the family, well, those are the hardest ones to work through."

"Or outside the family, if it's someone you care-for and they betray you."

"Like a woman?" Carrie had to know who had broken Josh's heart.

"Leah with the chestnut hair and honey-colored eyes. I took her to a dance, then went after two cups of punch. When I couldn't find her, I walked outside. She was out there with a drifter. He had his arms around her."

"It could have been completely innocent. Did you let her explain?"

"Nothing to explain. It was obvious they'd been meeting on the sly. Anyway, I lost my temper and punched the guy. I was lucky he didn't press charges. She married him a few months later. I chalked it up to experience. At least I found out before I did something stupid like propose to her. Katy, nothing hurts worse than when someone you care about deceives you."

Carrie swallowed hard. What would Josh do when he learned of her deceit? He had eventually forgiven his mother for what he'd considered betrayal. What about Leah? Had he recovered from unrequited love, or was he still bitter?

Carrie detected cynicism in his voice when he related the story. She had learned something important about Josh. Trust was a necessity in all his relationships.

"What about you? Have you ever been betrayed by someone you cared for?"

"Haven't we all?" Carrie wanted to confide in Josh about Blake, tell him about her parents' deaths and the promise she'd made to her mother. But she couldn't. She had defaulted on that promise to look out for her brother.

Josh cleared his throat. "Did you have . . . Do you have a guy in Arkansas, one you care about?"

"No. I never had time for a social life. I was too busy working." It was true. Between trying to raise Blake and working at the dress shop, Carrie had no free time.

"So you worked in the mercantile in Hope, Arkansas?"

Katy Davis did. Surely he wouldn't ask the name of the store. "When a girl's left alone, she has to find a means to support herself." At least she'd come up with a feasible explanation without fibbing.

"I understand you lost both your parents."

Carrie exhaled a ragged breath. "Yes." She had that much in common with Katy Davis.

"It must have been very hard on you as a young woman, having nobody to look out for you. I was twenty when my father died, twenty-three when Mother remarried and left, but I had Aunt Em. She's a godsend in many ways. I feel closer to her than to my real mother. That's why I wanted to get her help. She's getting on up in years and can no longer do the heavy chores alone."

JOSH UPENDED HIS GLASS, drained it, and stretched his arm across the back of the swing. His fingertips brushed Katy's neck as he repositioned them. She didn't flinch, but he felt her tense.

Tonight was magical. He looked up at the moonlit sky. "There must be a zillion stars out tonight. And the moon is full."

"Not yet," Katy corrected. "According to Aunt Em's almanac, tomorrow night is the full moon."

"Yeah. Just in time for the dance." That bothered him. Bad things happened on a full moon. And Katy was riding to the dance with Ben Grady. If he remembered right, the moon was full a year ago, the night he'd caught Leah in the arms of that worthless drifter.

When he'd asked Katy if she'd ever been hurt by someone she cared for, she'd evaded his question. Her reaction made him think she did have a beau in Arkansas. He could have broken her heart, given her a reason to flee. Why would anyone want to hurt a woman like her?

Katy was pretty with a childlike innocence. In all likelihood, she'd drawn the interest of several young men. The more he was around Katy, the more he wanted to be near her. She had the prettiest angelic face he'd ever seen, and she was kind to Aunt Em.

She turned her face toward him. "Are you going to the dance?"

"It'll probably be late when I get home." Since Leah, dances left a bad taste in Josh's mouth. Oh well, time to move on, forget about her. She hadn't loved him anyway. Leah had tried to explain that she thought of him as a brother. He wouldn't listen and kept trying to win her heart. Josh thought if he pursued her enough, she'd come to care for him in the same way he cared for her. His plan backfired.

He looked down at Katy's hands folded demurely in her lap. She wore a ring on her finger. He reached for her hand and lifted it. "What is this?"

"You mean the ring?"

"Yes. You said you didn't have a fiancé in Arkansas."

"No fiancé. This was my mother's wedding ring. Wearing it makes me feel close to her. She told me she wanted me to have it if anything ever happened to her."

"I haven't noticed you wearing it before."

"I don't often. I try to take care of it by wearing it only for special occasions."

Like the dance? Josh stroked the back of her hand with his thumb. "Your skin is soft."

She slid her hand from his grasp. "I just rubbed in some lotion your aunt gave me."

What an idiot thing he'd said and done! He had frightened her.

She rose. "I'd better go. It's past my bedtime. Good night. Dawn comes early."

"That it does." Josh rose and yawned. "I'm turning in too. Well, goodnight then."

The screen door slapped shut behind her. Josh raked through his hair. What had gotten into him? He'd have to watch himself around Katy. Her pretty eyes must have cast a spell on him.

Chapter Seven

The following morning when a lull came between the chores, Carrie asked Aunt Em for writing paper and a pen. She thanked her, went to her bedroom, and sat down at the desk. She'd waited long enough to tell her brother her whereabouts. Concerned about his welfare and the well-being of Big Jim Counce, she began to write.

> *Dear Blake,*
>
> *I hope this finds you well. I'm sorry I left suddenly, but I couldn't watch you destroy yourself and lose everything Pa and Mama left us. By now you've probably gambled away the house, including all my things. I hope you haven't let your addiction take you that far.*
>
> *I've found a domestic job on a ranch with a nice family. I help out with housework and other chores. They feed me, provide a roof over my head, and treat me well, besides paying my wages.*
>
> *I'll close for now. Take care of yourself and stay out of trouble. Make Mama proud.*
>
> *Love,*
> *Sis*

Carrie folded the paper and tucked it in an envelope without including the return address. She hoped she hadn't given away too much. Just enough to let Blake know she had started a new life. She didn't need him to show up at the Kramer ranch. She would mail the letter on her next trip to town.

Carrie found Aunt Em in the kitchen shelling purple hull peas. "Did you pick those yourself? You should have called me and had me do it."

The older woman flapped a hand. "Nonsense. I only picked enough for a mess for supper."

"I'll help you shell them." Carrie reached up on a shelf for a large bowl.

"And turn you thumbs purple? You most certainly will not! You have a dance to go to in a few hours and you'll want to look your best. The purple stain will stay with you for days, even after scrubbing with lye soap. Why don't you take that French-milled soap down to the creek and take a refreshing bath?"

Carrie hesitated. "Do you think Josh will get home in time to go to the dance?"

"Don't worry about him. I think Josh will show up, even if he is a bit late. You go on ahead with Nancy and Ben. I'm sure Ben will show you a pleasant time. I hear he's a good dancer."

Carrie chewed her bottom lip. Why was Aunt Em encouraging her to go to the dance with Ben Grady? After all, hadn't she advertised for a mail order bride for Josh? Wasn't Carrie supposed to fill that bill, whether Josh knew it or not? Poor Josh. At least she had the advantage of knowing his aunt's ploy.

Ben's sister would be riding to the dance with them, but it still made no sense. What was Aunt Em up to?

Aunt Em pointed at her. "Let's not forget, we have to fix potato salad for you to take along."

"That's right. It's potluck. I'll put the potatoes on and set the eggs to boil. Then I'll go to the creek."

When Carrie returned from her bath, the eggs and potatoes were done. "Sorry I was so long, but I washed my hair, too, and brushed it in the sun, to help it dry faster."

Aunt Em fingered a gold strand. "It's pretty—still damp— but it'll dry before the Gradys arrive."

Carrie peeled the eggs, mashed the potatoes, and chopped an onion. Her eyes watered. She pulled up the hem of her apron and wiped them. "There, that's done. I hope I don't smell like onions."

Aunt Em stood at the stove, stirring the peas. "Wash your hands real good with the French-milled soap, to get the smell off. Then scoot. Ben and Nancy will pull up within the hour. Oh, and you'll find a bottle of perfume on your dresser. That should cover the onion smell." She laughed. "Almenia Bailey gave it to me last Christmas. I think somebody gave it to her and she didn't want it. It smells like lavender, but me being an old woman, I've got no use for it. My courtin' days are over."

Carrie threw her arms around Aunt Em. "You're not old, but thank you! You've been too good to me. I don't know how I can ever repay you."

The older woman laughed, patting Carrie on the back. "I can think of one way, but we'll discuss that at a later date."

Carrie bit her bottom lip. Was Aunt Em still holding out hope for a union between her and Josh? She didn't see how it could happen. Josh had trust issues when it came to women. And after the truth came out about her, he would order her to leave. Carrie was certain of it.

CARRIE FLOATED into the living room wearing her new dress. White slippers adorned her feet and a string of imitation pearls circled her neck. She twirled for Aunt Em. "What do you think? Tell me the truth."

"Darlin', that dress is absolutely beautiful on you. You'll steal the hearts of every man there."

Carrie giggled. "You flatter me, Aunt Em." She held out the purse she'd made from the leftover material. "What do you think of this?"

"What a handy little bag. You can tuck your comb and hand-kerchief in it and whatever else." Aunt Em stood.

"Someone's comin'." She hurried to the window as a buggy pulled up near the porch. "Ben Grady's here in the one-seater buggy, and Nancy ain't with him. I don't know what he's up to, but I don't like it."

Carrie started to the door, but Aunt Em intercepted and handed her the bowl of potato salad. "Don't look eager. A gentleman caller should be allowed to knock on a lady's door."

She waited for Ben's knock, then counted to ten before opening the door. Ben doffed his hat and smiled at them. "Good afternoon, Mrs. Roberts . . . Katy."

Katy. The name constantly reminded Carrie of her treachery. "Good evening, Mr. Grady."

"Please call me Ben."

Aunt Em piped in. "Where's Nancy? Is she not feelin' well?"

"She's in perfect health, ma'am. Stuart Tucker escorted her to the dance."

"I see." Aunt Em might have seen, but she didn't look happy about the turn of events. "Does your ma and pa approve of the young man who came by for Nancy?"

"Yes, Stu's a good chap. We've been friends since college. He's over at our house a lot."

Southern custom said a young unmarried woman should have a chaperone when she went out with a young man after dark. Unless they were betrothed, of course. Customs were changing, but it was apparent to Carrie that Josh's aunt did not agree with the changes.

"You get this young lady home at a decent hour, you hear? No dawdling along the way."

Ben winked. "Of course. Are you ready, Miss Katy?"

If looks could kill, Aunt Em would have reduced Ben to a pile of dust. Carrie suppressed a giggle.

Ben offered her his arm. She clasped his elbow and turned around to smile at Aunt Em. Aunt Em glanced from her to the door. For a second, Carrie thought she might block their exit.

Instead, she crossed her arms over her ample bosom and glared at Ben's back.

"I'll be waitin' up," she warned.

They pulled out of the yard. Ben shook the reins, urging the horse into a trot. Along the way, he boasted about mischief he'd gotten into during his college years. Carrie listened quietly. She was not impressed. Like her brother Blake, Ben had some growing up to do.

Thirty minutes later, he turned the buggy into a narrow, grassy lane. Carrie 's heart pounded against her ribs. Where was he taking her? When a barn roof and house top appeared over the next rise, she released a ragged breath. Carrie admonished herself for suspecting Ben of bad intentions. After all, he had proven to be the perfect gentleman so far.

JOSH GALLOPED into the yard at dusk, swung down off his horse, and tramped into the house. All afternoon he'd thought of Ben Grady taking Katy to the dance. The more he did, the more he worried. Ben's sister riding to the dance with them didn't ease Josh's mind one bit. Because Ben would lose his sister after they reached the Coopers'.

Ben's wild streak was well known. He'd been a rebel even in grade school. In college, he'd run with the wrong crowd and gotten into trouble. While riding fence this afternoon, Josh asked Luke for his opinion of Ben. Luke's reply did nothing to ease Josh's mind. He said he wouldn't trust Ben in the same room with his sister. That Ben drank too much and boasted about his finesse with the ladies.

The screen door slapped to behind Josh. "Aunt Em, I'm home. Where's Katy?"

His aunt hurried toward him, drying her hands on her apron. "She's gone with that Ben Grady. I've been worried sick since she left. I've got a bad feelin' about that boy. And of all things, he showed up in his one-seater buggy, all alone."

"Alone? And you let her go with him?" Josh caught his breath while he tried to figure out what to do. "She had no business going anywhere with that cad."

Aunt Em threw up her hands. "What was I supposed to do, block the door? Katy's not my kin, and she's a grown woman. I don't have any say-so over what she does. I did give Mister Ben orders to bring her home at a decent hour."

"I thought Nancy planned to accompany them."

"She'd planned to, but Ben's college friend showed up and gave her a ride to the dance."

Josh marched to the kitchen. "Where's the soap? I'll take a quick bath in Elm creek, then head over to the dance."

He bent to kiss Aunt Em's cheek. "Will you lay out some fresh clothes for me, please?"

She nodded, sighing as she handed him the soap and a towel. "You'd best hurry. They left some thirty minutes ago."

"Will you get one of the hands to saddle Geronimo? I can make better time that way."

In less than ten minutes, Josh returned from the creek, blotting his hair with a towel. It was damp, but it would have to do. He needed to get to the Coopers. He splashed the musky cologne on his neck. He only used it for special occasions. After he'd put on clean clothes, he tugged on his Sunday-go-to-meetin' boots his aunt had shined, and headed out the door.

Aunt Em called after him. "Keep a rein on your temper, Josh, and bring Katy home."

"Don't worry; I will." The screen door popped to behind him. He hadn't promised to rein in his temper. Only to bring Katy home. He didn't want her with Ben any longer than necessary.

Josh urged Geronimo into a gallop, mentally kicking himself for not arriving before Ben did. The ground, unyielding due to a drought, made it harder to set the fence posts. In the spring, they'd had plenty of rain, but as summer approached, the rains had all but ceased.

~

THEY PULLED INTO THE COOPERS' yard surrounded by pecan trees and bur oaks. Carrie was relieved to see the large red barn and hear laughter and music drifting from it. Ben parked the buggy in the shade near the other buggies and buckboard and helped her down. He took her arm and led her toward the party.

When they reached the open door, Carrie spied a violinist playing a lively waltz. A few couples swayed across the floor. Hay had been stacked to make room. Chairs lined two walls, inviting folks to sit and socialize. Ladies attired in dresses of yellow, blue, and green occupied a few seats while some men sat on wooden crates. The seated ladies waved dainty fans to combat the humidity. Two tables butted together were spread with a checkered table cloth. Mouth-watering dishes made Carrie's stomach rumble. A crystal punch bowl, surrounded by matching cups and filled with orange punch, sat on a small table.

Ben squeezed her arm. "You must be thirsty after the ride. Let me get you some punch."

Carrie nodded. "Thank you. I am thirsty."

Carrie rearranged bowls on the table to make room for her potato salad while Ben strode toward the punch bowl. She scanned the crowd for Nancy and found her engaged in conversation with a man she guessed to be Stuart Tucker.

Ben nudged Carrie. "Your punch, m'lady."

"Thank you." She took the cup and sipped. "Delicious."

"Hey, there's Stu and Nancy. Let's join them." He urged her over to the couple. Ben seated Carrie next to Nancy sat down on the other side of Stuart. "We'll let you ladies talk girl talk."

Ben reminded Stuart of the time he poured glue in Professor Barker's chair. While the men laughed over college antics, Nancy introduced Carrie to several other young ladies.

When they returned to the men, Ben whispered to Stuart, and both men rose. "Excuse us for a moment, ladies. We shall return."

Nancy shrugged. "I suppose they want to talk privately about their college mischief. Things that aren't proper for a lady's ears. Let's get something to eat. Did you ever see such a spread?"

They filled their plates and reclaimed their seats. Carrie finished the last bite of her chocolate pie when Ben and Stuart returned. Ben reached for Carrie's plate and set it on the vacant chair next to her. "It's time we danced. I wouldn't want to miss this beautiful waltz." He pulled her onto the dance floor

"I don't know, I'm pretty rusty. It's been a long time since I've danced. And never a waltz."

"I'll teach you. Just follow me."

He coaxed her on the steps. "One-two-three, one-two-three. See, it's really very easy." Then he bent near her ear and whispered, "Enjoying yourself?"

Carrie caught a strong whiff of alcohol on his breath. He had been drinking. She wished she were wrong, but this wasn't the first time she'd been exposed to the scent. Her brother had come home drunk so many times she'd lost count.

Not wanting to cause a scene, Carrie kept time with Ben's steps as he swung her around the dance floor. When the song ended, he led her to a vacant chair. "You sit here while I fill my plate.

He returned with a full plate and ate as if he were starving. After forking in the last bite of pie, he smiled at her. "Please excuse me for a moment." Before she could reply, Ben had made his way to the door with Stuart following.

Carrie feared the worst. What if he drank too much? She refused to ride home with a drunken man, having learned the hard way that whiskey made them amorous.

Chapter Eight

❧❦❧

J osh trotted his horse to a grove of trees where buggies and wagons were parked. As he tethered his horse, laughter and festive music poured from the barn. The Coopers knew how to throw parties. He did a lively two-step on his way to the barn, whistling to the music.

Several couples swirled about on the dance floor. Katy and Ben weren't among them. The long table, loaded with every kind of food imaginable, made his stomach rumble. Josh hadn't eaten since noon. He scanned the barn until he found Katy and Nancy seated to one side, tapping their feet to the music. Where were their escorts?

Suspicion gnawed at him. Something was not right. Josh filled his plate, dipped a cup of punch, and stepped outside the barn and ducked into the shadows near the corral. He would keep out of sight, wait and watch. He forked a bite of potato salad into his mouth. Mm . . . mm. Then he nibbled on a chicken leg fried to perfection. Almost as good as Aunt Em's.

Josh cleaned his plate and remembered the chocolate pie he'd seen. The one with the fluffy meringue. Ben and his friend were probably inside the barn by now. Or maybe he'd overlooked them. He started to head back in for pie when a raucous laugh stopped him. He followed the sound with his gaze. Two men stood in the grove of trees near the wagons and buggies. The laugh sounded familiar. Ben Grady. The other man's voice he didn't know. What were they doing out here? Why weren't they inside dancing with the ladies? They were talking but he was too far away to make out their words. To hear, he would have to move in closer.

The only way to do that and stay out of sight was to keep to the shadows. Josh glanced from the barn to the house and back to where the men stood near a buggy. The house cast a long shadow most of the way to the barn. To hear the men without them seeing him, he needed to sneak behind the Coopers' house and emerge on the opposite side. If he could slip into the grove of trees, he would stay hidden until the time was right. That should put him twenty-some feet from Ben and the other man.

Josh set his plate and cup on a fence post before making his move. He made it to the side of the house without being seen. The hard part would be getting to the grove of trees. The slightest noise could alert the two men.

Their voices grew louder as he slipped toward the grove. If he could reach the large pecan tree he'd seen earlier, he'd hide behind it. A twig crunched beneath his foot. Josh paused. The men were still talking. He held his breath and stepped closer. A horse nickered. Six more feet to the pecan tree. He crept toward it then stubbed his boot on a fallen branch. He landed on the twig and it snapped. Face down in the leaves, he lay holding his breath, the only sound his heart drumming against the ground.

"What was that noise?" the stranger's voice asked.

"Ah-h, just a horse stepping on a twig. You sure you won't have a sip?"

Ben's voice.

"No, thanks. I don't want it on my breath. Nancy might catch the scent while we're dancing."

"I hate drinking alone, but if I must." Laughing, Ben held up a bottle. "Here's to our dates."

"We should rejoin the ladies. They may be getting impatient at our absence."

Ben laughed again. "I like my women impatient. And frisky. Makes for a good time."

That dirty, rotten scoundrel! I'll wring his neck. Josh seethed.

"I don't know, Ben. Katy is a pretty girl and she seems nice. Not the kind who would agree with your drinking. And you have to drive her home. Maybe you'd better lay off that bottle."

Josh swallowed his anger, rose, and carefully placed one booted foot in front of the other. Two more long steps and he would reach the pecan tree.

How far would Ben take his drinking? What were his intentions toward Katy? And no, she would not be leaving with him, if he had any say.

Ben chuckled. "I wouldn't have brought her if she was homely. I only court pretty women. Those who require my expertise when it comes to love."

Josh clenched his fists, anger boiling in his chest. It took every ounce of self-control to stay out of sight and refrain from punching Ben. The right moment would present himself if he could keep a check on his temper.

NANCY ROLLED HER EYES. "I declare. Those men disappear quicker than a summer shower. They've been gone a while this time. It's as if they've forgotten us."

Carrie sighed. She was disappointed in Ben. The dance was not going as she'd hoped, no fault of the Coopers. Everyone except Nancy and she seemed to be enjoying themselves. "What do you suppose they're doing out there?"

"I have no idea. Probably still swapping tales about college mischief."

Carrie leaned over to whisper to Nancy to voice her suspicions. "Did you detect anything on Stuart's breath?"

"Like what?"

"Like alcohol." Maybe Ben's friend didn't imbibe. "I detected it on your brother breath."

Nancy's eyebrows rose. "I didn't smell anything on Stu's breath. I don't think he drinks. Ben went through a wild stage and drank while he was in college. Most men do. I don't know if he still does."

"I'm sure it was alcohol I smelled on Ben's breath while we were dancing."

Nancy threw up her hands. "Do you think someone spiked the punch?"

Carrie shook her head. "If they had, you and I would be tipsy. We've had three cups each."

Nancy giggled. "I suppose you're right. Come on. Let's go find those deserters."

Moonlight cast a silvery sheen on the world, exposing everything to its glow as Carrie and Nancy ventured outside. Even a glass bottle raised in the dark glinted where two men stood in the grove amidst buckboards and buggies.

One man laughed. Ben. He raised a bottle to his mouth and upended it. It was all the proof Carrie needed. Ben was drinking something, and it wasn't orange punch.

Nancy called out as they approached, "Stu, Ben, how long are you men going to stay out here? Katy and I came here to dance. Listen to that wonderful music. So much of it has gone to waste while we sat in our chairs like wallflowers."

A horse nickered behind the men. Carrie thought she saw a shadow move between two trees. The bottle vanished before they reached the men. Where had Ben put it? Fear pricked her heart. She had to ride home with him. If he was drunk . . . The scene with Big Jim replayed through her mind. Would Ben try to force himself on her?

"Ah, there you are, pretty lady." Ben grabbed Carrie's hand, raised it, and kissed it. "You want to dance? We can waltz to the music under the stars."

Nancy tugged on Stuart's arm. "You two can stay out here if you like, but Stu and I would rather go inside and dance."

Carrie wanted to yell *Don't leave me!* as they walked away. When Nancy and Stuart were out of sight, Ben slid his arm around her waist and swung her around in a waltz. He stumbled and would have fallen if she hadn't steadied him.

"Please, Ben, let's go inside to dance."

"Why waste the night inside? We have the moon, the stars, and tree frogs to serenade us out here. Did I tell you that you look stunning in the moonlight?" He brushed his lips against her cheek.

She braced her palms against his chest and pushed back. "Please . . . stop. You're drunk."

He slid his lips to her face. "Aw, come on little lady, just one little kiss. I promise you'll like it."

A tall shadow flew toward them out of the trees and flung her out of Ben's clutches. Carrie stumbled, but caught her balance.

"How's this for a kiss, Grady?"

"Josh!" Carrie squealed.

Josh slammed his fist into Ben's jaw. Carrie gasped as he stumbled backward and fell.

Touching his jaw, Ben sat up and narrowed his eyes. "What are you all fired up about, Kramer? This woman doesn't belong to you."

"You don't know that. And if she does, it's none of your business."

"You are right." He picked up his hat and brushed off the debris. "You can have her. There are plenty more pretty ladies around looking for a refined gentleman."

Josh's fists clenched. "They won't find one in you. Since when does forcing his attentions on a young lady make a man a 'refined gentleman?'"

He grabbed Ben by the shirt collar and yanked him to his feet. "I strongly suggest you climb up in that buggy of yours and take your besotted self home."

Ben shifted his gaze from Josh to Katy. "But . . . I brought her here, so it's my gentlemanly duty to return her safely home."

"We've already established you're no gentleman, meaning the rule does not apply." Josh shoved Ben against the buggy. The horse nickered and shifted its feet. "Get going, before I lose my temper."

Ben held up his hands. "All right! Give me a chance."

He turned around and lifted one foot to step up in the buggy. He missed the step and fell backward. Josh caught him by his shirt collar. Gripping the seat of Ben's pants with his other hand, he swung the drunken man up into the buggy.

Ben landed faced down but managed to push himself upright. While Josh untied the reins, Ben seated himself. Josh dropped the reins in his lap and ordered, "Get going!"

Ben grappled for the reins and shook them. "Giddy-up!" The buggy rolled out of the yard and headed west with Ben swaying from side to side.

KATY GASPED BUT SAID NOTHING. Her hand shook as she wiped her eyes.

"Are you all right?" Josh asked. "Did Ben hurt you?" He wouldn't show up again if he knew what was good for him.

"Just a little shaky." Then a sob broke loose. "Oh, Josh! I couldn't stop him! Ben was too strong. He wouldn't let me go. I thought I could hold him off, but I couldn't. Just like when—." She began to weep.

"When what, Katy? Has a man done this to you before?" She hung her head but did not answer. Josh clenched his fists. "That sorry—" He wrapped his arms around Katy and pulled her close. She pressed her face against his chest. Warm tears soaked through his shirt. His heart ached for her.

"Shush. You are safe with me. Ben won't ever bother you again. I promise you that." She felt warm in his arms, like she belonged there. He hated to let her go.

Josh slid his hands down to Katy's elbows, cupped them, and stepped back. "I'll take you home if you're ready. I apologize for not bringing the buckboard. I was late getting in and had to hurry to get here."

Katy sniffed back tears and tossed a shimmering tress over one shoulder. "First, I need to let Nancy know I'm leaving." She wiped her eyes. "But I can't go in looking like this. She will know something happened. I don't want to embarrass her."

"Don't worry; I'll let her know that Ben left and I'm taking you home." He pointed to his horse tethered beneath a pecan tree. "Wait for me over there. I'll be right back."

A waltz ended, and Stuart led Nancy to a chair. Josh walked up to them. "Nancy, Stu, Ben decided to head home. He realized he'd drank too much. Katy is going home now, with me."

Stuart cleared his throat. "Is she all right?"

"A little upset, but she'll be fine."

"Let me get the bowl she brought. It's empty," Nancy offered and left the men.

Stuart asked, "What happened? Ben was drinking. I thought he had carried it too far. He doesn't know when to stop."

Josh sucked in his lips. "He tried to force himself on Katy, but I don't think he'll ever try it again."

Nancy returned with the bowl. Josh thanked her and doffed his hat. "Have a wonderful evening."

He found Katy stroking Geronimo's forehead and sweet-talking him. "You're spoiling my horse," he teased.

She hiked her chin. "A little affection never hurt either an animal or a person,"

"I'll remember that." Did her comment hold a double meaning? Josh was relieved that Katy's sass had returned. At least she'd stopped crying. The front of his shirt was already soaked. He didn't want the back soaked too. That would be twice as uncomfortable. "I hope you don't mind riding double. You're probably accustomed to a side saddle."

"I've never owned one." She spoke as if she was proud of riding astride.

It didn't surprise Josh. The young lady had gumption. He stuffed the empty bowl in the saddlebag and swung up onto his horse. Reaching down, he pulled Katy up behind him.

The air was muggy, making the warmth from her body uncomfortable in more than one way.

"I meant to tell you, your dress looks pretty, and fashionable."

"Thank you."

JOSH LIKED HER DRESS? Carrie's face warmed. He'd given her a compliment, or at least he'd complimented her dress. Wasn't that the same thing? Maybe not, but it still warmed her heart.

She adjusted her dress the best she could, pulling her skirt down as far as possible. At least they weren't in broad daylight where Josh could get a clear view of her partially exposed calves. The full moon showed them clearly enough to anyone who was looking. Since he was in front of her, that shouldn't be a problem.

Carrie hesitated, not sure where to place her hands. Could she figure out how to hold on without circling his waist?

Josh cleared his throat. "Katy, I'm waiting for you to wrap your arms around me so we can head home."

The impatient Josh was back. He'd been gentle and caring for a few minutes. Now he was barking orders. Carrie gave in and slid her arms around his taut midsection. He urged Geronimo to a graceful trot. She hung on, grateful to have the full moon to light their way.

"Josh, do you think Ben made it home all right? He was pretty drunk, you know."

"I'm sure his horse knows the way. If not, we'll find him along the roadside. Why are you concerned?"

"I don't know. I guess I worry about everybody whether they're good or bad."

"Well, stop worrying and relax."

"I'll try." She leaned against him. His back was warm, and the scent of his masculine cologne tantalized her nostrils. "I hoped you'd come to the dance. Why did you change your mind?"

"No reason in particular. I just thought I'd give it a try. I haven't been to a dance in a while."

"You didn't even get to dance. I hate that you had to miss the party on account of me."

"That's all right. I managed to eat. Your potato salad was delicious. I didn't know whose it was until Nancy handed me the empty bowl."

"Thank you. I'll take that as a compliment." She sat straighter in the saddle. "Josh, did you know Ben had a drinking habit?"

"Not until today, when Luke told me."

"Neither did I until I smelled it on his breath while we were dancing. He and Stu disappeared several times. Each time they stayed gone a little longer. Nancy said we should check on them."

"You danced with that drunken . . . ?"

"Just once. Did you come to the dance to check on me?" Carrie bit her lip. What was wrong with her? Had the full moon cast a spell on her, making her say things she wouldn't otherwise say?

Josh sighed. "If you must know, Aunt Em was worried about you. She ordered me to go after you and bring you home. She has a sixth sense about people. She didn't trust Ben."

Carrie's heart sank. Aunt Em had sent Josh, or he wouldn't have come. She'd hoped it had been his idea. Why should she be disheartened? He'd rescued her from the clutches of Ben.

"Oh. Well, thank you."

"You're welcome. There's a stream up ahead. Geronimo could use a cool drink. Do you mind if we stop?"

"Not at all." She felt safe with Josh no matter where they ventured. She suspected he exuded that effect on most folks. He was strong, brave.

Was she falling in love? Of course not! The matrimony plan

was Aunt Em's. Not hers. Carrie was content to help around the house. She didn't need anything more.

Josh pulled on the reins to head Geronimo off the road and down a grassy lane. Ahead, the moonlight shed its silvery light on the water she glimpsed beyond the trees. Strange that she felt safe with Josh but nearly panicked when Ben Grady turned his buggy down a narrow lane earlier.

When they reached the flowing stream, Josh reined in his horse and dismounted. He turned to swing Carrie to the ground.

WHILE GERONIMO SATIATED HIS THIRST, Josh splashed cool water on his sweltering face. He dried his eyes with his shirt sleeve and gazed up at the sky. An owl hooted in the distance. He turned his attentions to the night sounds. Another owl hooted a reply from the opposite direction. The tree frogs and chirping insects were having their heyday.

He closed his eyes. "Mm-mm . . . I could listen to this all night and let it soothe me to sleep."

"It's so peaceful. And there must be a trillion stars glowing. God has excelled tonight."

"I agree. His creation always amazes me."

"Me too. And the moon reflects off the water sparkling like thousands of tiny diamonds."

Diamonds? Was Katy focused on material things? Did she long for finer things, an easy life and a fine home with luxurious furnishings? Things she'd never had?

"What made you think of diamonds?" he had to ask.

"They are pretty. What else sparkles like them?"

"Polished glass, maybe."

Katy sighed. "Yes, but diamonds are rare and much prettier."

"Katy, life doesn't always turn out the way we would like it. We seldom get everything we want."

She frowned. "What do you mean? I didn't say I wanted

diamonds. I don't care about owning every beautiful thing I see. I get enjoyment by admiring them."

Was she being truthful or were her words a ploy? Josh didn't know how to take Katy Davis. She'd burst into their lives, bringing sunshine and sweetness. She'd been a godsend to Aunt Em, who had loved her the minute she'd set eyes on her.

Was Katy too good to be true? He'd kept his ears alert, listening for anything that made her appear to be a gold digger. What if he was wrong? What if she was the person she appeared to be? He needed to look at her through God's eyes and forget his own preconceived judgments.

Sure, Leah had hurt him. But that was in the past, and he should leave it there. And his mother? Had she really betrayed his father's memory by marrying again? What would his father have wanted for her?

I want your mother to be happy, to go on living and enjoying life.

Josh looked behind him. It was as if his father had spoken those words to his heart. The words he would say if he were standing here now. An eerie sense of peace enveloped Josh, lifting a heavy load from his heart. He laughed.

Katy flinched. "You scared me. What's funny?"

"I'm not sure. I think God, or my father, just spoke a message to my heart. I feel a ton lighter."

Screeeeeech! A large bird flew past them.

Katy shrieked and flew into his arms. Josh encircled her waist, pulling her close. "It's just a screech owl." Her heart beat against his ribcage, her breath coming in gasps. She shook like a leaf. He reached up one hand and stroked her hair as she lay her head against his chest. It was spun satin, as soft as he'd imagined. He could stand here forever holding her in his arms.

She stirred and lifted her head to gaze into his eyes. Her cat eyes threatened to melt his resolve.

"Josh . . ."

"Shh. No need to worry." Katy closed her eyes, and he bent to claim her lips. She put up no resistance. The hands she'd pressed against his chest slid up to encircle his neck. The kiss intensified. It held more sweetness than a wild honey tree, but without the bee stings. Katy went limp in his arms as their kiss built to a fervor. If he loosened his hold, she might slither to the ground.

Josh wasn't in any better shape. His heart drummed like a herd of stampeding cattle. He could have sworn fireworks exploded in front of his eyes. He had to stop before things got out of hand.

Just one more minute.

He kissed her again, savoring the wave of emotion raging through him.

What am I doing?

He straightened and peeled Katy's clasped hands from his neck. After rescuing her from one scoundrel, she'd think he was no better.

Katy stepped back and raised a shaky hand. She tucked a silky strand of hair behind one ear. "We should . . . be going. Aunt Em will be waiting up for us."

Still dazed, Josh stared at her. He managed break the spell when Geronimo nickered. He mounted the horse and pulled her up behind him. She sat rigid, avoiding any bodily contact, except for loosely linking her hands about his waist.

His heart still thundered.

The remainder of the ride home was sheer torture as he fought the urge to slide off his horse and pull Katy into his arms again. This time to kiss her until she ordered him to stop.

Chapter Nine

❦

They rode home in silence, questions swirling through Carrie's mind. Had their kiss meant anything to Josh? Did he have feelings for her? Why had she let him kiss her so soon after struggling with her intoxicated escort?

Easy answer. She was not threatened by Josh. The men were as different as daylight and dark. While Josh's touch was gentle and he'd treated her with respect, Ben had forced himself on her.

Carrie could no longer deny her feelings. She loved everything about this cowboy. The big question was what to do about it. If she revealed the truth about herself, she'd lose him. But if she didn't, Josh would find out sooner or later. How she hoped it would be later! Much later.

Carrie's heart soared. She needed more time to explore the strange feelings coursing through her. She didn't care about the future, only the now. Her one desire was to hold onto this euphoric feeling as long as possible, to embrace the memory of their ecstatic kiss. And not think of the consequences ahead.

Payday would come. It was only a matter of time. She could almost hear the clock ticking.

How long before this rapturous cocoon burst and she crashed?

Not soaring as a yellow monarch, but like a worm squirming in the Texas dust.

Geronimo trotted under the engraved wooden sign that read, *Kramer Ranch*. True to her word, Aunt Em waited. She stood on the porch waving a lantern while Josh helped Carrie off the horse and led him into the barn.

Carrie followed Aunt Em into the house. "What happened? Did Josh get into a fight?"

Carrie wasn't sure how much to tell Josh's aunt. How much did he want her to know? "I wouldn't call it fight. Maybe a scuffle."

"With Ben?"

Carrie nodded.

"Is Josh hurt?"

"No. Ben's jaw caught a blow, and he landed on his backside. Didn't even try to get up."

Aunt Em clicked her tongue. "Oh dear. I hate to face Louise Grady on Sunday. What did Ben do to instigate the fight? I know Josh had a reason."

"He tried to force his attentions on Katy." Neither had heard Josh walk in.

Aunt Em reached out and embraced Carrie, then stepped back. "I'm sorry, dear. Are you all right? He didn't hurt you?"

"I'm fine. Josh jumped in before things got ugly."

"And I assure you it could have gotten very ugly. I've heard tales about Mr. Grady that would not be appropriate to relate to you ladies."

Carrie sighed. "Ben had been drinking. I didn't know it until he pulled me onto the dance floor. That's when I caught a whiff of his breath."

Aunt Em clapped a hand to her mouth. "You don't say! The Coopers served alcohol at the dance? I'd never have thought it."

Josh hung his hat on a peg near the door. "No, Aunt Em. Ben brought his own bottle, hid it under the buggy seat, I'm sure."

"Well, I'm glad nobody got seriously hurt." She fingered

Carrie's sleeve. "Josh, what do you think of Katy's dress? Isn't it lovely?"

Josh's gaze raked Carrie. She could have sworn he blushed. "It's as pretty as any I saw at that fancy boutique."

Aunt Em cleared her throat. "Did you two have a pleasant ride back? I'm sure with the full moon . . ." Josh turned a suspicious gaze on Carrie. Her cheeks flamed. She gave her head a quick shake to indicate she hadn't told his aunt a thing. ". . .you could see the road clearer than most nights," Aunt Em finished.

Josh's shoulders visibly relaxed. He whooshed out a breath.

"Josh, did you dance with Katy?"

"I didn't get the chance. I did manage to wolf down a plate of food before the altercation with Ben."

"That's too bad. Well, all is not lost. There will be other socials." Aunt Em yawned. "You youngsters can stay up if you like, sit out on the swing a while. But I'm hittin' the hay. Goodnight to you both." She strode through her bedroom door and closed it with a thud.

Josh searched Carrie's eyes. "You won't say anything to her, I hope?"

"About what happened?"

". . . on the way back," he finished for her.

She shook her head. "Josh, I want you to know I don't usually, I mean, I've never let—"

"No need to explain. The full moon does crazy things to a man and woman. Get a good night's sleep. In the morning light, things will look different."

Maybe I don't want things to look different. Tears stung Carrie's eyes. She swallowed hard to keep from sobbing. Why would Josh say such a thing? Their kiss meant nothing to him? And why was he staring at her as if she had milk gravy smeared across her face?

"Good night!" She whirled around and ran for her bedroom.

"Katy, I was only trying to—"

Her door slammed, cutting off the rest of his words. It would be a long night. She doubted she would sleep a wink.

JOSH THREW UP HIS HANDS, rolled his eyes heavenward. "What did I say, Lord?" He was only trying to apologize for his behavior. He'd taken advantage of Katy while she was vulnerable. She'd been through enough tonight fighting off that lout without him forcing himself on her. He wanted to tell her he wasn't like Ben Grady, but she had run for cover like a scalded dog. If Katy had given him one minute, he would have explained.

Josh's hands clenched. If he ever caught Ben looking at Katy again, he'd knock him out cold. When he saw that scoundrel trying to hurt her, he'd lost his temper. He couldn't remember the last time he'd been that angry.

Oh, yes, he could. One year ago, at the same place. The Coopers' barn. He had escorted Leah to the dance and planned to propose to her on the way home. He'd looked at rings that day. In retrospect, he was glad he hadn't bought one. If he'd flipped open a box and presented the ring to Leah . . . talk about making a complete fool of oneself!

While he'd been inside waltzing with Nancy Grady, Leah had slipped outside to meet the drifter he'd seen her talking to in front of the livery stable the month before. Josh cut his dance short, followed Leah, and found her kissing the drifter at nearly the same spot Katy fought off Ben a little while ago. The difference was Leah enjoyed the drifter's attentions.

He'd pulled them apart and punched the man in the face. Then the drifter punched him in the stomach. Before they dove into each other again, Leah dashed between them, pressing her hands against their chests. She'd faced him with fire in her eyes. Josh still remembered her words.

"Stop it! Don't you understand? Steve has asked me to marry him. Josh, I've been trying to tell you for months that what I feel for you is only friendship. But you wouldn't—"

"I wouldn't what?" Josh had never been so humiliated.

"You wouldn't listen."

He'd picked up his hat and punched it down on his head. He'd replied with a sarcastic, "Congratulations. You two deserve each other" before nonchalantly swinging his leg over Geronimo and heading home.

~

ON MONDAY MORNING, Carrie set a bucket of tomatoes on the counter. Wiping her brow, she asked, "Do you think we could go into town and buy fabric to make your dress?"

The post office was located on the other side of the street and down a ways from the mercantile. After mailing her letter to Blake, she could scan the Wanted Posters on the wall. She was weary of losing sleep and worrying that a reward might have been issued for her arrest.

Aunt Em stood over the stove, stirring a pot of beans. "I reckon this is as good a time as any. Josh won't be home for dinner today. We can take our easy time and still get home before supper.

"I'll set these beans in the warming closet and change my dress. Josh doesn't like me to go to town alone. He frets like an old hen over me. Not that I pay him much mind. But there will be two of us plus the good Lord watching over. I reckon we'll be safe enough."

Carrie changed into a white print dress sprinkled with yellow flowers and tied on a yellow bonnet. She pulled the letter from the bureau drawer and tucked it in her drawstring bag. If Aunt Em saw it, she would ask questions. Carrie could not lie to her. Something about Josh's aunt demanded honesty. Watching every word she said had kept Carrie on her toes. She was weary from fearing Josh and his aunt would learn the truth about her.

Since Saturday night, she and Josh had spoken no more than two sentences to each other. His words had cut her. Admitting she had developed feelings for him was hard for her to swallow. She'd let him kiss her. She had never been kissed by a man. Not like Josh had kissed her. Then he had brushed it off by letting her know their kiss meant nothing to him. What kind of game was he playing?

She hadn't considered Josh might be a ladies' man, but she could be wrong. How many broken hearts did he have on a string? Her throat tightened, making it hard to breathe. Maybe the trip to town would lift her spirits.

When they finished hitching the horses to the buckboard and climbed up, Aunt Em laid the reins in Carrie's lap. "You can drive the team. I've got a touch of rheumatism in my hands."

The temperature had dropped to a comfortable level, bringing welcomed relief. Aunt Em tucked a wayward strand of hair beneath her bonnet. "Whew! I'm glad the Lord saw fit to give us a nice day for this trip."

"Me too." Carrie clicked her tongue and shook the reins. The horses took off at an easy canter. A red-tailed hawk screeched in the cloudless blue sky overhead while songbirds twittered in the bushes and trees. Cowbirds pecked for insects in a pasture to their right. They took flight as the wagon passed.

Carrie wanted to know everything about Josh— the mischief he'd gotten into as a child, his favorite foods. Because she and Aunt Em had been preoccupied with canning, cooking, and cleaning, or Josh had been in their presence, they hadn't had a chance for a private conversation.

She wanted to ask a dozen questions, but Aunt Em would not believe she was merely curious. Carrie bit her tongue. Josh's aunt wouldn't say a word, but she would give her that knowing look. What if she had fallen for the handsome cowboy? Aunt Em need not know. Besides, Josh did not feel the same for her. Her heart felt heavy.

Carrie had never been in love, unless she counted the crush she'd had on her teacher in high school. Half the girls in the tenth grade felt the same way about Mr. Evans. It wasn't as if she was the only one smitten. He was a tall, handsome man with slick, dark hair and gray eyes. It was probably lucky for him that he moved on after one year. Sally Gentry and Rebecca Newton cried when he made the announcement of his departure. Carrie managed to wait until the school bell rang and dashed home and threw herself across the bed and wept.

Mama explained to Carrie that she had nothing more than a schoolgirl crush. It might seem like true love, but it would pass. Carrie didn't believe her at the time but later admitted Mama was right. She'd attended a few dances over the next two years but met no one who interested her. Not one young man measured up to Mr. Evans. Soon after that, Mama and Papa died and Carrie took on a load of responsibility. Since, she hadn't had time to court.

Aunt Em cleared her throat, bringing Carrie out of her reverie. "You've been with us a while now. What do you think of Josh?"

How should she answer? She decided to try for nonchalance. "Josh is a good man. You have reason to be proud of him." *He is also handsome, and his dark eyes make my heart flutter.* Josh infuriated her at the same time. No, Carrie couldn't say any of it. She was glad Aunt Em could not read her mind.

"What else? How do you feel about Josh?"

Carrie bit her lip and released it. It was obvious Aunt Em's questions were intended to dig beneath the surface. "I can't tell you how relieved I was that he showed up at the dance Saturday night. I don't know what I'd have done if he hadn't."

Aunt Em patted her arm. "Hon, I'm sorry you had to go through that. I hope Ben learned his lesson."

Until the altercation with Big Jim Counce, Carrie thought she was strong enough to fend off an attacker. But she was wrong. Big Jim, and now Ben, had proven she was helpless.

"I don't mind admitting I was scared. The only option left was to scream. But I didn't want everyone to run outside to see what was the matter. It would've ruined the party. Thank God, Josh jumped out from behind a tree when he did, and put an end to Ben's pestering."

"And I thank the Lord you weren't hurt and neither was Josh. And that he didn't hurt Ben too bad."

Carrie agreed. Although, Saturday night after they got home, she wanted to throw a punch at Josh herself. The full moon makes people do crazy things? The nerve of him! It was Josh's way of saying he regretted their kiss. Tears stung her eyes as she relived the scene.

"I guess you noticed Ben's mother high-hatted me at church yesterday."

"No, but I noticed Ben wasn't there. I don't think Mrs. Grady meant to high-hat you. My guess is she was embarrassed by her son's behavior. Nancy probably told her what happened at the dance, when she returned."

"You may be right. I'm jumpin' to conclusions, and that's akin to passing judgment. We know what the Good Book says about judging. Lord knows, I'm not perfect. I need all the mercy I can get."

Carrie sighed. "As do I." *More so as the days go by.*

"I'm sorry you had to ride double behind Josh, the night of the dance, but it couldn't be helped. He was in a hurry to get there, and the buckboard would have made him later."

"He was in a hurry? Why?"

"When I told him Ben had showed up alone, he almost had a conniption. First, Josh wanted to know why I let you go with Ben without Nancy being present. After he calmed down, he told me to lay him out a change of clothes. Then he took a bath in the creek. He didn't waste any time on that bath. I'd be surprised if he washed behind his ears. I started to ask, but considered the mood he was in and thought better of it."

Carrie frowned. "Josh told me he had just learned about Ben's drinking habit."

"He didn't tell me. I guess he didn't want me to worry, since I let you go with Ben." Then Aunt Em winked. "Just an old lady's calculations, but I'm pretty good at figuring out Josh. And I think he's sweet on you."

If Aunt Em had heard what Josh had said afterward, she would change her opinion. He had no feelings for her. His heart was still frozen from Leah's betrayal.

Carrie squirmed. Time to switch to a safer topic. "Aunt Em, I know Josh's father died and his mother married again and moved to Sacramento, but what happened to his father?"

"Chuck died five years ago. Luke found him layin' flat of his back in the north pasture, a rock underneath his head. Doc Brown said from the looks of it, his heart stopped beatin' before he fell off his horse. It wasn't the fall that killed him, but a heart attack. Well, Josh refuses to accept the diagnosis. He thinks the horse spooked and threw his pa. He has it in his mind that if he'd been there, his pa would still be alive. Josh blames himself for Chuck's death and discounts the evidence.

"Josh was supposed to ride out with his pa to check fences that mornin', but he woke up coughin' and runnin' a high fever. Josh's mother talked him into going back to bed. He didn't need to be out checking fences, and him sick. I don't think Josh has quite forgiven her for that."

Carrie shook her head. "Carrying that kind of guilt weighs heavy on one's heart."

She had blamed herself when her parents died. She should have stopped them from going into town. They'd gone after her birthday present. She'd seen a pretty music box at the mercantile. Mama and Papa wanted to surprise her. On the way home, something must have spooked the horses. Their buggy overturned, and they were trapped beneath it. Unlike Josh's father, a rock had been the cause of her father's death. His head was lying against a boulder, blood oozing from his mouth. Her mother's neck was broken. Both were crushed beneath the overturned buggy.

Their neighbor, sweet old Evie Mason, helped Carrie through it with her wise words. The elderly woman explained that dwelling on "What ifs?" didn't change anything. She added, "We have to move forward and live our lives the best we can, considering each of us is given only a certain amount of time on this earth."

Carrie had taken those words to heart and strove to live by them. She'd tried to raise her fourteen-year-old brother to adulthood the best she knew how. She'd cooked, cleaned, and tried to teach Blake right from wrong. But it hadn't taken. Her brother rebelled.

She had managed to keep Blake in church for a while. It was what Mama would have wanted. But after a year of struggling with his strong will, she gave up.

It hadn't been too hard to keep him out trouble while he was still in school. But Blake quit in the eleventh grade. By then Carrie had lost control of him.

Where had she gone wrong? She'd done everything her mother asked. Now she had deserted Blake and become tangled in a web of deceit.

Carrie closed her eyes and silently prayed, *Lord, will you help me out of this mess?*

Aunt Em was studying her when she opened her eyes. "Katy, that day while you were beatin' the rug on the clothesline, you were whacking it like it was somebody you were mad at. Did you by chance leave a beau back in Arkansas?"

How much had she heard? "No, I was too busy working to have a social life."

"It's all right. You don't have to tell me a thing. It's just I've noticed you don't talk about your past." She patted Carrie's arm. "It helps to have someone you can talk to. Someone who won't judge you for what you may or may not have done. I just want you to know I'm here when you're ready to talk."

Warm tears threatened to spill from Carrie's eyes. "I know, Aunt Em. I appreciate that."

Now was not the right time. She wanted to find a way to reveal her true identity without upsetting Josh's aunt too much. If there was such a way. She hoped Aunt Em would be more understanding than Josh. She dreaded the day he discovered her deception. It would be a harsh payday.

CARRIE PULLED up to Wood Mercantile and tethered the wagon to a hitching post. Inside the store, they pulled out a dozen bolts of fabric and laid them on the table. Aunt Em exclaimed over one, then the other. When she'd narrowed it down to three favorites but still couldn't decide, the proprietor joined them and introduced herself to Carrie as Mildred Wood. "May I help you make a selection, Emma?

Carrie patted Aunt Em's arm. "I noticed the post office is across the street. Why don't I pick up the mail while Mrs. Wood helps you make up your mind?"

"Hmm. That's a wonderful idea. You go ahead and take your time. If you want to browse at another shop, go right ahead. I still have a grocery list to fill after making my fabric selection."

Carrie opened her reticule and pulled out the letter. She walked down the boardwalk past several stores, then crossed the dusty street. Not many people were in town. Mondays were slow in Denton too.

She waited in line at the post office. When she reached the window, she asked for two stamps besides the one she put on her letter. The balding postmaster gave her the stamps and took her money, staring over horn-rimmed glasses perched on his hawkish nose.

"Sir, may I have the mail for Josh Kramer and Emma Roberts?"

He frowned. "I'm not authorized to hand over mail to folks I don't know. Who are you?"

"Katy Davis." Her gut twisted at the lie, but she had no other option. "I'm Mrs. Roberts's domestic help." At least that part was true.

"I need proof. Got anybody to vouch for you?"

"Mrs. Roberts is across the street at the mercantile. Shall I go after her?"

"That won't be necessary," a masculine voice replied from behind her.

Carrie whirled around to find Ben Grady. "Ben!" She wasn't sure what kind of welcome she would receive after the incident at the dance. The right side of his chin was splotched with a purplish bruise. Otherwise, he looked fine.

He waved at the postmaster. "Mr. Donovan, this is Katy Davis. I'll vouch for her. She's staying at the Kramer ranch, hired on as Mrs. Roberts's help."

The postmaster nodded. "That's fine, Ben. I trust your word. He ducked below the window and came up with a stack of mail."

The postmaster trusts him? If he only knew how Ben treated the ladies. Carrie accepted the mail and turned around. "I appreciate you vouching for me, Ben."

He whispered near her ear, "The least I could do after the way I behaved the other night. I hope you'll forgive me considering my condition." He waited for her answer.

"Of course." Ben could make what he wanted out of her reply, but she would never again be caught alone with the likes of him. Not if she could help it.

Carrie moved out of the line to allow Ben to step up to the window. Wanted posters on the wall to her left caught her attention. She stepped closer to peruse them. Three were of grisly men. Two were beady-eyed with thick mustaches. The other man was clean-shaven with a scar down the right side of his face. The poster below of a tough-looking woman with blonde stringy hair, made her shiver. She was part of a gang wanted for bank robbery. She bent forward for a closer look. The woman could be her if—.

"Carrie!" a high-pitched voice squealed.

She jumped as if someone had shot her. Before she could turn, a hand grabbed her arm. "It's me—Molly Taylor. We met on the train."

Carrie placed a hand over her drumming heart and gasped. "Oh, yes. How are you doing, Molly?" She scanned the post office, breathing easier when she spied Ben heading for the door and the postmaster missing from his window. Hopefully, neither heard Molly yell her real name.

Molly and the lanky cowboy hanging onto her arm were the only ones in sight. Molly pulled the smiling man forward. "This is my husband, Slim Hanks. We just got married at the justice of the peace. We came to Buffalo Gap because it has more restaurants than Baird, and a nice hotel where we can spend our honeymoon." She giggled at Slim's flushed face.

Carrie smiled. "Congratulations." They appeared to be in love. At least they had taken a little time to get acquainted before tying the knot.

Molly smiled. "Did you find a job here? You were hoping to be hired at a dress shop."

"No, I haven't found a job at a dress shop. I'm working as domestic help for a local family." She prayed Molly would not ask which family. Had her friend heard from Katy Davis? She wanted to ask, but if she did, the Kramer name would surely come up. So she kept silent.

"Did you find Josh Kramer waiting at the depot and give him Katy's message?"

Here it comes. "Yes, I found him."

"How did he take it?

"I'm not sure." It was true. Josh's poker face was hard to read.

She patted Carrie's arm. "Oh, he'll soon find another woman and get over her. It's too bad about you not finding a job. Have you checked at Sonja's Boutique? It looks to be a nice place."

The more time Carrie spent with Molly, the more likely she would let her secret slip. Her friend's questions, though asked out of concern, made her nervous.

Carrie excused herself. "Thank you. I'll head to Sonja's Boutique now. It's been good seeing you again, Molly. Nice to meet you, Mr. Hanks. I wish you both the best."

The slim-faced cowboy bared his protruding teeth. "Thank you, ma'am. Same to you."

Chapter Ten

Carrie hurried down the boardwalk and crossed the street. It shouldn't take long to see if the boutique was hiring. The scent of heavy perfume filled her nostrils as she entered the shop. A few ladies browsed through the dresses hanging on the racks and other finery folded and stacked on tables.

She walked up to the counter where an exquisitely dressed woman pinned price tags to blouses. "May I speak with the owner, please?"

"I am Sonja Devereaux, the owner. What do you need, mademoiselle?" The woman spoke with a foreign accent.

"I wondered if you were hiring."

"Do you have recommendations?"

"No, but I'm sure I could get one from my former employer, Mrs. Johnson. I worked at her dress maker's shop in Denton."

"Would that be Rose Johnson?"

"Yes, then you've heard of her?"

"I've visited her shop a few times. She carries the latest fashions. Her seamstresses are exceptional. They create the most exquisite dresses."

Carrie's cheeks warmed. "I was one of those seamstresses. I made the dress I'm wearing."

Sonja cupped her chin to study Carrie's dress. "Hmm. May I check the stitches?

"Yes, ma'am."

Sonja walked around the counter, knelt, and turned up the hem. Then she checked the stitches on the collar and the set of the sleeves. "Please turn and allow me a view from the back."

When Carrie twirled, Sonja said, "The bustle is perfect. This dress shows beautiful craftsmanship and a unique design. Although the fabric is not what I would have selected." She tapped a finger against her chin. "I wonder if we could create this dress in satin, or even silk."

Carrie smoothed her dress. "I'm sorry to hurry you, Miss Devereaux, but someone is waiting for me. I came to ask if you are hiring at this time."

"No, not at the present; but one of the young ladies who works for me will soon marry. She plans to quit and start a family. Please check back in a few weeks."

"Thank you. I will." Carrie turned and walked out, gripping the mail in her hand. She glanced down at the letter on top, slid her thumb to one side.

It was from Leah, addressed to Josh. She slid her thumb an inch farther and uncovered Leah's last name. Rollins. Josh's former sweetheart? Rollins must be her married name. Why had she written him? She'd broken his heart, rejected him, and married another. Carrie's stomach twisted in a knot. She walked blindly, taking deep breaths to quell her tumultuous thoughts.

It's no business of mine if Leah woos Josh back. I've no chains on him. He is a free man.

Thunk! Carrie slammed into a brick wall and stumbled. No, it was a husky cowboy.

"Excuse me, miss," the grinning man offered. "I didn't mean to run into you."

Carrie swayed and he reached out to steady her. "Thank you." Had Josh so preoccupied her mind that she had paid no attention to where she was going? "I'm sorry, sir. It was I who ran into you."

"My pleasure. All is forgiven." He doffed his hat and walked on.

Carrie read the sign above her head and the name across the bat wing doors below. *The Barbed-Wire Saloon.* Had she passed the mercantile already? An older man crossed the street and headed toward her. When he reached the saloon, she asked, "Sir, will you point me to Woods' mercantile? I seem to have lost my way."

He pointed. "Miss, it's a few doors behind you. Read the signs. You can't miss it."

She thanked him and retraced her steps. What a silly thing to do! All because this letter to Josh had upset her. She held it up and studied it. If she tossed it in the trash, Josh would never know Leah had written. When Leah didn't receive a reply from Josh, she would think he had rejected her.

If that woman wanted Josh back in her life after what she'd done—. It was wrong. Leah should not expect him to take her back. She had no right to Josh after she'd betrayed him.

Carrie whooshed out a breath and stuffed the mail in her skirt pocket. She would give the letter to Josh's aunt and let her do with it what she liked. The letter was not hers to decide.

Lord, forgive me for my evil thoughts. "I want to do the right thing, but I don't want to lose Josh."

Her mind taunted, *He's not yours to lose.*

But he might be one day if . . . "Stop it! Control yourself," Carrie admonished herself. She glanced around to see if anyone had heard her. To her relief, nobody was within hearing distance.

She made her way along the boardwalk, her mind still warring. Josh had no tolerance for deception. Leah had made him believe she loved him, then she'd rejected him. But Carrie was no better. She had tricked Josh and his aunt into believing she was someone else.

Carrie traipsed into the mercantile. Two bolts of fabric lay on the counter. Aunt Em clapped her hands together. "I couldn't decide between these two—they're both lovely—so I bought them both." She snickered. "I'll have two new dresses."

Carrie fingered one, then the other. "Both fabrics are lovely. I can't wait to start on them."

Aunt Em paid for her purchases and nodded at the clerk. "We'll be back soon to buy material for this young lady."

Carrie picked up the bag and started to the door with Aunt Em following. When they were outside, Aunt Em asked, "Did we get any mail?"

Carrie reached into her skirt pocket and handed it over. Aunt Em frowned at the letter on top. "Hmm, what does Miss Leah want with Josh after all this time? I've a good mind to toss it in the wood stove."

Carrie stifled a giggle and cleared her throat instead. She and Aunt Em had the same thought. "We can't. It belongs to Josh. He has a right to read it."

Aunt Em snorted. "You *would* have to remind me. It's temptin' to accident'lly drop it along the way. I'd like to protect him from her. She's hurt him enough. I don't want him hurt any more. But as you said, Josh has a right to read it."

"Why would she write him now?"

"I wonder if her marriage is in trouble."

Carrie wondered the same thing, but they would not know unless Josh chose to reveal the contents of the letter. Considering his penchant for privacy, she doubted he'd reveal it to anyone, except maybe his foreman. According to Aunt Em, Luke was a very good foreman. And the two were as close as brothers.

On their way out of town, Aunt Em asked, "Where all did you go?"

Carrie shook the reins. "To the post office, then I dropped by Sonja's Boutique. Not to buy. Just to look."

"When you get paid, you'll have a little money to spend on pretty things."

"Aunt Em, I wish you wouldn't pay me. It's enough to have a place to eat and sleep."

"Nonsense. You're a big help to me. You're a hard worker, young lady."

"You are too." Carrie fixed her eyes on the road. "I saw Ben Grady in the post office. He apologized for the way he acted at the dance. He even admitted he'd had too much to drink."

"I hope you aren't considerin' letting him court you. Josh won't like it."

Carrie's heart warmed. She couldn't stop the smile from spreading across her lips. "You don't think he would?"

Aunt Em arched her brows. "I know he wouldn't."

As Josh dried his hands, Aunt Em reached into her apron pocket. "This came for you."

His brows knit together as he stared at the envelope. "I'll be right back."

He left the kitchen with the letter and returned empty-handed as if nothing unusual had happened. Aunt Em studied Josh through narrowed eyes, showing her disapproval that he had not opened Leah's letter and revealed its contents.

Josh's gaze raked the platter of beef roast and full serving bowls. "The food smells delicious. Is supper ready? I'm starving."

When they were seated, Aunt Em announced, "I'm starting a new custom in the Kramer household. We've done this before, but I want us to join hands every time we pray." She stretched one hand toward Carrie and the other toward Josh. Carrie clasped Aunt Em's extended hand. Josh hesitated then clasped her other one.

His aunt nodded. "Now Josh, take Carrie's other hand." Carrie extended her free hand.

Josh's mouth twisted to one side. Carrie would bet he wasn't keen on his aunt's new bidding. He hesitated, then reached across the table. His strong, callused hand enfolded hers.

Bowing his head, he said grace. "Heavenly Father, we thank You for Your protection and for the bounty you have provided. For the garden vegetables and the new calves. We also thank you for the hands which prepared this food. In Jesus' name. Amen."

Josh's long, knotty fingers squeezed Carrie's. When he slipped his hand away, she felt she'd lost something precious.

Aunt Em kept the conversation going while Carrie either nodded or agreed. Josh only grunted his responses. Carrie's effort to avoid eye contact with Josh was wasted since he kept his gaze on his plate.

Since the night of the dance, he'd spoken to her twice and only out of necessity. In church, he'd slid down the pew, putting an extra foot between them. Carrie was sure Aunt Em noticed the change in their behavior. It would be only a matter of time before she brought it up. She didn't put up with what she called nonsense.

Aunt Em grabbed a piece of cornbread and plunked the plate down on the table. "All right, which one of you wants to tell me what's goin' on?"

Carrie eyed her, then Josh. Oh, dear. She had wasted no time taking them to task.

Josh's sullen gaze raked Carrie before he turned it on his aunt. "What do you mean?"

"Nobody is talkin'." She threw her napkin on the table and leaned back in her chair. "I'm tired of being the only one around this table who doesn't grunt or simply agree with what's being said. Out with it! What's goin' on between you two? And don't say, 'Nothin,' because I wasn't born yesterday."

Josh winked while patting her hand. "You took the word right out of my mouth. 'Nothing."

"Sweet talkin' won't work with me, boy. I want the truth. You've acted strange since the mornin' after the dance. Don't think I didn't notice how you slid halfway down the pew in church. You'd think Katy and I had smallpox."

Neither Carrie nor Josh spoke, allowing Aunt Em to continue. "If I don't get an explanation out of both of you sittin' here at this table, I'll talk to you separately later. The only way around not tellin' me what the problem is, is to start being civil to each other."

She slid her chair back, rose, crossed her arms over her chest. "Josh, you go saddle up Geronimo for yourself and saddle up that sweet pinto for Carrie. There's still an hour of daylight left. You two can take a leisurely ride for as far as you like. Take as long as necessary. However long it takes to put smiles back on your faces and get you two speakin' to one another."

Carrie hopped up, protesting, "I need to do the dishes."

"No. You do as I say. I've washed these dishes for more than two decades without help. I can do it one more time." Josh strode out of the kitchen. Aunt Em thumbed toward Carrie's bedroom. "Go change into that ridin' skirt you showed me."

Carrie threw up her hands in surrender and walked to the bedroom. The screen door slammed. Josh's boots clomped across the porch and thudded when his feet hit the ground. What good would it do to take a horseback ride with him? He would probably clam up, wasted effort.

Carrie pulled on a white eyelet blouse and the split riding skirt she'd made. After tucking in the blouse, she walked back to the kitchen. Aunt Em turned from pouring steaming water in the dish pan. "Do I look all right?" She twirled.

"You look pretty." Josh's aunt took a deep breath. "If it's any comfort to you, I figure this standoff isn't your fault. Josh inherited a stubborn streak from his Pa. He comes by it natural. I was born with a generous dose too. I guess it runs in the family. My advice to you, sweetie, is don't prod him too much or he'll balk. Josh will open up and talk when he's good 'n ready."

JOSH CINCHED the saddle on Geronimo. Of all the crazy tricks for his aunt to pull, sending him and Katy horseback riding before sunset had to be the craziest. How did she know something wasn't right between them? Had Katy told her about their kiss?

No, that didn't sound like her. Katy and Aunt Em might be close, but she wouldn't disclose anything that private.

Since Saturday night, Josh's mind had been preoccupied to the point he couldn't focus. Luke had to repeat several things before he could get his attention.

Josh had never experienced anything like the sweetness of Katy's kiss. Now all she had to do was look at him and his face flamed. Cowboys weren't supposed to blush, but Josh couldn't be in the same room with her without mentally replaying their kiss.

The full moon had beamed down on Katy's face, rendering an ethereal glow. Josh could still feel her arms circling his neck and her heart beating against his ribs. How had she ended up in his arms? Had he tried to comfort her? He shook his head. That part of the scene was a blur.

Because Josh was attracted to Katy and didn't know how to cure himself, he had started avoiding her as much as possible, even ignoring her across the table during meals.

One year ago, he promised himself he would never again allow his heart to become involved. Not after his bad experience with Leah. Josh had always been level-headed, seldom letting his heart rule. He'd let his guard down that once and gotten burned. What went wrong?

Josh's rational side wanted to kick himself for letting Katy get to him. His irrational side wanted to pull her into his arms and replay that kiss again and again.

Shaking his head as if to clear it, he hefted a saddle on the pinto's back. The mare was gentle, not easily spooked. With the bridle in place and the saddle cinched, they were ready to ride. May as well get this over with. If he refused Aunt Em, he'd never hear the last of it. It would probably be a silent ride, but at least it would appease his aunt.

He tramped upon the porch, stuck his head inside the screen door. "Horses are ready. We'd better hurry, not much daylight left."

Katy walked out wearing a white eyelet blouse and a blue riding skirt. He'd bet she made both. The lady had talent when it came to sewing.

"Need some help mounting?"

She was in the saddle before he could move. "Pretty horse." She patted the pinto's neck.

Josh swung up into his saddle. "Her name is Cloud. She's a gentle horse."

∽

CARRIE COULD FEEL Cloud's restlessness beneath her. The mare hadn't been ridden since she'd been at the Kramer ranch. She made trips to the barn a couple of times each day to pet the horse and brush her, occasionally bringing her a carrot. She and the horse weren't strangers.

"I'll lead the way," Josh announced.

When Josh's horse trotted out of the yard, Carrie dug in her knees. Cloud flew down the road, kicking up dust. She laughed as she passed a surprised Josh. The wind on her face sent her long braid flying. A rush of freedom engulfed her has she urged the pinto to full speed.

Rapid hoof beats pounded the ground behind her. Carrie turned to see a determined set to Josh's jaw as he urged Geronimo forward. He grinned when he reached her side. They slowed their horses to a trot.

"That was invigorating," Carrie whispered.

Josh fixed her with a mock stern glare. "You gave me a scare. I didn't know you could ride like that."

"I've been on a horse since I was three. Pa taught me and — my pa taught me to ride." Carrie bit her tongue. Her brother's name had almost slipped off it. It would have been her undoing. Josh would have asked questions, and Carrie would have had to come up with a good answer. One that might be her undoing.

How she wished she was free from this deceit. No more avoiding questions or changing the subject to protect herself. She could then talk freely with Josh about her past, her joys and her struggles, without worrying the wrong thing might slip out and her true identity be exposed.

Carrie and Josh trotted side by side in a comfortable silence. Was he thinking about the letter from Leah? Shock registered on his face when Aunt Em handed it to him. He hadn't said a word, just took it to his room.

She would love to read the letter. Was Leah happily married to the drifter, or had he abandoned her? If he was out of the picture, would Josh take Leah back? Josh didn't strike her as a man who offered second chances. Not good for her, not good for Leah. Trust was high on Josh's list of values. When a person let him down, the relationship was over. She didn't need anyone to tell her.

This was why, as much as she wanted to tell him the truth, she could not do it. Carrie prayed every morning, "Please, Lord, I need a little more time. I'll tell him soon. Just not yet."

But would the time ever be right?

Josh broke the silence. "We'll stop up ahead and let the horses drink from the stream. It's beyond that grove of trees. Sometimes I go there when I need to think."

They trotted up under the trees. Josh dismounted and turned to help Carrie down, but she'd beat him to it. "Follow me." Josh led Geronimo down a well-worn path to a meandering stream. She stayed close behind, gripping Cloud's reins.

When they reached the stream and the horses began to drink, Josh reached for Carrie's hand. "Follow me and watch out for tree roots. They can trip you."

He led her to a log at the edge of the water downstream and gestured for her to sit. He sat down beside her within arm's length. Birds twittered on a limb above them. A kaleidoscopic sunset of peach, lavender and baby blue peeked through the trees on the opposite side of the stream. "This is the spot where I do my serious thinking."

"I see why. It's serene, the perfect place to think." Carrie reached down, flipped off her shoes.

Josh frowned. "What are you doing?"

"Cooling my feet." Carrie stuck her toes in the stream, swirled them around in the water. "Mmm . . . it's refreshing. Take off your boots."

He hesitated, made a face. "They're hard to pull back on when my feet get wet."

"Aw, come on. The water feels wonderful."

He reached down, pulled one boot off, then the other. His teeth chattered as he placed one foot then the other in the stream. "Oo-oh, th-a-t's co-o-l-d."

Carrie giggled. "It'll be all right once you are adjusted to the temperature."

A minute later he admitted, "It does feel good."

Carrie looked up at him. "What do you want to talk about?"

"Talk? Do we have to?"

"Yes. You know Aunt Em's instructions. We can't come home until we're both smiling."

Grinning, Josh tweaked her nose. "I don't know what to think about you, young lady. You're full of surprises."

She threw her braid over one shoulder. "Life would be boring without an occasional surprise."

"You're right." His expression sobered. "Katy, I haven't been fair to you. Since my experience with Leah, I've had a bad attitude toward most women. She all but destroyed my confidence."

Carrie whispered, "You must have loved her very much."

Josh shrugged. "I'm not sure anymore. I wonder if my pride was more involved than my heart."

Carrie was dying to know what was in that letter. His aunt's warning words echoed through her head. *Don't prod Josh too much. He'll balk.*

Was the letter the reason he'd been quiet at supper? He hadn't talked much since the dance, but tonight he'd seemed more distant, as if something weighed on his mind.

Josh popped off his hat to scratch his head. "I was too thick-headed when it came to our relationship. I thought I could change Leah, make her care for me. I bought her gifts and tried to charm her."

Carrie couldn't imagine the serious cowboy acting silly over a girl. Evidently Josh possessed a side to his personality that he kept hidden.

He tugged his hat on again. "When I think about it, I was as much at fault as Leah. I tried to push her into feeling something she didn't feel, when she only thought of me as a friend."

"I'm sorry she hurt you."

"Don't be. I learned a good lesson from the experience. One I will not soon forget. Never try to force a person to feel something for you. It's no good unless the feeling comes of its own accord."

Josh had admitted that forcing a person to feel something they didn't, ended in disaster. What Carrie wanted to know was if he still carried a torch for Leah. If not, did she stand a chance with him?

What was wrong with her? She had deceived him. When he discovered who she really was, she would be history. He would throw her and her bag out in the yard and order her to leave.

Josh cleared his throat, pulling Carrie back to the present. "I'd like to apologize for whatever I said Saturday night. I don't know exactly what I said that upset you. Maybe you will explain."

Carrie ducked her head and watched the water trickling between her toes. Explain what? That she'd fallen in love with this tall, handsome cowboy, and that his blaming the full moon for making him crazy, had crushed her? As if he had to be crazy to kiss her! No, she wasn't explaining any of it.

Josh was waiting for her reply. She had to say something. But what could she say without revealing her growing feelings for him? Her heart was at stake. What if she told him how she felt and he said he didn't feel the same? She'd be devastated.

Carrie focused on two chattering squirrels high up in the gum tree on the opposite bank. "Josh, a girl doesn't know how to take it when a man apologizes after he kisses her."

"Why not? It's only proper if he's taken advantage of her while she was vulnerable." Josh yanked off his hat again and raked shaky fingers through his hair.

"You didn't."

"A few minutes after that heel forced himself on you? I . . . well, I shouldn't have done it."

This was not what Carrie expected. She had not been vulnerable when Josh kissed her, but she was now. "Apology accepted." If he knew his kiss had touched her soul, he might repeat Leah's death knell sentence on her.

I think of you only as a friend.

She closed her eyes and swallowed past the lump in her throat. Those words were the last ones she wanted to hear from his lips.

∿

JOSH TURNED TO FACE HER. "You said I shouldn't have apologized. Then are you saying you didn't mind my kissing you?"

Katy's luminous eyes shimmered with an emotion he couldn't define. He struggled with wanting to pull her into his arms and replay their kiss. First he needed assurance she wouldn't resist.

The hint of a smile tugged at the corners of her mouth as she flicked a ladybug off his shoulder. He covered her hand with his. Katy sighed. It was all the encouragement he needed. Josh scooted closer and pulled her into his arms. When she looked up at him, he claimed her lips. She slid her hands to his shoulders, then up and around his neck.

As the kiss intensified, fireworks exploded in his head. Did Katy see them too? Josh released her to steady his erratic breathing. She laid her head against his chest. He couldn't help thinking how nicely she fit in his arms. Like she belonged there. Sweet and trusting. He feathered kisses along her temple and cheek and breathed, "Katy, Katy, what are you doing to me?"

She tensed and pushed against him. He straightened to look at her face. Fear registered in her eyes. Fear and an emotion he couldn't name vexed him.

Katy reached for her shoes, pulled them on and stood. After

dusting her riding skirt, she walked to where the horses were teth-ered. "We should go. The sun will soon be down."

Josh needed a moment to get his bearings. What had he done now? He sucked in air, rose and made his way toward her. Was she afraid of him? He would never force himself on her. She needed to know he wasn't like Ben. Before she could mount, he touched her shoulder. "Katy, look at me, please."

She turned, met his gaze. "I would never do anything to hurt you. Do you believe that?"

She ducked her chin and nodded. "Yes, I believe you."

He hadn't imagined the tension between them. It was real. "Then what did I do wrong?"

She swallowed hard. "I can't explain. We should go."

They could continue the conversation later. Josh wanted answers. He glanced up at the remaining streaks of color in the sky. "Won't be long before it's dark." As if to back up his words, an owl hooted in a nearby sweet gum tree.

Josh held Katy's stirrup until she was settled on the horse and swung up in his saddle. Someone must have broken her heart. He silently questioned for the hundredth time why a pretty young woman would travel this far to answer an ad for domestic help. Couldn't she find a job near her hometown? Something had forced her to leave home. What, or who? He intended to find out. For the time being, he would let it rest.

He turned to face Katy. "We had better be wearing smiles when we get back. Aunt Em will be watching us like an eagle."

Katy inhaled and let the breath out. "I'm sure she will. I will do my best. But how will we slip by her direct questions?"

"We'll figure out something. Maybe if we describe the stream, the birds twittering, and the squirrels chattering in the sweet gum tree, we can get her sidetracked."

"I doubt it. Then she'll want even more details."

Like, "What were you two doing down by the stream?" Josh felt his face flush. He was relieved the dusk hid it. "Aunt Em is persistent, for sure."

Katy laughed. "Like a dog with a bone. She clamps down on it and there's no letting go."

Josh kneed his horse "We'd better get a move on."

She glanced up. "Yes. No full moon out tonight."

Was she thinking about the night he'd taken her home after the barn dance? His face burned again. "Come on. I'll race you."

He took off at a gallop, but Katy quickly caught up. They raced neck in neck until they reached the ranch. Geronimo could have easily outrun the pinto, but Josh didn't push him.

They slowed to a trot when the house came into view. Aunt Em stood on the porch, waving. "Ah, you're back. I was beginning to think you wouldn't make it before the sun sank."

He climbed off his horse and helped Katy down. Aunt Em walked out to meet them. Josh bent to kiss her cheek. "Well, we did. Ask Katy how fast Cloud can run."

Katy glanced from his aunt to him and winked. "Faster than Geronimo."

"Don't tell me you two were racin' on the way back. That's dangerous in the dark."

Josh grinned. "You wanted us back before the sun set. We aimed to please."

Aunt Em shook her head. "Well, did you two have a pleasant ride?" She directed her question to Josh but studied Katy "It looks like the fresh air did Katy good. The color's back in her cheeks."

"The ride was invigorating. I didn't realize how much I missed horseback riding."

"Even Josh has a healthy glow," his aunt noted. "And he's smiling for the first time in days. If I'd known horseback ridin' would cure the mully-grubs, I'd have suggested it sooner."

JOSH LED the horses into the barn while Carrie and Aunt Em entered the house. A sweet aroma engulfed Carrie as they entered the kitchen. "Mmm, something smells delicious."

"Fried peach pies." Aunt Em cleared her throat. "Did you and Josh get things cleared up between you? Did he say anything about the letter?"

"We talked a little. No, he didn't mention the letter, and I didn't want to pry."

"My goodness, young lady, you won't learn a thing until you ask. You know my nephew."

This might be Aunt Em's way to get answers, but Carrie lacked the courage to interrogate Josh. Time to change the subject. "Do you need help with anything?"

Aunt Em scanned the kitchen. "Pour three glasses of milk while I serve up the pies. The milk should be cold by now. I just drew the jug up out of the cistern."

Josh stopped in the living room and sniffed the air. "Mmm, someone's been baking. When the kids are away, the cook will play."

When both Carrie and his aunt made a squeamish face, he shrugged. "That's an original Kramer twist on an old saying."

Aunt Em shook her head. "I fried some peach pies. They're hot and just right for eatin'. Katy is in the kitchen pourin' up the milk."

Josh rubbed his stomach. "Yum! I could eat at least two." He turned to Carrie. "How about you?"

"Maybe half of one."

He winked. "Good. Then I'll eat my two plus your other half."

Aunt Em rolled her eyes. "I declare, boy. you oughta' be as big as a barn."

"I can't help it if I'm a growing boy."

"Humph. And I'm Annie Oakley."

Josh winked. "You could be. You shoot like her."

Aunt Em hurried toward the kitchen. "Hush. Katy don't want to hear about that."

By Josh's smirk, Carrie knew she was about to hear an amusing tale. "Hear about what?"

"About the red-tailed hawk circling the chicken yard and how Aunt Em grabbed the rifle to scare him off."

"What happened?"

Aunt Em slid another fried pie onto the plate. "If you must know, I shot a squirrel's nest out of the large oak behind the barn. Don't worry, there weren't any squirrels in it. But that bloomin' rifle has a kick to it. It rammed against my shoulder and threw me on my backside."

Carrie shook with laughter. She set the milk jug on the table to prevent spilling it and waited until the laughter dissipated. When Josh fixed her with an admonishing look, she started convulsing again.

He raised a finger and shook it. "Oh, the tales I could tell on my sweet Aunt Em."

His aunt hiked an eyebrow. "Don't forget, I know several on you."

Carrie poured another glass of milk and set it in front of Josh. "Was Josh a mischievous child?"

"Mischievous doesn't do it justice. One day he wondered what the White Leghorn rooster would look like with red tail feathers."

Carrie clicked her tongue. "Josh, you didn't."

He shrugged. "I thought a bright Indian headdress on his back end would give him a dignified air. I got a walloping for that, but the old rooster wore his colors proudly all summer."

They sat down to enjoy their peach pies. Josh and his aunt swapped several more funny tales throughout the meal. Carrie couldn't remember when she'd laughed so much.

As soon as the pies were eaten, Josh's expression sobered. He took a swallow of milk and plunked the empty glass on the table. Carrie didn't have to wait long to find out why his mood changed.

"Tomorrow, the vote comes up on whether to keep the county seat in Buffalo Gap or move it to Abilene. Buffalo Gap has lost a lot in businesses and population since the railroad ran north of us two years ago. Everyone I've talked to is afraid it will move to Abilene. I just hope our townspeople don't take matters into their own hands if the vote goes that way. Listening to several business owners, I'm afraid the townsfolk are stirred. All over town, people were huddled in groups. Some whispered and others were ranting."

Carrie shifted her gaze from Josh to Aunt Em. "Why would they move the county seat?"

Aunt Em laid her fork beside her plate. "Before the railroad came through, Abilene didn't exist as a township. After it came, the town burst at its seams, almost overnight. Then Abilene began to pull people and businesses away from Buffalo Gap."

Josh nodded. "In two years' time, Abilene's population has overtaken that of Buffalo Gap. It's bursting at the seams and still growing. Before the railroad, Buffalo Gap was a thriving town. Settlers moved here by the droves. The population had grown to twelve hundred by the time the railroad came. Businesses popped up all over. Today, Buffalo Gap has dwindled to six hundred residents.

"People traveled from the South and the East to Abilene because the land around it was divided into plots and sold off to first comers," Josh explained. "Like Aunt Em said, Buffalo Gap has lost both businesses and residents to Abilene. There's bad blood between the towns.

"The locals are not happy about losing businesses. We stand to lose more if the vote goes in favor of Abilene. Four commissioners are set to decide the fate of our town. If the vote ends in a tie, Judge Murray will break that tie. No one knows how he will vote, but if he votes against Buffalo Gap . . . well, I look for trouble whichever way the vote goes."

"Is it possible that Judge Murray would vote to move the county seat?" Carrie asked.

Aunt Em refilled Josh's milk glass. "No tellin' how he might vote. I just know it don't take much to get folks riled when their livelihoods are threatened."

Josh nodded. "The town has been on edge two years, since the railroad ran north of us."

Carrie's eyes widened. "What will happen if the vote goes to move the county seat?"

Josh shook his head. "It's hard to say. Let's hope it doesn't come to that."

Aunt Em slid her chair back and stood. "Well, I'm goin' to bed young'uns. Katy, do you play checkers? Josh might want to take you on."

"Yes, my bro— moth-er and I used to play." Did either Josh or his aunt hear her slip? They might ask probing questions. No, they were still discussing possible scenarios about tomorrow's vote.

"I probably won't be home until late afternoon," Josh announced. "I plan to be there firsthand to see how the vote goes. I don't know how long it will take. From what I hear, the court-house will be jam-packed. I pity the judge if he votes against our citizens' wishes."

"You'd best get some sleep tonight then. Tomorrow will be a trying day."

"I'll go to bed after I beat Katy in a couple of checker games." He stared down his nose at her. "How about it? You up to it?"

She raised her chin. "I'm up to it. I just hope you are."

Josh arched an eyebrow. "I'll get the checkerboard."

Aunt Em yawned. "Good night, young'uns. Sleep tight, and don't let the bedbugs bite."

Josh set up the game on a small table and placed a chair on either side. "I must warn you, I'm a shrewd player."

Carrie flitted her lashes. "I can be pretty shrewd too."

He snorted. "Oh, I'll bet you can."

Did his words have a double meaning? Carrie took one of the chairs. "All right. Let's play. I'll take red."

One hour later, Josh had clobbered her in two games. Carrie barely won the third one.

Josh slid his chair back and groaned. "I'm through."

"Oh, come on, let's play one more. I deserve a chance to break even."

He rose and stretched. "I need my sleep. I can beat you another time."

Carrie curled up her lip and eyed him. "Ha! You're just afraid I'll beat you."

He chuckled as he swaggered toward his bedroom.

~

CARRIE LAY in bed reminiscing about her family, the good times she'd shared with them as a child, and how much she missed her parents. Nothing was more precious than family. A good one stuck together through thick and thin.

If only she'd done a better job raising her brother, maybe he wouldn't be wild now. Although, for the life of her, she couldn't figure out where she'd gone wrong, why Blake was reckless and irresponsible.

Not long before her parents' fatal accident, Carrie overheard their conversation as they sat on the porch. She knew they were discussing Blake when her pa said, "Some are born with a wild streak and there ain't nothin' in tarnation a body can do about it. Nothin' 'cept pray for 'em, raise 'em by the Good Book, and hope it takes."

Carrie punched up her pillow and rolled to her side. She had failed on her promise to keep her brother out of trouble. And she'd done wrong hopping on the train after she'd walloped Big Jim Counce. If that wasn't bad enough, she'd added deception to her list of wrong-doings.

Carrie's feelings for Josh and Aunt Em made her plight worse. If she hadn't grown fond of both, her predicament wouldn't be half as convoluted. How could she confess what she'd done without angering Josh, hurting Aunt Em, and breaking her own heart?

She closed her eyes and whispered, "Lord, you know the intents of my heart. I didn't do any of these things intending harm to anyone. It just happened, and now that it has, I can't see my way out clearly. Please show me how to set things right. I don't like living a lie.

"I don't know if Big Jim is looking for me or if he's even alive.

Maybe the law is looking for me. I didn't mean to hurt him, but he kept bothering me. I was trying to get past him to coax Blake out of the saloon before he squandered his paycheck again."

Josh and Aunt Em had become like family to Carrie. The Kramer ranch house felt like the home she'd had before her parents died. "Please don't ask me to tell them who I really am. Not yet. I don't know where I would go if they made me leave.

"Lord, I'm weary of trying to stay strong. I need to rest a while, to lean on someone else's strength."

Josh was her protector for the time being, but that could not last.

Chapter Eleven

When Josh sat down to breakfast, he reminded his aunt, "I won't be home until late afternoon. The court decision shouldn't take long once the arguments are over, but the arguments could go on for a while. The commissioners and judge have had plenty of time to make up their minds. Most of the town has promised to be present when the decision comes down. That is when things could take a turn for the worse."

Aunt Em slid a plate of scrambled eggs, steak, biscuits and milk gravy in front of Josh. "You be extra careful, you hear? When tempers flare, people can get hurt."

Josh swallowed a bite of steak. "I will. Hopefully, no one slips inside with a gun."

Carrie dropped a fork and clapped a hand to her mouth. "Could that happen? Aren't guns banned from the courtroom?"

Josh chewed his eggs and sampled the gravy. "Yes, but you never know when somebody will sneak one in." He wiped his mouth. "Mmm, this gravy is delicious. Best I ever ate."

Aunt Em winked. "Katy made it. She's a real good cook too."

Carrie's face warmed. "I'm glad you like it. Want some more?"

Josh shook his head. "I'd better not. I really need to get going."

The screen door rattled. "Boss, are you in there? I need to talk to you. It's urgent!"

Aunt Em whirled around. "What in tarnation?" Josh paid her no mind as he tramped out to the porch to meet his foreman.

Their voices drifted through the window to reach Carrie's ears. "Luke, what's the trouble? Did a bunch of javelinas cut our fence?"

"No, boss. It's the townspeople. They're madder than hornets. Dave White sent word by his foreman that two dozen armed men from Abilene are on their way to Buffalo Gap to make sure the town doesn't interfere with what they call justice. If the vote doesn't go in Abilene's favor, no tellin' what'll happen if those heathens show up in the courtroom. And if it doesn't go in favor of Buffalo Gap, there will still be hotheads to contend with. Either way, somebody from one side is sure to show out. Mr. White wants us to meet him at his ranch as soon as possible. He has a plan and needs more reinforcements."

Josh walked inside for his Stetson and a rifle. He turned back to Luke, who stood holding the screen door open. "Round up Hank and Charlie. I'll meet you at the White ranch."

Luke jumped off the porch and hopped on his horse while Josh grabbed cartridges for his rifle. Aunt Em wrung a dishtowel in her hands. "Where are you goin'?"

"To try to talk sense into those Abilene rowdies before innocent folks get hurt, or worse."

"Please, don't go, Josh! You'll be outnumbered," Carrie pleaded.

Josh gave her a crooked half-grin as he loaded his rifle. "Don't worry. White's hired hands plus mine will make the odds much better."

When he dropped extra cartridges into his shirt pocket, Aunt Em wiped perspiration from her brow with a trembling hand. "You, Luke, Hank and Charlie, plus Dave White and his ranch hands? That still ain't enough to fight against two dozen angry men."

The dirty plates and silverware clattered as she gathered them.

Carrie picked up the fork that clanged to the floor as Aunt Em marched to the dishpan with her load.

Carrie's shoulders rose and fell. "Josh, do you know what you're walking into?"

Aunt Em dunked the plates in the hot water. "Ain't no use tryin' to talk him out of it. He's a Kramer. You'd be wastin' your breath." Without turning, she said, "We'll be prayin' for y'all."

"I appreciate it, as will the rest of the men." Josh tugged on his hat and marched out of the house toward the barn, his rifle resting across one shoulder.

Carrie shrieked, "We have to stop him!"

Aunt Em shook her head. "Gal, don't you know there's no stoppin' a Kramer once he's set his mind to somethin'? Josh is as stubborn as his pa was."

Carrie flew out the door and into the barn, her shoes kicking up dust. She found Josh cinching his saddle around Geronimo. His clenched jaw and veiled eyes told her any attempt to change his mind would be futile. She walked closer, laid her hand on his arm. "Josh, I'm afraid for you. Are you sure you have to do this?"

He exhaled. "Katy, my pa taught me to stand by my convictions. I can't cow down and let a bunch of hooligans ride roughshod into Buffalo Gap and harm those who get in their way."

Tears stung her eyes. She brushed them away. "I know." Her pa had been the same way. And her brother, even though he'd taken the wrong path, would not back down either.

"I'll be all right." Josh gave her shoulders a squeeze and patted her arm.

"Please, be careful." Carrie stood on tiptoes, wrapped her arms around his neck, and pulled his head down to kiss his cheek.

Before she knew what had happened, Josh slid his arms around her waist and drew her closer. When she looked up at him, his eyes smoldered. She closed hers, and he bent and claimed her lips. Fire coursed through Carrie's veins as the kiss intensified. Her knees turned to jelly. When Josh let her go, she stumbled backward against the stall. She grabbed hold of it to steady herself while her breath came in gasps.

Josh fingered a lock of her hair and winked. "That was a little something for you to think about until I return."

Carrie touched her pulsating lips and watched the handsome cowboy gallop away on his horse, kicking up a cloud of Texas dirt. At his retreating back, she whispered, "Lord, please protect him. I love him so much."

~

AUNT EM DRIED the last plate and handed it to Carrie. "If you don't mind, I'd like you to start on my dress today. It'll take our minds off Josh and those hooligans. We've been prayin' for thirty minutes. I reckon the Lord has heard us by now. Sunday is our homecoming day. I'd like to see Almenia Bailey's eyebrows slap her hairline when I walk into church wearing a new dress in the latest style. She always has a new outfit for the occasion and gets to wallow in the compliments. For once I'd like to hear them exclaimin' over my dress."

Carrie giggled. She'd never have guessed Josh's aunt possessed even a trace of vanity. She needed something to keep her mind from straying to Josh's kiss. Had Aunt Em noticed her flushed cheeks? They still burned. "I'd like to start on it, but you need help canning tomatoes."

Aunt Em waved her away. "Shoo, I can handle that half-bushel by myself. This is the last of 'em, the garden's about gone. It won't take long to get these in jars. You milked the cow and fed the chickens this mornin'. There's not much else to do since Josh won't be in until late. I'll have to start supper after a while. Besides the cannin', we're caught up on chores."

She patted Carrie's arm. "I'll show you where I keep the patterns and notions and get your opinion on which style will most flatter my figure. I want the lavender print made up first."

When they reached the bedroom, Aunt Em lifted the lid on

the cedar chest. The pungent scent stung Carrie's nostrils. The older woman reached inside and pulled out fabric and a stack of patterns. She dropped the lid and lined up the patterns on top.

"Which style do you think would suit me best? Be honest with me."

Carrie scanned the selection. "They're all pretty." She tapped one of the packages with her forefinger. "For the lavender print, I like this one with the slightly puffed sleeves. It has a trim waist, and the bustle isn't overly exaggerated, which will make it slimming."

Aunt Em laid the folded fabric across Carrie's arms. "There you go. You'll find scissors, pins, needles, and everything else you need inside the sewing basket. Let me get my thimble and a needle out of the basket first. I need to mend a couple of Josh's shirts. That young'un is hard on his clothes. A sleeve is comin' loose on one. Two buttons are missing from the other. You can cut the pattern out on the kitchen table."

Aunt Em would always think of Josh as a boy. But his taut biceps enfolding Carrie, and his warm lips pressed against hers, proved otherwise. She'd better take control of her thoughts.

Carrie pulled the tape measure from the sewing basket. "Let's measure you first, to see if the pattern runs true to size. The sizes can differ depending on the manufacturer."

When Carrie had jotted down Aunt Em's measurements, they marched back to the kitchen. Aunt Em set the box of canning jars on the small worktable while Carrie spread the dress material across the table.

She was in her element, pinning pattern pieces to the material so as to not waste one more square inch of material than necessary. Pins protruding from her mouth, Carrie hummed along with Aunt Em's rendition of *Work for the Night Is Coming*.

When all the pieces were pinned, Carrie asked the question that had weighed on her mind since the trip to the post office. "Has Josh said anything about the letter from Leah?"

Aunt Em laid a towel over a hot jar and tightened the lid. "Not one word. I suspect her marriage to the drifter went sour."

Carrie had thought as much. "Do you think she will try to win Josh back?"

"Good luck to Leah, is all I have to say. That gal's chances are zero to nothin' because Josh rarely gives second chances. She hurt him. And when his heart's involved, forgivin' is next to impossible."

No second chances with Josh? That didn't bode well for Carrie.

"But I wouldn't put it past her to try to win him back."

Aunt Em's words left a bad taste in Carrie's mouth. Leah had no right to Josh after betraying him. She would never betray a man like Josh if he were her beau.

Yet, hadn't she betrayed him in a different way?

Picking up the scissors, Carrie prepared to cut out the dress. "What is Leah like? What did you think of her before she hurt Josh?"

With her back to Carrie, Aunt Em covered another hot jar with a towel and lifted it from the canning pot. "I can read people pretty well, and what I read about Leah didn't bode well from the start. Oh, she was all right for Josh to take to social events. But to court Leah with matrimony in mind . . . I still can't imagine those two ever bein' happily married."

She set the jar on the worktable and pointed at Carrie. "On the other hand, you and Josh would make a lovely pair. Don't think I haven't noticed the way you look at one another."

Carrie's hand trembled. Fearing she'd slash through the sleeve she'd cut out, she laid the scissors down. She decided not to reply. Aunt Em was too observant and outspoken. She didn't think twice before speaking her mind. Sometimes her frankness put Carrie on the spot.

Josh had mentioned his aunt's eagle eyes. Honestly, Aunt Em didn't miss a thing. She had correctly guessed the looks she gave Josh. But she was wrong about Josh returning those looks.

If only it were true!

No, that would make matters worse. If Josh cared for her, he would be even angrier when he discovered she'd tricked him.

Aunt Em filled another jar with tomatoes, humming as if she'd said nothing out of the way. Carrie took a deep breath and picked up the scissors. Was is possible Josh did feel something for her? She cut out another sleeve and laid it aside. "How does Josh look at me?"

"Don't tell me you haven't seen his eyes light up when he looks at you. Other times a sad puppy-dog expression crosses his face, like he's longin' for something precious he can't have."

How had Carrie missed that look? No, she wouldn't have seen it because lately she'd avoided eye contact with him as much as possible. Then why had she rushed out to the barn and practically thrown herself into his arms?

Nothing made sense. Her emotions were all over the place. She'd let Josh kiss her. Or had she kissed him? And what were his words before he hopped on Geronimo and rode away?

That was a little something for you to think about until I return.

Carrie's face warmed as the memory of the kiss flooded through her. Thank goodness Aunt Em's back was turned as she twisted lids on jars. Did she suspicion Josh had kissed her, not once but three times? The way she'd acted lately, and things she'd said, made Carrie wonder. And sending them off on a sunset ride to make up. How did she know they'd had an argument?

Not a real argument. Josh stating that the full moon had made him act crazy still stung. Either he meant what he'd said, or he was denying any feelings for her. Either way, it hurt.

Soon all the dress pieces were cut out and lying on the table. Carrie stacked the smaller pieces on top of the larger ones and laid them atop the sewing basket. "I'm off to the sewing machine. It won't take long before we will have an idea what the dress will look like."

Aunt Em clapped her hands together. "I can hardly wait."

"Neither can I." Carrie laughed at the older woman's happiness. It warmed her heart.

"Katy, something's been puzzlin' me since the day you arrived."

Carrie's gaze darted to Aunt Em's now somber face. Her heart pounded against her ribcage. *Uh-oh, here it comes.*

"I don't know how to ask this . . ."

Carrie froze. "What is it?"

"Let's sit a spell." Aunt Em laid the towel on top of the jars and gestured for Carrie to take a chair at the table. Aunt Em sat down at her usual spot at the head.

When they were settled, she began. "In your letters, you sounded eager to meet Josh. But when you arrived, you acted as if you weren't sure you wanted to go through with the marriage. What made you change your mind?"

Carrie kept her head down mentally searching for a noncommittal answer. She settled on, "Meeting someone is not the same as writing letters."

Aunt Em propped an elbow on the table and cupped her chin with her hand. "I understand why you'd be upset with me. I misled you, and it was wrong. I'm sorry I had to do it behind Josh's back, but I feared he would never have trusted his heart again if I didn't help things along. Leah hurt him real bad."

Carrie swallowed hard. "I don't know what to say." She honestly didn't. Telling the truth now would mean a sudden end to the life she'd come to love, the people she'd come to love. Tears stung her eyes. She wanted to weep for what she stood to lose—and would—when the truth came out.

Aunt Em continued. "I figure you pulled back because I told you how I'd tricked Josh by placing ads for him a bride. I couldn't blame you if you were upset. I worried that you'd pack up and leave on that account. You had every right to expect to get married right away. That's the reason I sent Josh into town with you the next mornin'. Not only because I feared you might try to leave, but I hoped you two might get better acquainted. But you didn't leave. It made me wonder if you saw somethin' special in Josh."

What would Aunt Em say if she knew Carrie's plans had been to find a job at a dress shop in Abilene and a room in a boarding house? What would she have thought of her if she had suddenly changed her mind about their arrangement?

Josh's aunt didn't wait for a reply. "My nephew is a good man. He gets moody now and then, but he gets over it. You need patience handlin' him. I see you're already makin' progress." She patted Carrie's hand.

"Josh is handsome, to boot. I don't think you're gettin' cheated in that area. He's loyal to his friends and quick to defend a cause or a person he believes in. Ask anyone who knows him. They'd trust him with their lives." Aunt Em chuckled. "I doubt that includes Ben Grady anymore."

She talked as if Carrie already had Josh bagged. Far from it. What his aunt didn't know was, although she was hopelessly in love with him, Josh did not reciprocate those feelings. And after he discovered she was living a lie, Carrie would be on the next train to who knew where.

Carrie smiled. "I think you are right about Josh's feeling toward Ben."

Aunt Em cleared her throat. "I hope you'll forgive me for not lettin' you in on my real plan through the letters. I figured to get you here first. Then Josh would take one look and be smitten. It appears he is, even though he seems to be movin' slower than a turtle stuck in a bog."

Carrie averted her gaze to look through the window and offered no comment.

Aunt Em sighed. "That letter from Miss Leah could throw a cog in the wheel. But let's not jump to conclusions. Could be there's nothin' to it. Just a friendly howdy. When Josh is good and ready, he'll reveal the contents."

Would he? From the impression Carrie had gotten, Josh was a private person. He stayed out of other people's business and expected them to stay out of his. "I hope you are right."

"I believe he will. What it comes down to is, if Josh had known I was lookin' for a bride for him, he'd never have let me place the ads." She chuckled. "And if I'd told you how he felt about matrimony, I doubt you'd be here now. Would you?"

"I'm not sure." Carrie might have come anyway. She had become frustrated with her brother, threatening to leave him, even before the run-in with Big Jim.

Katy Davis, on the other hand, had sensed something was wrong through the correspondence. According to Molly, it was why she'd backed out of the marriage proposition. Katy had read between the lines. She could tell through Josh's letters—no, his aunt's letters—that important personal information was being withheld.

"I guess it boils down to this. If you're interested in Josh, you need to show him. We don't want Leah stealing him away. At least not without puttin' up a good fight."

What would Aunt Em say if Carrie told her she hadn't originally planned to come to Buffalo Gap or to seek a husband? The domestic job suited her fine. At least it had until the night of the barn dance. Being Aunt Em's hired help was enough until that magical night, the same night Josh punched Ben Grady's jaw to protect her.

The moon had been full, shedding an ethereal glow over the earth. Carrie had ridden home behind Josh, happy and secure, her arms hugging his midsection while warmth radiated from his back. About halfway to the ranch he'd stopped at the creek to let Geronimo drink. An owl screeched, Carrie flew into in his arms, and he had kissed her.

Carrie's cheeks burned from the memory. If Aunt Em noticed her color rise, she made no comment as she rose except, "Well, I'd better get back to cannin'."

Carrie stood, keeping her back to the older woman. Aunt Em was adept at reading minds by observing facial expressions. If the older woman saw her face now, she would ask questions.

Aunt Em had read Josh wrong. Carrie was the smitten one, not him. Josh still licked the wounds inflicted by Leah and loved her in spite of her treachery. Maybe Josh had not forgiven the woman who had betrayed him, but he still had feelings for her.

Carrie felt at home at the Kramer Ranch. She had a roof over her head and three delicious meals a day. Aunt Em, and now Josh, treated her like one of the family. If only it could last. Her heart ached for Josh. What if she were forced to leave and never saw him again?

If she were allowed to stay, could she make him forget Leah? Was it possible to convince Josh that she would never betray him like Leah had, that her feelings for him ran much deeper?

Carrie's conscience stung. She closed her eyes. *No, you didn't betray him. You deceived him instead.* Were betrayal and deception equally atrocious in God's eyes?

She wanted to believe what Leah had done to Josh was much worse than her deception. But looking through Josh's eyes, she wasn't sure that was true. Carrie stood a strong chance of losing him. Honesty ranked high with Josh. Probably higher after his bad experience with Leah.

When the right moment presented itself, Carrie would tell the truth. She would beg Josh to hear her out. She would make him understand why at the train station she hadn't persisted in trying to explain that she was not Katy Davis.

Would he accept her explanation? Would he be angry? Those were questions she dared not contemplate.

DAVE WHITE and Josh rode lead. Six miles north, Luke pointed to a thick cloud of dust on the road ahead. "There they are. Over the rise."

Dave raised his hand, a signal for his men to halt. He twisted around in his saddle and gestured at the riders behind him. "Barricade the road."

When the road was blocked using wagons, Josh ordered, "Get out your rifles, but hold your fire."

The men pulled their rifles from their scabbards and laid them across their laps. The approaching riders galloped closer and closer, barely visible through the thick, red dust. They reined in, slowing to a trot when they saw the barricade.

"Whoa there!" Dave yelled. The men on both sides eyed one another with curiosity.

"Who are you, and where are you men headed?" Dave asked.

A large, dignified man who appeared to be their leader, raked the Buffalo Gap men with his stern gaze. "I'm Clabe Merchant from Abilene, and these are my men. We're headed to Buffalo Gap to ensure the vote on the county seat is upheld when the decision comes down."

Dave walked his horse closer and extended his hand. "I'm Dave White. These men and I are Buffalo Gap residents. Our vested interest is to ensure no innocent blood is shed over the vote. Why don't you men turn around and head back to Abilene?"

A tall, beady-eyed man sat taller in his saddle. His steely gaze bored into Dave and Josh. "We've come to see that justice is carried out, and that's what we're gonna do."

Josh hiked his shoulders and glared back through hooded eyes. "At the cost of innocent lives? Listen to us. You're riding into a trap. The Buffalo Gap men are armed and ready, at least a hundred of them. Both our towns have a vested interest in this decision, but getting into a shootout won't change a thing. Even if you come out in one piece, you could do prison time."

Josh yanked off his hat and wiped sweat from his brow. "Look, I'm sure most or all of you have families. Do you want your wives to become widows and your kids to grow up with no father over what could be settled peaceably?"

"Josh is right. This can be settled peaceably," Dave said. "You're all welcome to enter the courthouse if you promise to leave your guns outside."

Clabe Merchant turned to face the Abilene riders. "When we get to the town, you wait outside the courthouse. I'll go in and check things out. Then I'll come for the rest of you. Are we in agreement?"

The Abilene men nodded. All but one. He groused, "You sure this ain't a trick?"

Clabe pointed at Dave and Josh. "Mr. White and Mr. Kramer are honorable and highly respected men. I've heard tell they own ranches west of Buffalo Gap." He then spoke to Dave and Josh. "You have my word that no shot will be fired."

Dave nodded, and Clabe extended his hand. The men shook on it.

Then Dave White turned to the Buffalo Gap men. "All right, boys. Move the wagons and let them by."

As the Abilene riders galloped toward Buffalo Gap, Dave looked to Josh. "Should we trust them?"

Josh watched the riders disappear in a cloud of dust. "We will follow them into town, just in case. It would be best to divide up in pairs. Let the first pair get a good fourth-mile head start and the others do the same. If we don't all ride in together, we won't draw as much attention."

Dave clapped him on the shoulder. "Good idea. Boys, Josh and I will go first."

When Josh and Dave reached Buffalo Gap, the town was in a stir. The courthouse was packed. People hung out the windows. Nervous men huddled outside in groups with six-shooters strapped to their waists or rifles in their hands.

True to his word, Clabe Merchant told his men to wait outside and entered the courthouse. In a few minutes, he returned. "Leave your guns out here and come in." The Abilene men obeyed and tramped into the courthouse behind Clabe. Josh and Dave walked in behind them.

Judge Murray struck his gavel. "Silence, please! Order in the court!"

A few minutes of discussion ensued over the pros and cons of the county seat's location. Toward the end of the discussion, a court officer walked up to the judge and whispered in his ear. Judge Murray rose to address the crowd. "Excuse me, please."

They watched the judge and attendant disappear into the back room. The door closed behind them. Whispers echoed across the courtroom. The whispers grew to mutterings. Before tempers could flare, the attendant returned, holding an envelope. He handed it to the sheriff. The sheriff pulled a paper from the envelope and stood. "All rise, please."

Benches scraped across the wooden floor as the people stood. Silence prevailed as the verdict was read. "It has been decided by a vote of three to two that Abilene will become the new seat of Taylor County."

An angry male voice shouted from the back of the courtroom, "You haven't heard the last of this!"

Several in the crowd shouted, "It's not right!"

Another voice yelled, "Where's our cowardly judge?"

Another shouted, "We'll tar and feather that traitor!"

The sheriff raised his hand to silence the crowd. "Listen to me, good folks. We don't want any trouble. I suggest you all go home and cool off. We don't need a lot of hotheads shootin' off their mouths or their guns. This is a law-abidin' town, and we aim to keep it that way."

The throng pushed and shoved its way outside the courthouse where several appointed deputies stood guard. People muttered, then broke off and went their separate ways.

Josh stopped on the courthouse steps and wiped his brow. "Do you think this is over, Sheriff?"

The sheriff scratched his whiskered face. "I don't know, boy. But I sure hope it is."

Dave clapped Josh on the shoulder. "I'll collect my hands and head back to the ranch. We've already lost half a day's work. No use losing the other half."

Josh agreed. "This takes more out of a body than digging post holes. A section of my fence is down in the south pasture."

Josh walked across the street and found his hands at the

drugstore. Luke, Hank, and Charlie looked up from their bar stools, finishing off sarsaparillas.

Luke said, "We heard how the vote went. I figured we didn't have any business in the courtroom. I'm not fond of crowds anyway. Instead, we came over here for refreshments."

Josh's mouth watered at the foamy sodas. He could use something to drink too. He slid onto a bar stool beside Luke and snapped his fingers to get the attention of the man behind the counter. "George, make me one of those too." Turning back to his hired hands, he said. "You boys go on ahead and start digging the post holes. I'll be there soon. I have an errand to run after I finish my sarsaparilla."

Chapter Twelve

Josh tucked the green satin ribbons into his saddlebag, mounted his stallion, and trotted out of town. He'd admired the sea green dress with tiny white flowers Katy had worn to church last Sunday. These hair ribbons would match it perfectly. He hoped to see Katy's warm smile and her eyes light up when he handed her the ribbons.

She'd made a beautiful dress from the pink fabric he'd bought her the day they had rode into Abilene. Aunt Em was still in the dark about who purchased the material. Apparently, Katy hadn't let on that it had been a present from him. If she had, Aunt Em would be finalizing wedding arrangements by now.

Wedding arrangements? Hmm . . . the notion was beginning to appeal to him. He could do a lot worse. "Katy Kramer." He said it aloud and laughed. It had a nice ring to it.

Josh shook his head. He must be addled to let her get to him. He'd vowed to stay away from the ladies since Leah had burned him. Females spelled trouble. Then what had gotten into him this morning? Why had he grabbed Katy up in his arms and claimed her lips like a ravenous wolf after its prey?

Was it her pretty eyes filled with concern for his welfare, that moved him? Josh had intended to give her a quick hug to assure her he'd be all right. She threw him off balance when she wrapped her arms around his neck and pulled his lips down to meet hers. He forgot everything except his desire to express what was in his heart in one kiss. And what a kiss!

Where did that thought come from? What *was* in his heart? Had the kiss he shared with Katy resurfaced feelings he'd thought were dead and buried, feelings he'd thought Leah destroyed?

Leah? Josh tried to visualize her face, but it was a blur. He tried to conjure up feelings for her, but they either lay dormant or had dissolved. Was Katy responsible for these changes in him?

Yesterday, Aunt Em handed him a letter from Leah. First, he took it to the study and crushed it into a ball. Then he tossed it in the trash. On second thought, he pulled the envelope from the trash can and smoothed it. The letter might contain important information. Since he wasn't ready to read it, he hid it under a stack of papers in his desk drawer.

Leah wasn't the one occupying his thoughts lately. It was Katy. Something about her made him want to protect her. It was Katy's wide-eyed innocence that brought out the warrior in Josh. He would defend her against a cougar with his bare hands, if necessary, or any person who was a threat to her. His teeth clenched.

Including that self-proclaimed womanizer, Ben Grady.

Josh pulled his thoughts back to the daily grind. The Kramer land spread before him as far as the eye could see. He turned his horse toward the south pasture where the fence was laid over. Whether flattened by Kramer cattle or men who raged against fenced land, it had to be repaired.

JOSH TROTTED his horse into the barn, emotionally and physically weary. He was uneasy about leaving town while people were muttering and promising to get revenge on Judge Murray. Since most meanness occurred after dark, he'd eat supper, rest a little while, and ride back into town. That would give him an idea whether tempers had cooled or become more riled.

He hefted the saddle off Geronimo, picked up the brush, and began to stroke him. "Boy, do you know you're lucky? You don't have to deal with ill-tempered people or worry every year if there will be enough rain to grow hay to feed the cattle. All you do is haul me around and eat from your trough."

Geronimo tossed his head and nickered. Josh chuckled. "Yes, you know you've got it made." He put the brush down. "I'd better get inside before those women come after me. They'll be wanting all the details on the ruling and everything that was said in the courtroom."

"Josh!" Carrie stood at the barn door, several eggs folded in her apron. "I didn't hear you ride in."

"Yeah, I just got here." He sighed. "It's been a long day. We lost the vote."

"Oh, no! How did the people take it?"

"Not well. Tempers appeared to have cooled when we left town, but . . ." He shrugged not wanting to upset her.

She looked at him, her green eyes filled with compassion. Or was it something more? "You think there will be trouble?"

"I hope not, but I'm uneasy about it."

"You look tired. Come on in. Supper should be ready."

Josh filled the ladies in on the vote and the disturbance in the courthouse as they ate. "Judge Murray disappeared into the back room just before they brought in the envelope with the decision. The sheriff was the one who read it to the court." He hiked his eyebrows. "The people were not happy. Not happy at all."

"I'm not happy, either, but looks like we'll have to live with it. Maybe the people will calm down," Aunt Em offered.

"In time they will." Josh figured it wasn't over by a long shot, but he didn't want to worry the womenfolk. He rose and walked to the stove. When he'd lifted the heavy water pot and set it on the stove, he said, "I think I'll rest a bit. I'm bushed." He dragged himself to the bedroom and closed the door. After pulling off his boots and shirt, he lay down on top of the covers and instantly fell asleep.

~

"Josh! Josh!"

"What in the world?" Josh sat straight up, trying to get his bearings. Twenty minutes after five. Was it morning? Had he overslept? He threw his legs over the side of the bed and grabbed his shirt. Now he remembered. He'd lain down to rest after supper. "What is it, Katy?"

"The ranch hands rode up. Aunt Em's talking to them. There's a disturbance in town. It has to do with Judge Murray. They thought you should know."

Josh rushed out of the bedroom, carrying his boots in one hand, buttoning his shirt with the other.

Katy stepped out onto the porch behind him. Luke paced back and forth on the porch while Hank stood on the bottom step, fidgeting with his hat.

"What is it Luke? What's happened?"

Luke stopped pacing. "Charlie just rode in from town. He says there's talk in the saloon about forming a welcoming committee and heading over to the judge's house. The talk will get rougher as the men get more whiskey in 'em."

"They're callin' the judge a traitor," Hank added.

"Where is Charlie?"

"In the barn saddlin' a fresh horse. His is lathered."

Josh sat down on the porch swing and tugged on his boots. Raking his hands through his hair, he turned to Katy. "Will you get my hat and rifle?" The rifle was loaded and ready.

Katy returned with the items. Tears trickled down her cheeks. "Josh, please don't take any chances. If they form a lynch mob, they won't care who they lynch."

He wiped a tear from her cheek, fighting the urge to kiss her.

"I'll be careful. You and Aunt Em, start praying. God will protect us."

"You know we will. Don't do anything foolish."

Charlie led Geronimo and a chestnut mare out of the barn. The men swung up in their saddles. Josh turned around and pointed at Katy before they rode away. "Don't you forget. I'm the checkers champion."

Her eyes narrowed. "That's not fair. You didn't give me a chance to even the score."

He winked at her and turned to his men. "Come on, boys, let's get going."

THE SUN HAD SUNK HALFWAY below the horizon when Josh and his men rode into town. A curtain moved at the window of the Woods's house before their teenaged son dashed outside and intercepted them. "Mr. Kramer, a bunch of angry men rode over to Judge Murray's house a little while ago! You've gotta stop them."

"How long ago, Ted? Were they armed?"

"Almost an hour, I'd say. They had rifles. We heard shots comin' from that direction."

Josh's heart lurched. A lot could happen in an hour. He silently prayed, *Lord protect the judge, if it's not too late.* "How many men would you say?"

"Six or eight."

"Thanks for telling us." Josh kneed his horse. "Let's go, boys!"

The judge's place was located a half-mile south of town. The men galloped toward it. A loud commotion reached their ears before they reined in their horses. The white frame house sat dark and silent, but raucous laughter and hollering emanated from behind the house. It sounded as if they were celebrating. What had those men done?

Josh and his hired hands dismounted and tethered their horses to the white picket fence surrounding the yard. Josh took a deep breath and pulled his rifle from its scabbard. His men followed suit. "Let's see what's transpiring."

They walked through the open gate, stepping closer to the dark house. Josh turned to his men, pressed a finger to his lips, and whispered, "Follow me. Stay close to the side of the house and don't make a sound."

They raised their rifles, pressed their backs against the house, and inched to the corner. Josh peeked around and spied a dozen men seated around a campfire enjoying a feast. One man held what appeared to be a chicken wing to his mouth, while another nibbled on a drumstick. They were a jolly bunch.

Josh gestured for his ranch hands to stay put.

A bearded man tossed a bone in the yard and laughed. "Won't the judge be surprised when he comes back."

Josh exhaled. The judge was alive. *Thank you, Lord.*

A short, stocky man shook his head. "Yep! It's the best roasted chicken I ever did eat."

A lanky man stood and ordered in a raspy voice, "Let's all sing *She'll Be Comin' 'Round the Mountain.*" As he waved a drumstick to direct the rag-tag orchestra, a stocky man pulled out a harmonica and started playing. The others joined in singing.

The men were well on their way to becoming drunk. How far along, Josh couldn't tell. When they sang out, "We will kill the old red rooster," he smothered a laugh and turned to Luke. "Come on, I think it's safe." They lowered their rifles and walked out to join the circle around the campfire.

Edward Rice from the feed store raised a chicken wing and slurred, "Hel-lo, Mr. Kramer, won't you join us? We're having a mighty fine feast."

"No, thank you, Mr. Rice. We're looking for the judge."

"So was we, but you won't find him here."

Josh glanced toward the house. "Where is he?"

"Don't know. He and his family was gone when we got here."

The tall man interjected, "Yep. Judge Murray ain't just a traitor, he's a coward to boot."

The stocky man made a sound of a cackling chicken and the others laughed.

Edward Rice slapped his knee. "You got that right, Tom. The judge is a chicken. Well, he won't find none in his hen house when he gets home"

The men joined in a chorus of cackling. Everyone except a slim, bearded man who swallowed a bite of his drumstick and explained, "The deputy came by and said the judge was escorted out of town before court adjourned. Murray had armed men on both sides of his carriage. He had this planned, for sure, and took his fam'ly with him."

A slim-faced man shook his finger at the others. "That's why he slinked into the back room before they read the verdict. If you'll remember, he never did come back out. Murray took the coward's way out and let the sheriff read the rulin'."

Josh scratched his chin. It made sense, but was probably for the best. The judge knew the people would be angry when the ruling was read and had taken measures to escape.

He scanned the yard. "Where did you get all this roasted chicken?"

The feed store owner thumbed toward the chicken house behind him. "It's the least the judge could do to pay penance for his traitorism, if that's a word."

Josh's jaw dropped. "You mean all this roasted chicken—?"

". . . was walking around on two legs and cluckin' when we got here," Edward finished. "The judge had six plump hens and a mighty fine lookin' red rooster. We're enjoyin' a fine feast." He held out a platter stacked with several plump pieces of chicken. "Sure you won't join us? There's plenty to go around."

Josh shook his head. "No, thanks."

The short, husky man sighed. "Well, it's too bad the judge ain't here to enjoy the party. When, or if, he does come back, he'll be mighty surprised to find his chickens have flown the coop."

The man slapped his knee and laughed at his own joke.

Edward Rice wagged a finger at the men around the campfire. "Naw, you're wrong. They didn't exactly fly off."

Josh pulled off his hat and scratched his head. They had roasted all the judge's chickens? He should be relieved. Things could have been a lot worse if the judge had been home.

He nodded at the flour mill owner, the only man who appeared to be stone sober. "Robert, be sure the fire is out before all of you leave."

"Will do, Josh. Tell your aunt this roasted chicken is good, but it still don't hold a light to hers."

"I'll do it." He yawned. "Well, it's been a long day. I'm heading on home. You men be careful." He turned to his ranch hands. "Let's go, boys."

Luke reached into the platter for a drumstick. "Suits me."

CARRIE AND AUNT EM tried to relax on the porch swing while they listened for hoof beats and prayed for the safety of Josh and the Kramer ranch hands. The sun had sunk an hour before.

Carrie huffed. "I don't know how much longer I can wait. If they don't come home soon, I could take the buggy and go after them."

"No, dear, we'll wait. God will bring them safely home. We have to put this in His hands."

Carrie slapped at a mosquito on her arm. "At least it's cooler tonight. If I wasn't so nervous, I'd work on your dress. But my hands are shaking so that I'm afraid I might stitch through my finger."

"Work on it tomorrow. We still have plenty of time to finish it before Sunday."

Carrie-sat up straighter. "Listen! I think I hear hoof beats." A minute later, four riders trotted their horses into the yard and dismounted.

"Josh, is that you?" Aunt Em called out.

"Yes, it's me and the hands." He handed his horse over to Charlie and walked toward the house while Luke and Hank led theirs into the barn.

Carrie ran out to meet Josh, fighting the urge to throw herself into his arms. "Thank God, you're all right. Aunt Em and I never let up praying. What happened?"

"I could use a glass of milk and a slice of apple pie before I get into the details."

She detected the weariness in his voice. It had been a long, exhausting day for everyone. "Come in and sit down while I get it for you."

Aunt Em rose and cupped her hands around her mouth. "The rest of you men, come on inside and have a slice of apple pie," she called out. "There's plenty to go around." She turned to Carrie and Josh. "Josh, get inside. Carrie and I will dish up the pie and pour the milk."

Carrie set three extra places and poured milk into tall glasses. While Aunt Em scooped slices of pie on four plates, the ranch hands wiped their feet on the doormat and entered.

Carrie couldn't sit still, and she could tell by Aunt Em's frequent sighs she was holding back. Would the men ever finish eating?

Finally, Josh pushed his empty plate away and wiped crumbs from his mouth. "That was delicious."

"Sure was," Luke, Charlie and Hank chimed in.

"Anyone need more milk or pie?" Aunt Em asked.

All shook their heads.

Aunt Em propped her hands on her hips. "Then it's high time you told Katy and me what happened tonight."

The ranch hands looked at Josh. He cleared his throat. "Apparently the judge left town with his family, straight from the court-house this afternoon. I think it would be a good idea if he moved to Abilene since it was his vote that lost the county seat position for Buffalo Gap. The townspeople could be riled for a long time."

"It's hard to believe our own judge voted agin' us," Charlie chipped in.

"But he did," Luke commented.

Carrie could wait no longer. "What happened in town with the angry mob?"

Josh folded his arms across his chest and leaned back in his chair. "The mob beat us to the judge's place. They were having a party in his back yard."

"Feastin' on roasted chickens," Hank offered. "The judges' chickens."

Aunt Em frowned. "They roasted Judge Murray's chickens in his own yard?"

"Yep. All of 'em."

Josh shook his head. "They had a campfire built and a platter of chicken piled high. Aunt Em, before I forget, Robert from the flour mill said to tell you the judge's chicken didn't hold a light to yours."

Aunt Em blushed. "That was sweet of him."

Josh continued. "The men had come straight from the saloon. You can imagine their condition."

Charlie chuckled. "The thang that tickled my funny bone most was when the men started sangin', 'We will kill the old red rooster when she comes.'"

Carrie giggled and clapped a hand over her mouth. "I'm sorry. I mean, I hate that the judge lost his chickens, but the song struck me as funny."

"I'm just thankful nobody got hurt," Aunt Em added. "Now we can all go to bed and rest. Worrying over this vote has kept the town torn apart for too long."

"Speaking of rest . . ." Josh yawned. "I think I'll hit the hay."

"No checker competition tonight?" Carrie teased.

He arched a dark eyebrow and pointed at her. "Ha! You know I'd be easy prey tonight. Don't you worry, I'll take you up on the challenge at a later date. Meanwhile, I still retain the championship."

Carrie raised her chin and made a face at him. "I will be ready."

Chapter Thirteen

Aunt Em preened in front of the free-standing mirror in her bedroom. "I do declare. This dress gets prettier every time I try it on." She stuck her head out the door and yelled up the hall, "Katy, will you come here a minute?"

Carrie appeared in the doorway. "Sure. What do you need?"

"Advice. Which do you like best with my lavender print, this pearl necklace or the cameo?"

"The strand of pearls goes better, in my opinion."

"All right. The pearl necklace it is." Her gaze raked Carrie. "You'd better hurry and get dressed. We leave in thirty minutes. I don't want to be late on homecoming day."

Carrie grinned. What Aunt Em really meant was she wanted to get there, with time to spare, to flaunt her new dress before the service began. "I just finished putting our food in the picnic basket. I'll head to my bedroom now."

"All right then." Aunt Em pivoted for a side view in the mirror. "I love this bustle. It's a perfect size." Carrie had diminished it to flatter Aunt Em's full figure.

Josh pulled into the churchyard and parked their buckboard next to the other wagons and buggies. The horses were tethered farther away to make room for the tables of food. Josh helped

Carrie and Aunt Em out of the wagon. Carrie picked up a jug of fresh lemonade and walked toward the tables. Josh followed with the picnic basket.

"Is Almenia here yet?" Aunt Em twisted this way and that searching for her.

Carrie pointed to a wagon pulling up. "I believe that's her now."

"Yes, I do believe it is." She cleared her throat. "If you two will excuse me, I think I'll go meet her, see if she needs help with her basket."

Josh shook his head. "Those two have competed since I was knee high. When we have the church bazaar, both Aunt Em and Mrs. Bailey enter pickles, jellies, and pies in the competition. They alternate between winning first prize on their entries. Whoever takes second prize stays miffed at the other for a month afterward."

Carrie sighed. "And today it's a dress competition."

Josh laughed. "You did a wonderful job on Aunt Em's dress, if I do say so."

"She seems to like it."

"I don't know when I've last seen her act like a giddy schoolgirl. With your talent, it's a wonder you haven't opened a style shop."

Carrie rolled her eyes up at him. "It's a dream of mine, but you know, it takes money to run a business. Besides, Sonja Devereaux probably wouldn't appreciate it."

"Katy!" Nancy Grady waved from the church steps. "Come here. I need to talk to you."

Carrie patted Josh's arm with her gloved hand. "Excuse me. I'll see what she wants."

Carrie stepped up on the porch, and Nancy said, "Follow me."

She led her to a back room where colored drawings hung on the wall. "Do you suppose you could help me with the young children? On homecoming day, we have double or triple the number. It's hard for one person to keep them under control when it's half that many."

"Of course. What do you do to keep them quiet?"

"I tell them a Bible story, then we sing a few songs. When it's pretty like today, I take them outside afterward."

"Let me tell Aunt Em," Carrie said.

"You can tell her inside. First we join the rest of the congregation for a Scripture reading, a song, and a prayer. Just help me herd the children out of the pews and follow me when the prayer is over." Nancy hung her head. "I haven't had a chance to apologize for my brother's behavior." She glanced toward the door and whispered, "I didn't know he'd brought liquor to the dance."

"It's all right. You didn't know. Drinking often makes people do things they're ashamed of later. Anyway, Ben has already apologized."

"Oh? Where did you see my brother?"

"I—" Josh stood in the doorway, scowling. How much had he heard? Carrie hadn't told him she had seen Ben in town. The last thing she wanted was to stir up a hornet's nest.

Josh nodded at Nancy and her. "Aunt Em sent me to tell you ladies the service is about to begin.

JOSH TRIED to put on a pleasant face as he joined the congregation in singing, *I Love to Tell the Story.* Anger boiled in his chest, burning his throat. He paused on the second verse to cough.

Katy saw Ben again? When? Where? And why? It had to have been that day she and Aunt Em rode into town without him. Josh swallowed hard and glanced at Katy who stood serenely beside him, as if nothing was wrong. He wanted to grip her shoulders, make her look at him and give a full account.

Then he would say, *Woman, have you lost your ever-lovin' mind? Ben Grady is a heel! He doesn't give a hoot about you or any other woman. They're all just playthings for him.*

Josh had thought Katy had enough sense to stay away from that sorry excuse for a human being. Until now. No telling what

Ben would have done to her if he hadn't intervened that night outside the Coopers' barn. None of it made sense. Ben had forced himself on Katy. She'd fought, pleaded for him to release her.

Then he'd punched Ben so hard his knuckles throbbed. And Katy had met with him again? What was she thinking? Josh couldn't believe he'd judged her wrong. He'd always credited himself as being an exceptional judge of character.

He whooshed out a breath when Katy slipped out of the pew to help Nancy round up the children and herd them toward the Sunday School room. Her nearness made him uncomfortable. On one hand, Josh wanted to pull her into his arms and plead, "Katy, forget that Cad. He's not worth it." On the other hand, he wanted to shake sense into her.

What business was it of his anyway? Why should he care who Katy Davis courted? She was his aunt's hired help. Nothing more. Even as the thought entered his mind, his conscience shouted, *"Liar!"*

He didn't know exactly when, but he'd come to care for Katy. And he wasn't solely interested in her welfare or being her friend. Josh wanted more. He wanted what Leah could not give him. A future together, blonde-haired babies.

He had been bitter too long over Leah's treachery. Then Katy came along with her sweet personality, enchanting green eyes, and a smile warm enough to set his heart on fire. When he tried to dredge up feelings for Leah, he couldn't. Not only had the embers cooled, but the only thing left was a pile of cold, dead ashes.

Josh shifted again, thumping the back of the pew. Aunt Em sent him an admonishing look like she had when he was a fidgety child in church fighting pent-up energy. He had better pay closer attention to the sermon, or when his aunt grilled him on it later, he'd be in trouble. He could only recall bits and pieces of what Pastor Grissom had said. The sermon dealt with judging others, pointing out the speck in your brother's eye, but refusing to acknowledge the log in your own.

When the congregation finally stood and sang, *It Is Well with*

My Soul, Josh felt like a hypocrite. He mouthed the words, but his insides were sick with jealousy.

Jealousy? Yes, admit it. Too angry to think rationally, he closed his eyes and silently prayed, *Lord show me what to do, how to overcome these feelings.*

Pastor Grissom cleared his throat. "How can we not forgive our brother his sins against us when we consider how dark and how numerous were ours before Jesus took them on himself? For if you forgive not your brother his sins, neither will Your Father in Heaven forgive you."

Whoa. Strong words.

PLATES IN HAND, the congregates lined up on either side of a twenty-foot long picnic table nailed to two Bur Oaks, one at each end. The food smelled delicious, but the gall boiling in Josh's throat killed his appetite. He scanned the churchyard for Katy and spied her up ahead, behind Nancy and Ben Grady.

That did it. He stepped out of line and walked into the shade surrounding a giant pecan tree. Folding his arms over his chest, he reclined against the tree trunk and closed his eyes. Let the congregation fill their plates. Then he'd fill his, if he could find his appetite in the meantime.

"Josh."

He opened his eyes. Aunt Em stood before him, her hands propped on her ample hips, looking at him as if he'd slipped the last cookie from the cookie jar.

"What in tarnation's the matter with you? You jerked so much during the service, I thought you'd contracted Saint Vitus's Dance. Look! Katy's almost filled her plate. She's at the front of the line with Nancy and Ben Grady."

Josh glanced toward the far end of the long picnic table where Aunt Em pointed. "I can see her. So, what?" Katy was wedged between Ben and Nancy. Another reason not to get in any hurry to get in line.

"Well, what are you going to do about it?"

He shrugged. "About what?"

Aunt Em huffed. "Boy, I do declare. Sometimes I wonder if you've lost your marbles."

Josh threw up his hands. "What business is it of mine if Katy wants to eat a homecoming meal with the Gradys?"

"You have to ask that after what Ben tried to do to her?"

"Apparently she enjoys his company. Or she wouldn't be eating with him."

"I declare! Josh Kramer, I know you've got better sense than that. What makes you say such a thing? Katy is with Nancy only because she helped her with the young'uns. She's made a new friend. Ben just happens to be along because he's Nancy's brother."

Josh didn't buy it. His mind swirled with images of what might have happened between Katy and Ben the day the ladies went to Buffalo Gap. "When you and Katy went to town, did you see Ben?"

"I didn't, but Katy did. I browsed through bolts of fabric at the mercantile while she was gone."

Just what he'd feared. While his aunt shopped, Katy took off to meet Ben Grady. Did they have lunch together at the hotel? When had they planned the meeting? The previous Sunday? They hadn't seen each other outside of church services since the dance. Strange, he hadn't seen Katy talking to Ben once since the incident, even at church. And Ben had made himself scarce there.

Josh stroked his chin. "Whose idea was it to go to town that day?"

"Mine. I asked Katy if she was ready to make me a new dress. Ain't it pretty?" She whirled so he could view it from every angle.

"It's very becoming, Aunt Em."

This didn't add up. If his aunt suggested the trip to town, Katy couldn't have planned a meeting with Ben. "Where did Katy see Ben?"

"Why are you askin' all these questions?" Aunt Em clapped a

hand to her mouth. "Oh . . . you think . . . Josh Kramer, you've got better sense than to suspect Katy would give that man a second look. What do you take her for? She'd be crazy to cozy up to him after—." She paused to scan their surroundings. "I'd best watch my mouth. Someone could be eavesdroppin'."

Josh's face burned. His aunt had read him well. He couldn't get a thing past her.

Aunt Em adjusted her hat brim. "To clear things up, Katy didn't meet Ben. He just happened to be at the post office when she picked up your letter from Leah. Why don't we discuss that?"

"The letter?" Josh whooshed out a breath. "There's nothing to discuss."

"What's that supposed to mean? Leah didn't write you for nothin'. We both know that."

He shrugged. "I haven't opened it."

"You mean, you haven't even looked at it while Katy and I have worried ourselves silly over the bloomin' thing?"

Josh drew his eyebrows together. "Why would you do that?"

"Young'un, if you don't know the answer by now, get somebody else to explain it. And while I'm at it, I'll give you my opinion concernin' Miss Leah." She took a deep breath. "First, Leah can't hold a light to Katy."

Josh didn't need his aunt to tell him that. "You think Leah wants to lure me back in? Is that it? It won't work. I'm not interested, plus I'm sure she and her drifter are very happily married."

"You don't know that since you ain't read the letter. Some women have wiles about them that a man don't catch onto until he's trapped. Katy's not that kind."

"I agree. I've acted like a fool." *A lovesick fool.*

"No, you just jumped to conclusions before first asking Katy. Josh, you're lettin' what Leah did, taint your view of all womenfolk." She nudged him. "Now, quit sulkin' and get over there and fill your plate before the food gets picked over. Then march over there and join Katy." Aunt Em pointed to where Katy sat on a wedding ring quilt with Nancy and Ben. "I've a feelin' if Ben's hangin' around waitin' for Katy to warm up to him, he won't hang around long after you show up."

Josh gave his aunt a peck on the cheek. "Come to think of it, I am getting hungry."

He piled his plate with meats and vegetables and strode over to where Katy sat. Ben had his knees drawn up, hands clasped around them, staring off into the distance while Katy and Nancy discussed fashions.

Nancy wrinkled her nose. "I don't know if that style would flatter me."

"It would look perfect on you," Katy declared. "You and I are about the same size. Come over one day and I'll let you try on the dress I made from that pattern."

"Excuse me, may I sit here?" Josh didn't wait for an answer. He plunked down next to Katy, moving Ben aside. "Our church has the best cooks in the South."

Ben's scowl was aimed at him. "I wouldn't know. I seem to have suddenly lost my appetite."

"Too bad," Josh retorted nonchalantly. "That means more for someone else."

Ben rose, balancing his plate in one hand. He dusted off his pants. "If you ladies will excuse me, I see someone I must speak to."

Josh flapped his hand. "You're excused. Enjoy yourself."

With no backward glance, Ben strutted off to join a circle of men under an elm tree.

Josh turned his gaze on Katy and Nancy. "How did it go with the kids?"

Katy clapped her hands together. "We had a wonderful time. The kids were funny. Our Bible story was about Abraham preparing to sacrifice Isaac to the Lord. After Nancy finished reading, a little blond boy raised his hand and asked, 'Which Abraham?' A dark-haired little boy was quick to jump in with, 'Lincoln, you moron.'"

Josh threw his head back and laughed while Katy giggled.

Nancy clucked her tongue. "Kids are spontaneous. You never know what will come out of their mouths. Johnny Stokes was the blond boy, Amos Malone the dark-haired one. Those boys are inseparable, but you can't tell it from the way they talk to each other."

Her expression sobered as she studied Josh. "I'm sorry my brother ruined the Coopers' party for you. You didn't even get a chance to dance. I promise I didn't know he was imbibing. If I had, I would have insisted Katy come back inside with Stuart and me."

"You don't need to apologize. No one can take responsibility for another person's actions. We make our own choices, and we each reap consequences from those choices." Josh didn't regret cuffing Ben. He was sorry Katy had been subjected to Ben's drunken behavior.

Nancy's gaze flitted from Katy to Josh. "Did Ben become . . . violent?"

Josh grunted. "He was beginning to. I didn't let it go very far."

Katy closed her eyes, opened them, and looked at Nancy. "Not exactly. He tried to kiss me. When I struggled to free myself, he wouldn't let me go."

"That's when I hit him," Josh interjected. "I won't stand by and let any man take advantage of a young lady."

"But, Ben did apologize," Katy inserted, "the day I saw him at the post office."

Josh leaned back and propped himself up on his elbows. Katy had run into Ben at the post office, nothing more. He should have trusted her. Aunt Em was right. Katy wouldn't give a man like Ben a second chance.

"The singin's about to start. Mind if I join y'all?"

Carrie looked up to see Aunt Em standing over them. "Not at all. You can sit here." She patted a spot beside her on the quilt and moved aside to make room while Josh stood to help his aunt descend modestly.

Aunt Em folded her legs in a comfortable position rearranged her dress to cover her ankles. "I can't get over how pretty this dress is."

Carrie smiled. "Thank you. I'm pleased you like it. I'm never happier than when I'm sewing."

"God gave you that gift, Katy. I enjoy having a talented seamstress in the house. I'm countin' on you makin' me another dress before long."

Carrie's face warmed. "I can hardly wait."

"It pleases me to hear that," Aunt Em replied. She studied Josh. "I guess you know I'll need help gettin' back up."

"That's no problem. Are you comfortable?"

"As comfortable as a body can be on the hard ground."

Pastor Grissom stepped up on a large stump. "Let me have your attention, ladies and gentlemen. Our featured group is the Gordon Family. Before they bless us with their beautiful voices, I will ask Leonard Wainwright to play a special song on his violin."

A stocky, middle-aged man seated behind Carrie and Josh cupped his hands around his mouth. "It's called a fiddle! Preacher, we don't call 'em violins in Texas."

The pastor smiled. "It depends on whether one is playing square dance music or Beethoven."

A twangy male voice near them whispered, "Bay who?"

Carrie giggled and coughed to cover it. "Sorry. It just popped out." Josh hiked his eyebrows and fixed her with a mock stern glare.

Aunt Em leaned close and whispered in Carrie's ear. "That was Andy Conroy. He's not real educated."

Mr. Wainwright took his place on the stump, drew the bow across the strings, and began to play, *Fairest Lord Jesus*. Carrie closed her eyes to let the sweet melody seep into her soul.

After the song ended, followed by a lengthy applause, Pastor Grissom introduced the Gordon Family. "These folks came all the way from Baird to be with us today. Dan and Margaret Gordon and their four children. Let's give them a big Texas welcome."

The people applauded. When the music started, Carrie relaxed. She reveled in the harmonious blend of the group's voices as they sang one song after another. Until today, she hadn't realized how much she'd missed attending church services over the past five years. Without realizing it, her heart had become an empty vessel waiting to be filled.

Carrie leaned back on her arms and closed her eyes, allowing herself to become saturated with the message in song. She didn't know how close she was to Josh until he breathed in her ear.

"Beautiful, isn't it?"

She could only nod while her heart fluttered. No man had ever affected her this way. Josh Kramer's smooth voice and his dark, somber gaze seemed to penetrate her soul. The lopsided grin that often appeared without warning warmed her heart. Carrie held her breath to calm herself. She had better keep her thoughts in check. Letting them stray could prove dangerous.

After an hour of singing, the Gordon Family took a break. During the intermission, a man stepped up on the stump, pulled out a harmonica, and played, *What A Friend We Have in Jesus*. Aunt Em clapped heartily when the instrumental ended.

TWO HOURS LATER, Carrie, Josh, and Aunt Em gathered their belongings into the picnic basket and headed home. The weather was perfect. Small, puffy clouds drifted in a periwinkle blue sky.

Aunt Em must have forgotten to question them about the sermon. Carrie couldn't have told her a thing since she had been in the back room wrangling a dozen children.

Aunt Em finally spoke, though not about the sermon. She went on about Almenia Bailey's reaction to the new dress Carrie had made for her.

"I've never seen a woman so shocked when she got her eyes full of this lavender print. She turned as pale as an old white leghorn hen when I walked up to greet her."

Carrie had seen the woman's eyes pop, a funny sight indeed. Aunt Em and Mrs. Bailey might be rivals, but when push came to shove, Carrie knew they would be there for one another.

Aunt Em huffed. "Then Almenia stuck her nose in the air and asked, 'At which fancy shop did you buy that dress, Em?' Ha! Like I would waste money buyin' one from a fashionable shop like Sonja's Boutique. You should've seen her scowl when I whispered, 'Psst! That's my little secret.'"

Josh shook the reins and clucked his tongue. "I don't know what to think about you, Aunt Em. Did you ever tell Mrs. Bailey that Katy made the dress?"

"Not yet, but I will. I'll let her fume for a while. I'll bet she dashes to Sonja's Boutique to see how much I paid for it."

Carrie snickered. "Can't you see Almenia flipping through the racks searching for a replica of your dress?"

Aunt Em rolled her eyes. "And imagine how flustered she'll get when she can't find it."

While the ladies laughed, Josh groaned. "Aunt Em, you should be ashamed. You taught me to always tell the truth."

"This doesn't count. Anyway, I didn't fib to Almenia; I just didn't say." She turned to Carrie. "Did you enjoy yourself today? I know your hands were full with a dozen young'uns in that backroom."

"They were a handful, but I enjoyed every minute. It took both Nancy and me to keep them calmed down enough to listen to the Bible story. But we managed."

Carrie also enjoyed the time she had spent seated beside Josh on the quilt, even though they weren't alone. She'd caught him studying her and wondered what he was thinking.

Ben Grady had apologized for his behavior, but he still made her uncomfortable, even while in the presence of others. Relief swept over her when Ben had excused himself and left. Carrie hoped she would never again find herself alone with him.

Ben seemed to possess two opposite personalities—polite and charming when he was sober—but when the liquor took control, he transformed into a beast. The same way strong drink had transformed Big Jim Counce.

Carrie's chest heaved. Big Jim Counce was another problem she would have to face. As if revealing her true identity wasn't enough. Blake would know if the man had survived. But he couldn't reply to her letter since she'd omitted the return address. It was best no one from Denton—especially Blake— knew her whereabouts. Still, she worried about what she might have done to Big Jim.

"Did you have a pleasant day?" Josh asked, interrupting her thoughts.

"Mm-hmm, it's been a perfect day. I wish it would never end. When the violinist played *Fairest Lord Jesus,* I was swept into another realm."

Aunt Em nodded. "And didn't Ken Barker do a good job of playin' *Rock of Ages* on his harmonica?"

"Yes," Josh agreed. "I liked the quartet too. Their voices had a harmonious blend. Who were they, again?"

"The Gordon Family," Aunt Em replied. "They were wonderful. We'll have to invite them back next year."

Carrie's breath caught in her throat. Next year? It seemed eons away. Where would she be this time next year? She could carry this sham only so long before her world crashed around her.

She hadn't planned to fall in love with Josh. Leaving the Kramer ranch was supposed to be easy. If only she'd kept her heart intact, at least she could have walked away with no scars. As it stood, her heart would break when her time of departure arrived. It was only a matter of time.

Carrie was not ready to dwell on the impending grief after the glorious day she'd shared with Josh and his aunt. She closed her eyes to erase the pain.

Tomorrow would come soon enough. She would dwell on it then. Not now.

Chapter Fourteen

✤✤✤

"We're starting roundup today," Josh announced after breakfast Wednesday morning. "We'll have some mighty unhappy calves tonight."

Puzzled by his words, Carrie asked, "Why?"

"Because they'll be separated from their mommas for the first time," Aunt Em replied. "The little ones will bawl and raise a ruckus, as will their mommas."

"That is sad. It sounds like a terrible thing to do to them."

Josh pulled his hat from the peg by the door and popped it on his head. Tilting his head to one side, he said, "Katy Davis, you have a very soft heart." He shoved a pair of gloves in his pants pocket and added, "This is one part of cattle ranching that isn't fun, but it is necessary."

"I know. I just hate to see the calves miserable."

Josh tweaked her nose. "Me either." He gave his aunt a peck on cheek. "Don't hold the noon meal for me." After patting Carrie's shoulder, he headed out.

When his horse had galloped out of the yard, Aunt Em poured a kettle of hot water into the dishpan. "How are you and Josh progressin'?"

Carrie was not sure "progressing" was the right word. "We're getting along fine. Why?"

Aunt Em pressed on. "Just wonderin'. He didn't like it none, Ben sittin' with you on the quilt."

"I must confess that Ben makes me uncomfortable, even when Nancy's nearby. I was relieved when Josh sat down with us."

Aunt Em chuckled. "I noticed Mr. Grady got up and left pretty quick after Josh joined you." Her expression sobered as she set the kettle on the stove. "Katy, you've been with us nigh onto two months now. What do you think of Josh? Does he appeal to you in a matrimonial way?"

Carrie had gotten over her shock at Aunt Em's straightforward questions, but revealing her true feelings to the woman made her uncomfortable. So she turned the tables. "The big question is, what does Josh think of me, and do I appeal to him?"

"I'd bet my new dress you do, sugar. But he's not one to show it. I don't know what it will take for him to admit his feelins'. You should've seen him sulkin' Sunday when he saw you in line with Ben. He started askin' all kinds of questions about our trip into town last week."

"Why would he do that?"

"He thought you had it all planned to meet with Ben, the best I can figure."

"Oh. Now I understand why he acted strange when he walked into the Sunday School room while Nancy was showing me around before church service began. I had just told her I'd run into Ben in town when Josh stuck his head in the door. He must have thought — But until that day, I hadn't talked to Ben since the dance."

"That's what I told him. Then he asked whose idea it was to go into town. I told him it was mine. After I'd thought about it later, I realized I'd fibbed. But I didn't tell him any different."

"Hmm. He thought I had arranged a date with Ben?"

"At least he suspected it. I'd say that ol' green-eyed monster has raised its ugly head."

Her back to Aunt Em, Carrie smiled as she stacked the dirty plates. Josh was jealous of Ben? A rush of heat warmed her face. Jealousy suggested he had feelings for her. Her heart warned her not to jump to conclusions. Josh's feelings might not be the kind that led to the altar. On the other hand, they were not the feelings a brother had for his sister, or he wouldn't have kissed her. She hoped Josh's affection for her would grow to half what she felt for him.

But what would happen when he discovered she'd tricked him? Carrie couldn't keep pretending to be Katy Davis. If she were blessed enough to eventually marry Josh, she would be forced to sign the marriage certificate as "Katy Davis," making their union illegal. On the other hand, if she confessed who she really was, she would never have to worry about a marriage certificate.

Dear Lord, I'm between a rock and a hard place. What am I to do?

Carrie couldn't imagine the heartbreak that would come with losing Josh. To see the spark of affection in his eyes turn to fiery darts of anger would be more than she could bear.

Carrie pushed the thoughts from her mind and carried the dirty plates to the dish pan.

IN THE LATE afternoon Carrie heard thundering hoof beats, cattle bawling, and loud voices barking orders. She reached the window in time to see Josh hop down from his horse near the corral. He unlatched the gate, swung it open, and stepped aside. The herd consisting of several hundred cattle, poured into the corral through the gate. All except one renegade steer that broke loose and ran toward Josh, knocking him down. He tried to dodge, but when the dust cleared, he lay flat on his back.

"Josh has been trampled!" Carrie yelled to Aunt Em as she flew out of the house. She reached him first and dropped down beside him. His eyes were closed. She gently shook his shoulders. "Are you all right? Please, Josh, open your eyes."

Luke dropped to his knees on the other side of Josh and lightly slapped his cheeks. "Boss, wake up."

Carrie sighed when Josh opened his eyes and groaned. "My foot. I think it's broken. That renegade . . . stomped it hard." He waited until Charlie secured the gate on the corralled herd. "Charlie, rope that steer before it gets away. We can't afford to lose one." He closed his eyes again and muttered under his breath, "This is no time to get hurt."

"Don't worry, boss," Luke soothed, "I have to ride into town anyway to hire drifters to drive the herd to Abilene. I'll hire one extra."

"Help me get up and into the house, Luke. It looks like I can't do it on my own."

With Carrie supporting Josh on one side and Luke on the other, they managed to get him to his feet. After a couple of stumbles on the porch steps, he was inside the house and on the sofa.

Aunt Em bustled about the living room, tying on her bonnet. She had changed into a Sunday dress. "I'm going after Doc Sullivan. Carrie, you stay with Josh. Luke, tell one of the boys to hitch up the buggy. I'll make better time in it than the buckboard."

Luke hurried out, letting the screen door slap to behind him.

Carrie ran trembling fingers through her hair. "Aunt Em, if you will give me directions to the doctor's office, I'll bring him back."

"No, it will be quicker for me to go than to explain the directions to you. You take care of Josh's foot." She hurried to the kitchen, rummaged through a cabinet, set a large wash pan, Epsom Salt, and a bottle of liniment on the table.

"I wish you two would quit fussing over me. I'll be all right." Josh groused. Then he tried to wiggle his toes. "Ow-ww!"

Carrie threw up her hands. "All right. Aunt Em, tell me what to do."

"Roll up his pants leg and check his foot. If it's swelled, pour a half cup of Epsom salts into the pan filled with warm water. Mix it good and have him soak his hurt foot thirty minutes. After that, dry it off gently, and rub both his foot and ankle with liniment."

"All right." Carrie sighed. "I can do that." She knelt to roll up Josh's pants leg. "The foot is swollen."

"I figured as much." Aunt Em laid a shawl across her arm. "Autumn evenings are getting nippy."

Charlie called through the screen door. "Your buggy is ready, Mrs. Roberts."

"All right, young'uns. I'm leavin'. Take care. I'll return before dark."

Carrie walked to the stove, touched the sides of the kettle. The water was warm. She lifted it and poured some into the large metal pan before stirring in Epsom salt. After refilling the kettle and setting it on the stove to heat, she knelt in front of Josh's injured foot.

JOSH GRITTED his teeth and watched Katy, every muscle in his body taut. His foot throbbed so hard it brought tears to his eyes. He sniffed them back. Katy didn't need to know the extent of his pain. Grown men didn't cry. Not cowboys, for sure.

When she stooped to roll up his pants leg farther, he winced. Her lovely, green eyes held compassion.

"I'm sorry. I didn't mean to hurt you."

He took a deep breath and exhaled. "It's all right. It had to be done."

"Can you raise your foot and place it in the pan, or do you need me to lift it?"

"Let me try." He tried and set it back down. "Ouch!"

"Let me try. Relax now and don't try to help me."

Her touch was gentle as she cradled the weight of his injured foot in her hands, supporting his heel. When she lowered it into the pan of warm water, he bit back a whimper.

"See? That wasn't so bad."

If she only knew.

His head pounded with every throb of his foot. "No, it wasn't," he fibbed. "I hope that doctor isn't off somewhere in Timbuktu."

"You and me both. Wherever he is, I'm sure Aunt Em won't come back without him."

"I hope you're right." Josh leaned back into the sofa cushions. "The warm water feels good."

Katy gazed up at him with those pretty, wide eyes. "Try to relax." She cupped her hands, dipped them into the solution, letting it drizzle through her fingers onto Josh's foot.

He managed a slight grin. "Has anyone ever told you, you have a soothing touch?"

She blushed and ducked her head. "No."

"Well, you do." He cleared his throat. "Katy?"

"Yes?"

Josh couldn't finish it. The timing was all wrong. His foot was bunged up and throbbing. If he confessed his love now, she might respond likewise, but her feelings could be rooted in sympathy. He would wait until he was back on his feet, then profess his love for Katy Davis.

"I just wanted to say I appreciate all you do for Aunt Em and me."

She rose from her kneeling position and sat beside him on the sofa. "Well, that's what I was hired to do."

"True, but you go above and beyond your duties."

"Because I love . . . what I'm doing." She stared through the window. "I hope you'll write me a good recommendation when . . ."

"When you leave? Why? Are you thinking about leaving?" Her reluctance to look at him told Josh he'd guessed correctly. What had he said or done to make her unhappy here? She had melded well into the household.

"I don't want to go." She faced him. Her eyes begged him to give her a reason not to.

He wished he could. Not yet. All in due time. "I— We don't want you to leave. Aunt Em thinks of you as the daughter she never had. She told me that. Think how it would hurt her if you left."

Katy searched his face. "And you?"

Josh held her gaze, debating how to reply. It wouldn't be fair to put her on the spot in a moment of weakness. He decided to take the easy way out. "You got any more hot water in the kettle? This is getting cool."

Tears pooled in Katy's eyes. His heart ached for her. He reached out, pulled her into his arms. She lay her head against his chest and sniffed. He stroked her silky hair. "It's my turn to say I'm sorry, and I didn't mean to hurt you."

She tensed. "Sorry for what?" When he didn't answer, she sat up straight and pulled back. "Sorry you can't feel about me the way you feel about Leah?"

"Leah?" What did Leah have to do with anything? And why was she on Katy's mind? The letter? Aunt Em mentioned she and Katy were curious about it. Josh still hadn't opened it. Not because he was afraid of its contents, but because he didn't care to know anything about Leah.

Katy stood, smoothed the wrinkles from her skirt. "I'll check the kettle. The water should be warm." Glancing at the clock on the mantle, she added, "You still have ten minutes to soak."

When the soaking time was up, Katy helped Josh lift his foot from the pan. She gingerly wrapped a towel around it and his ankle, patting to absorb the moisture. Uncorking the liniment bottle, she made a face. "Shew! The way this smells, it ought to fix anything that ails a body."

She took the clean cloth Aunt Em laid out and soaked it with the medicine. "Do you want me to apply this, or would you rather do it?"

Josh blew out a breath. "You do it. You have a gentler touch."

Katy knelt on the floor, touched the saturated cloth to his foot. He flinched a couple of times during the application. The liniment burned as it soaked into his skin, but it was a healing burn.

She rose to her feet. "Let me get the footstool. Keeping your foot elevated will help keep the swelling down." Katy retrieved it and propped it under his foot.

Now all he could do was wait for the doctor.

"Aunt Em and I made fried peach pies. Are you hungry? I put them in the warming closet."

"A fried peach pie and a glass of milk? Mmm. If my foot didn't feel like somebody was pounding it with a hammer, I'd think I was in heaven."

~

Doc Sullivan 's buggy pulled in ahead of Aunt Em's. Doc's piercing blue eyes examined Josh's foot. "Looks like this young lady did a fine job doctoring you."

He squatted and cradled Josh's throbbing foot in his hand, pressing various spots. "Does this hurt?"

"Oww . . . oww!" Josh moaned. "Every place you touch hurts."

"Son, this feels like a fracture, but I don't think your foot's broken clean through. I'm going to wrap it tightly to prevent further injury. You'll need to rely on a crutch for a few weeks to keep the weight off it."

Josh slapped the sofa. "A few weeks! I have a ranch to run, Doc."

"I say, put your foreman in charge. Luke's a good man, at least from what I hear. I can't stress enough the importance of staying off this foot. Bones take time to knit back together." He shook his head. "It could have been a lot worse. You're lucky that steer didn't trample on the rest of you."

The doctor finished wrapping Josh's foot and ankle and rose to his feet. "My work is done here. The rest is up to you, boy. Don't put any weight on that foot for at least a month. Then you can gradually increase the pressure." He scratched his beard. "Now, do you have a crutch?"

Aunt Em pointed through the window. "There's two hangin' in the barn from when Josh's pa broke his leg a few years back."

"Good. Two will be better." He turned to Carrie. "Young lady, will you get them, please?"

Carrie looked at Aunt Em. "Where are they?"

"Hangin' on the barn wall to the right as you go in. Behind the door."

Carrie returned with the crutches and handed them to the doctor. He propped them against the fireplace and turned to his patient. "Stand up, son, and hold onto the mantle. I need to see if the height is correct."

Carrie and Aunt Em helped Josh rise and hop over to the mantle. Doc Sullivan held a crutch to Josh's arm pit. "Perfect fit. I'd guess you and your pa were about the same height."

Aunt Em agreed. "And same build too."

Carrie took the pan of water and liniment to the kitchen while the doctor made out a bill. She returned as he handed it to Aunt Em. "You can drop by my office and pay me when you get to town."

"No, I'll pay you now." She sashayed toward the kitchen, returning with the money and something wrapped in brown paper. She smiled at the doctor. "This is for when you get hungry."

He winked. "I hope it's a fried peach pie. You make the best, Em." He stuffed it in one coat pocket and the money in the other. "Thank you. Well, I'd better get going. I have rounds to make. The Conner baby is due any time."

When his buggy pulled away, Josh propped the crutches under his arms and hopped to the door.

Aunt Em blocked the door, folding her arms across her bosom. "Where do you think you're goin'?"

"To talk to Luke."

Carrie peered through the window. "There he is, leaning on the gate. I'll get him."

She ran out to the corral where the foreman had a foot propped on the gate. "Luke, Josh wants to see you."

He nodded. "How is he? Is his foot broken?"

"The doctor says it's fractured, but he's to stay off it completely for a few weeks."

Carrie trailed Luke to the house. "Luke, I'm in here," Josh called from the study. He was seated behind the large, walnut desk, his crutches propped against the book case behind him. "Close the door behind you."

The door closed, blocking any words that might reach the ladies' ears. Carrie bit her lower lip. What was so private about running a ranch that Josh Kramer could not allow his aunt to overhear?

THE NEXT MORNING after an early breakfast, Luke rode in with six new hired hands to help with roundup and the cattle drive. Carrie dried a plate as she peered through the window. Luke walked into the bunkhouse, while the men dismounted. One man looked familiar. Light brown hair, square shoulders, short and stocky. Even his stance made her think of someone.

No, it couldn't be. Carrie was letting her imagination run wild. She closed her eyes, opened them and looked again. It was Blake! What was her brother doing here, and how did he find her? She'd purposely left her return address off the letter she'd mailed him. He must have noticed the postmark and somehow tracked her here.

Her heart kicked against her ribcage. She glanced toward the study door. Josh had closed himself in to go over accounts. Aunt Em had gone out the back door to feed the chickens. Carrie dropped the dishtowel and plate on the table and ran outside. She had to inform her brother of her predicament before he talked to Josh and exposed her.

To Carrie's relief, Blake stood apart from the other men, watering his horse. She slowed her pace and casually walked up to him.

Recognition dawned in his eyes as she approached. "Carrie!"

She fixed him with a warning glare, stopping in front of him. The other cowhands stared at them, their eyebrows raised.

With her back to them, Carrie tapped a finger against her lips, signaling Blake to let her speak first. "Hello, Mr. Franklin. I thought I recognized you. I came out to make sure." She extended her hand. "I'm Katy Davis. I believe we've met before. Will you be working for Mr. Kramer?"

"Uh . . . yes." Blake's brows knit together. He yanked off his hat and scratched his forehead before whispering, "Carrie, are you in some kind of—?"

"Katy," she interjected. "Katy Davis."

"Are you in some kind of trouble?" he muttered under his breath.

She clenched her teeth and whispered, "No, but I will be if you don't start calling me 'Katy.' I can't explain now, but to everyone here, I'm Katy Davis, the domestic help. Please . . . remember that."

He lowered his voice. "Sure thing, sis." Raising his voice, he announced, "Oh yes, I do remember you. Didn't you sing at the Golden Spur saloon in Denton?"

Carrie's face burned. How dare Blake play games with her reputation when one slip of the tongue could alter her life? She glared at him. "No, sir. I've never worked in a saloon." In a lowered voice she hissed, "Don't call me 'sis,' either. Call me 'Katy.'"

Blake rubbed his chin, feigning deep thought. "Wait. Maybe we met at a dress shop."

"Yes, I did work at a dressmaker's shop." At least that wasn't a fib.

Why in the world had her brother shown up now? His timing couldn't have been worse. Blake would surely be her downfall. She whispered, "Call me 'Katy,' or 'Miss Davis.'"

Blake doffed his hat. "Miss Davis, isn't it?"

She nodded. Carrie's gaze darted toward the bunkhouse, then back to Blake, worried that Josh's foreman might mention her conversation with Blake. But Luke was nowhere in sight.

"How did you find me?"

Carrie's brother kept his head down and his voice low. "Easy. I noticed your letter was postmarked Buffalo Gap. I took the train out yesterday morning. When I got here, I asked around town for a woman fittin' your description. The snooty old lady at the mercantile said the Kramer ranch was the only place she knew that had recently hired a young blonde woman with green eyes. I knew it had to be you."

Blake patted his horse. "Then this mornin', the foreman of this mighty fine spread rode into town lookin' for extra hands to help with the roundup." He shrugged. "So here I am. Aren't you happy to see your little brother?"

Carrie crossed her hands over her chest. "You know absolutely nothing about ranching. What did you tell Luke to get this job?"

A mischievous grin split his face. "I might've said I'd had some experience with roundups."

Carrie's chest heaved. "You told a fib to get hired?"

Blake's eyes shot daggers. "Now don't you get all high and mighty with me. It looks like you've done some fibbin' yourself."

Carrie couldn't call him on that. She glanced toward the bunkhouse again. Still no Luke. "What happened to our house?"

Blake hung his head. "Our house? Look, sis, I'm really sorry about that, but it couldn't be helped. Cage Ames called my bluff on a high-stakes poker game. I lost the house."

"You bet our house in a poker game?" Carrie sucked in a deep breath, forcing herself to stay calm when she wanted to flog her brother.

"I had to hand over the deed. Cage won it fair and square. Do you have any idea what his men would do to me if I didn't pay up? That's why I'm here. I didn't have anywhere to live, so I figured why not look you up."

Carrie hissed, "I can't believe it. Everything Pa and Mama worked for, you lost in a poker game."

Luke swaggered out of the bunkhouse, looked at her and Blake, and nodded. She returned the nod, ducked her head, and whispered to her brother, "We'll discuss this later, in private."

Pasting on a smile, Carrie spoke loud enough for all to hear. "It's been nice to run into you again, Mr. Franklin."

Blake tipped his hat and winked. "It was my pleasure, Miss Davis, is it?"

"That is correct." Carrie flipped a lock of hair over one shoulder. "Now, I must get back to those dishes."

Curious looks passed from one cowhand to another. Keeping her shoulders hiked, Carrie marched toward the house. She had bought herself a little time. How much time, she didn't know.

Her future depended on Blake's silence. If he slipped up, her life would change quickly and drastically and not for the better. When she'd first come to live with Josh and Aunt Em, she had planned to reveal her true identity at the right time. But the right time had never come. Not that she would have recognized it when it did.

Was her brother's appearance God's way of urging her to come clean, to tell Josh and his aunt that she'd taken on the identity of Katy Davis? Was it a nudge for her to bare her soul?

When Carrie had first arrived, telling the truth would have been easier. Since then she'd grown fond of Aunt Em and fallen in love with Josh. Today, the truth would crush her. Not the truth itself, but the consequences that would follow her disclosure.

Her heart would break when Josh fixed her with a cold glare and ordered her to pack her things. Besides, she had no place to go. Blake had gambled away their home. She'd heard rumors that he had been boasting he would do just that before she left Denton, but she'd hoped they were only rumors.

Carrie knew what she had to do, and it had to be done quickly. Before the truth came out.

Chapter Fifteen

Two days later Aunt Em washed dishes while Carrie sat on the floor wrapping a fresh bandage around Josh's foot. "Katy, would you mind going into town for groceries?"

"Not at all." She'd worried herself sick how to broach Josh or Aunt Em about taking the buggy into town. Now Josh's aunt had provided a solution.

"Why don't you both go?" Josh grumbled. "I'm not a complete invalid."

Carrie patted the fresh bandage against his ankle. "No, you aren't, but you need to keep this foot propped up."

Aunt Em shook her finger at him. "And one of us needs to be here to make sure you do it."

Josh rolled his eyes. "I feel suffocated from all the mothering these past few days. I have a ranch to run, but I lie around the house like an infant, getting waited on hand and foot. It's nothing personal, but you two are smothering me. I can't breathe. Why don't you just hold a pillow over my face?"

Aunt Em clicked her tongue, "My, aren't we getting impatient."

Carrie giggled. She picked up the bandage roll and scissors and rose. "I wouldn't say that. You've gotten the hang of those crutches and manage to get around the house by yourself. Still, you need to keep that foot elevated at frequent intervals."

Josh exhaled a long breath, shaking his head. "I can't win an argument as long as there's two conniving women working against one helpless man."

The buggy was easier to handle than the buckboard, and being the only passenger, she'd have plenty of room to stash groceries.

The autumn morning air had a nip earlier, but had warmed to a pleasant temperature by the time she took the reins in her hands. Carrie hadn't talked to her brother since the day he was hired, although she'd seen him through the window each morning walking out of the bunkhouse with the other hands. She needed to ask Blake about Big Jim Counce.

She wouldn't rest until she knew if the man was alive. If he wasn't, she'd go back to Denton and turn herself in to the sheriff. She was tired of running and of her conscience keeping her awake at night. Surely a judge would rule the case as self-defense.

According to Josh, who met with Luke in the study every evening, the cowhands had finished separating the calves from their mommas. Tomorrow they would drive the herd to the stock-yards in Abilene. It would be a long, exhausting day for the hired hands.

Carrie pulled into town and drove up the street to Sonja's Boutique. She tethered the horse to a hitching post and walked up the boardwalk and through the door. A bell jingled overhead.

"Yes, may I help you?" a female voice with a French accent inquired.

Carrie followed the voice to the far side of the shop where she found Sonja stocking shelves with ladies' lingerie. She turned to face Carrie. "Miss Devereaux, since I had to come into town today, I stopped by to see if the job opening was available yet."

Sonja's gaze raked her from head to toe. "Oui, I remember. You are the young lady who is an expert seamstress. The young lady I told you of, who planned to wed, has broken off her engagement. Therefore, I have only a temporary opening through the holidays.

The Christmas season will soon be upon us and will bring an influx of customers. I do hire extra help every year around this time."

She glanced at the calendar. "Let me see. If you could start the Monday before Thanksgiving, that would be good."

Almost two weeks. Carrie nodded. "Do you know a good place to rent a room?"

"Indeed, I do. Mrs. Owen runs a reputable boardinghouse not far south of town, on the right side of the road. It's a lovely white house surrounded by a white picket fence and pretty rose bushes. I believe I saw a vacancy sign out when I drove past this morning."

"Thank you."

"Mademoiselle, I suggest if you will be afoot when you leave my shop at closing time, that you not walk in that direction. It gets dark early now, and the walk to the boardinghouse requires you to pass the saloon. It's not so bad Monday through Thursday, but on Friday and Saturday evenings it gets—shall we say, lively?"

The saloon? Carrie owned neither horse nor buggy. She didn't relish a second encounter with a drunken brute. Which reminded her, she must ask Blake about Big Jim's condition.

"We open at nine in the mornings and close at four-thirty, fall through winter. Please arrive thirty minutes early in the mornings to help open. Also, the girls take turnabout staying late to restore order to the shop. That includes restocking shelves and general cleaning."

When Sonja informed Carrie of the wages, she was surprised to learn Josh paid her almost the same, and that included room and board. She would have to pinch pennies to rent a room in town. The savings she'd put back would buy her a little time until she contemplated her next move.

Hopefully the boardinghouse wouldn't be too expensive. The price normally included two meals, breakfast and supper. "Thank you, Miss Devereaux. I'll give you an answer by the end of next week."

"Call me Sonja, please. That will be good, but I cannot promise to hold the job for you."

"I understand. Good day, Sonja."

Carrie clucked to the horse and turned the buggy around to head to the boardinghouse. Her heart felt like a lead ball suspended in her chest as she shook the reins. She easily found the place and got out to knock on the door. A round-faced, elderly lady with graying hair opened it and smiled warmly. "Have you come to inquire about the room?"

"Yes, ma'am. What do you charge for a month's rent?"

"Do come in for a cup of tea."

Vying scents of lemon oil and cinnamon filled Carrie's nostrils as she entered the house. The doily-covered furniture and staircase had been polished to a high gleam, explaining the lemon oil. The cinnamon aroma seemed to waft in from the back room, probably the kitchen.

Mrs. Owen led her to a room where blue-flecked wallpaper covered the walls. She gestured toward a comfortable chair. When Carrie was seated, the woman excused herself. "I'll only be a minute."

The older woman returned as promised and sat in a winged-back chair across from Carrie. The maid brought the tea and disappeared through a door which Carrie guessed was the kitchen.

"Now, let us begin." Mrs. Owen sipped from her cup, and set it down before revealing the price of the room. It sounded reasonable since two meals were included.

Then Mrs. Owen asked questions about Carrie's background—if she had a job, and where she came from. Carrie told her about the prospective job at Sonja's Boutique and that she'd come from Denton.

Finally, Mrs. Owen laid out the rules. "No pets, no male visitors except in the parlor where we are presently seated. All visitors must vacate the premises by eight p.m." She sipped from her cup and set it down. "When we finish our tea, I'll show you the vacant room."

The bedroom Mrs. Owen showed her was neat, with a white Chenille bedspread and a vanity. Slightly faded wallpaper with lavender flowers adorned the walls. Carrie couldn't give her a definite date when she would need the room. Although her mind whirled from the possible outcomes of each decision she would soon make, Carrie held onto a grain of hope that Josh would forgive her after she revealed her identity.

She climbed up in the buggy, smoothed her skirt, and shook the reins to get the horse moving. Fear rose in her chest, choking out her breath. Her life was about to change.

Payday for her deception drew closer with each passing day. Carrie had made up her mind to tell Josh the truth soon. It was the right thing to do, although not the easiest. Due to Josh's accident, now was not a good time. He needed her to change his bandage and help him get around, though he had begun to move around a bit. She'd seen him slip out to the barn once.

Carrie would have to face the consequences. The worst thing that could happen would be if Josh heard the truth from someone else. Namely, her brother.

She wouldn't put it past Blake to try to exhort money from her to keep him quiet. Well, he wouldn't get one red cent! Not after he'd lost their house. Anger rose in her chest as she recalled how casually he'd admitted it.

She refused to play the blackmail game. She would own up to her wrongdoing and not allow her brother to lord the bad deed over her head like a hangman's noose ready to drop.

Carrie picked up the mail and stopped at the mercantile to purchase the groceries on Aunt Em's list. She had plenty of time to think about the consequences of her decision as she headed back to the ranch. Breaking ties with Josh and his aunt would leave her scarred emotionally.

On the ride back, she took in the purple and yellow wildflowers along the way. Some varieties had died off, but a few hardy ones held on to brighten her drive. Halfway to the ranch, she spied the pecan tree near the creek where Josh had kissed her for the first time. Her face heated as the emotions resurfaced. A screech owl had sent her flying into his arms that night.

When Carrie entered the house, she found Aunt Em preparing supper. The study door was open as she passed it. Josh bent over his desk working on ledgers.

His brows knit together as he penciled in figures. "Is that all? If so, I have work to do."

Someone was in the study with him. Who? Carrie took a step aside to get a better view.

"Yeah, boss. Luke said we would move the herd to market tomorrow."

"Thank you, Blake. You can go now."

Blake! Why was he in there? Had he ratted on her? Was her head already on the chopping block? Carrie sucked in a deep breath. *Stay calm. Don't jump to conclusions. This was probably an innocent conversation about ranching,* she told herself.

"Katy, will you mash the potatoes?"

She flinched. "I'll be right there, Aunt Em." She turned around and marched to the kitchen. Aunt Em slid a bowl of steaming potatoes toward her and handed her the masher.

THE DAYS WERE GETTING SHORTER, Josh had noticed. The autumn evenings were perfect for sitting on the porch. When the dishes were done, Aunt Em suggested they do just that.

When Josh started to rise, Katy rushed to his side, passed him the crutches, and helped him to his feet. He tried to get around with as little assistance as possible.

She walked ahead to hold the door open. Katy was sweet like that, but it was all Josh would let her do. He didn't like being dependent. He sat down in the swing, folding his arms across his chest. "Tomorrow is the big day. The herd is off to market."

Aunt Em eased down in the cane back rocker. "Moving the cattle to Abilene is a big job. It takes an entire day to get them there and get back. But it's always a relief when it's over."

Josh winked. "The relief comes when that bank draft is in my hand."

Katy propped his crutches against the house before she sat down beside him in the swing. She'd been unusually quiet during supper. After a day in town, she should have something to talk about. She had seemed preoccupied.

"The garden's gone, and the hens have slowed down layin'. A sign winter's comin' on."

"Do you get any snow here?" Katy asked.

"Not enough you'd know it. One January, when Josh was little, it snowed two inches. He got all excited because he thought Santa was comin' back."

Josh's face grew hot, and Katy smiled but made no comment.

After a few minutes of talk about the weather and ranch work, Aunt Em pushed herself up. "Well, young'uns, I'm goin' in. I hear a mystery book callin' my name."

When she was out of sight, Josh slid his arm across the back of the swing and fingered Katy's locks. "It looks like gold and feels like silk."

She let her gaze slide to the western sky. "The sunset is pretty. Swirls of rose, peach and baby blue."

"Katy, is something wrong?"

"Just tired from a long day, I guess."

He figured there was more to it, but didn't push her. "Do you like it here? I mean, living on a ranch isn't what you were used to."

"I'm used to hard work. When my parents were alive, we raised a garden, had chickens, and a cow. There's not much difference, at least in the women's chores."

Josh squeezed her shoulder. "You've brought so much joy to our home. I can't believe I suspected you of being a fraud when you first arrived. It's obvious now that you hadn't planned to trick me. You aren't that kind of woman. You are too honest and too sweet to enter into deception."

He lightly traced her cheek with his index finger. "I'm sorry I made your life miserable at first. I hope you aren't still upset with me. I want you to be happy here."

Josh reached into his shirt pocket. "Before I forget it, these are for you." He pulled out the green satin ribbons he'd bought the day Buffalo Gap lost its title as county seat. "I hope they match the pretty green dress you wore to church a couple of weeks ago."

She took the ribbons and stroked them. "Thank you. They appear to be a perfect match."

Katy studied him as if she wanted to say something more. For a split second fear flashed in her eyes then vanished. He slid one arm around her, pulling her closer. But when he started to kiss her, she pulled away and jumped to her feet.

"I should go in. It's late and I'm tired." After a swish of her skirt, the door slammed behind her.

Was Katy afraid of him? What had he done to frighten her? This was not the giggling, vivacious woman who had stolen his heart.

Josh leaned back in the swing and sighed, letting his gaze skim the yard and barn. When it fell on the paddock, he thought a silhouette moved into the shadows. Yes. It moved again.

"Who's there?" he called out.

A man stepped out into the moonlight. "Just me, boss."

That Franklin kid. He spelled trouble. Josh couldn't put his finger on it, but he didn't trust the boy any farther than he could throw him. He reminded Josh of Ben Grady. "What are you up to?"

"Just smoking my cigar. The others don't appreciate the scent of a fine cigar. They held a vote and I lost, nine to one. So, me and my cigar came out here to enjoy the wide-open spaces."

"Just be sure you put it out when you're done."

"Sure thing, boss."

"Goodnight, Franklin."

"Goodnight, boss."

Josh grabbed his crutches and propelled himself inside the house. He clomped down the hall to his room and dropped down on the bed. Aunt Em's breaths came at regular intervals, signifying she was sound asleep. He wished sleep would come for him. It wouldn't tonight. His concern for Katy unsettled him. He couldn't fathom what had gotten into her this evening.

He needed to think what he was doing, if he was making the same mistake with Katy as he had with Leah. Becoming pushy, not listening to what she was *not* saying. He'd missed those clues with Leah. In retrospect, she'd given him signs. She had never mentioned love or a future together and always changed the subject when he'd hinted at matrimony.

While Josh thought about her, he pulled Leah's letter from the drawer and opened it. When he'd lit the lantern, he unfolded the stationery and read:

DEAR JOSH,

Conroy and I wanted to tell you our news. We are so happy to announce that we are going to become parents. Our first child is due in March.

We wish you all the best in the future.

Sincerely,

Leah.

WELL, what do you know? Leah was going to be a mother. And it didn't bother Josh one bit. He felt no anger, no jealousy. He was happy for her. Josh was finally over Leah. He had Katy to thank for that. Sweet Katy, with her pretty smile and wide, green eyes.

Josh's throat was parched. He ought to get a drink before lying down. He propped his crutches under his arms. The light under Katy's door shined brightly. She must be reading *The Lady and the Law*. Aunt Em said it was a good suspense novel.

Josh swung himself toward the kitchen as quietly as possible, trying not to awaken anyone. He filled his glass and sat at the table. A cool breeze drifted through the windows, fluttering the curtains. Maybe they would get some rain to remedy the drought. It had rained plenty in the spring, then cut off in the summer.

The full moon shed its silvery light across the barn, the corral, and everything in sight. It seemed like ages since the full moon when he'd punched Ben Grady for his less than gentlemanly treatment of Katy. He grinned recalling the stunned look on Ben's face.

When Josh had slaked his thirst, he set the glass on the table. The floorboard creaked where the living room joined the hall. Someone was walking up the hall. He sat in the shadows and waited for the figure to emerge into the moonlight. Katy. Was she thirsty too?

He watched her slip to the front door, unlatch it, and quietly step out onto the porch. Should he join her? No, he'd let her have her quiet time to think about whatever troubled her.

Josh closed his eyes and silently prayed, *Lord, whatever is bothering Katy, give her peace about it. If it's me, help me restrain myself and give her a little time to think.*

The chain on the porch swing jangled as she sat down. He might as well go to bed and let her be. Josh picked up his crutches and started to rise. When he looked through the window again, a man loitered near the paddock gate. That Franklin kid? Was he still out there smoking his cigar?

Josh moved to the window, careful to stay out of sight. Going to bed was out of the question while that guy wandered about and Katy sat on the porch.

~

CARRIE SETTLED in the porch swing with a sigh. She'd tried to concentrate on the book she'd been reading, but for the life of her, she couldn't. After re-reading the same page three times, she'd tossed it aside in hopes that the cool, night air might clear her jumbled thoughts.

Gazing heavenward, she whispered, "Lord, what do you want me to do? I don't want anyone to get hurt when they learn the truth about me, but I know that's impossible. What I did was wrong. I won't make any excuses for myself. I ask Your forgiveness for deceiving Josh and Aunt Em. Please show me the best way to tell them. And please, Lord, help them find it in their hearts to forgive me. I never meant to hurt anyone."

Carrie had come to love not only Josh and his aunt but also her life at the ranch. She felt like she belonged here. The wide-open spaces, cottonwood trees, the sweet scent of honeysuckle and the lonely call of the whippoorwill had cast a spell on her.

Her gaze slid from the cottonwoods to the corral and to the surrounding hills. Everything shimmered in the moonlight. She would miss this place. Since her parents' deaths, the ranch had felt more like home than the house her parents had left her and Blake.

Carrie looked up at the starlit sky and the moon. The first full moon since the barn dance. Memories of that night flooded back. The same night Josh first kissed her. Heat flooded through her veins, warming her from the slight chill in the air. "I don't want to leave Josh," she breathed. "If only there was another way."

Something moved near the paddock gate. Was it her imagination, or did she see a man standing there? A sense of foreboding engulfed her. Whatever it was moved. She felt the shadowy figure watching her. Carrie rose to go inside when a familiar, but barely audible voice spoke.

"Sis."

Blake!

Why was he lurking in the dark? He should be asleep. The men had a long day ahead of them tomorrow. This was her chance. She needed to ask him about Big Jim's condition. Josh's bedroom overlooked the back yard. He wouldn't see them. And Aunt Em was sleeping like a log, if her heavy breathing was any indication.

"Come out here!" he yelled.

Against her better judgment, Carrie hurried out to meet him. If he didn't lower his voice, he would awaken Josh and Aunt Em. Then she would have some explaining to do. She planned to tell them, but not tonight. She didn't relish packing her bags and walking to town in the dark.

One foot propped on the gate, Blake took a long draw off a

cigar and blew out a stream of smoke. "Keep your voice down," Carrie warned when she reached him. "Do you want to wake up the entire house? And when did you take up smoking?" Like he didn't have enough bad habits.

Blake reached out and tugged her hair. "Aw, sis, is that any way to greet your little brother you haven't seen for a good while?"

"What are you doing out here?"

"Smoking my cigar. The boys don't appreciate the aroma of a fine cigar. They insisted I go outside to indulge my habit."

Carrie folded her arms across her midsection. The robe she'd pulled on was thin and the air had become nippy. "I want to ask you something."

"Fine. Then I want to ask you somethin'."

"How is Big Jim Counce?"

"Up and around, last time I saw him. He wasn't for a couple of weeks there. Why are you interested in his welfare?"

Carrie closed her eyes. *Thank you, Lord. He's alive.* "Because I overheard two men talking about him at the depot the morning I boarded the train. They talked as if he was seriously hurt."

Blake shrugged. "That must've been the same night that woman attacked him." He chuckled. "Big Jim let a feisty woman get the best of him. It's an on goin' joke. She must have been a tough one. Lanky Stevens found Big Jim lying on the ground next to the boardwalk outside the saloon. He saw a woman runnin' away, but didn't get a good look at her. It took three men to haul ol' Jim off to jail so he could sleep it off. The sheriff would have charged him with public drunkenness if he hadn't felt sorry for him. Big Jim said he was just mindin' his own business and a woman pushed him off the boardwalk. She must've been a stout dame."

Minding his own business, indeed! "Did he know her?"

"All Big Jim recalled was a feisty woman shoved him hard and he fell backwards. The poor fella doesn't know if she hit him with a club or his head struck a rock when he hit the ground. He can't remember much about it. The fall gave him partial amnesia."

Carrie exhaled a sigh of relief. "That's good." When Blake sent her a puzzled look, she hurriedly added, "..that Big Jim is all right."

"He had a goose-egg size knot on the back of his head." Blake crossed his arms over his chest. "You seem awful interested in Big Jim's welfare. You wouldn't be the woman—"

"Blake, I'm moving into town soon," Carrie interjected. "I've been offered a job at a dress shop."

He shook his head. "That doesn't make sense. You've got it made here, sis. If you play your cards right, you could become Mrs. Josh Kramer, I'm told. And as your brother, Kramer might let me move my things into the house."

Carrie clenched her teeth. "How dare you suggest such a thing!"

"So, why are you pretendin' to be someone else?"

"It happened by accident. I don't have time to explain, now. I'd better get back inside before someone wakes up." She turned to go. Blake grabbed her arm.

"Wait." He released her and tugged off his hat. Fiddling with the brim, he cleared his throat. "Could you loan me a few bucks? Just until payday."

Carrie narrowed her eyes. "You will get paid the same time as the other hands. After you return from the cattle drive, when Mr. Kramer writes out the checks to all his hands."

He bristled. "Don't you get all high and mighty with me! I'm flat broke. I need money now! I'll need enough to buy somethin' to eat once we reach Abilene."

"Drink, you mean. You should have thought of that when you gambled away everything we owned. I won't give you one cent. You will have to wait until payday, just like the others." She whirled around and ran toward the house.

"Payday could come quicker than you think!" he yelled after her. "Sleep on that."

Carrie froze but did not turn around. Her heart drummed against her ribcage. Surely he wouldn't follow through with his threat. If he did— No! She wouldn't even consider it. She hurried toward the house, her legs shaking like jelly. At the bottom of the steps, Carrie focused on planting one foot in front of the other until she reached the porch. Inside, she slipped to her bedroom and collapsed on the bed.

What trick did Blake have up his sleeve? Would he really expose her if she didn't give him money? It would be better if she told Josh the truth before her brother made up his own version of why she had taken on Katy Davis's identity."

She punched her pillow. Another sleepless night.

JOSH COULD NOT BELIEVE what he'd seen. Two figures stood in the moonlight near the paddock. It reeked of a secret meeting in the dark. What reason did Katy have to meet Blake in the dark, after he and Aunt Em were in bed?

"Payday could come quicker than you think."

Those were the only words he'd heard. The menacing tone of Blake's words made his skin crawl. What kind of hold did that Franklin kid have over Katy? Was he blackmailing her? For what? Was she running from the law?

Josh shook his head. None of it made sense. Maybe Franklin was her beau and she'd left Arkansas to get away from him? How had he found her?

Josh wished they hadn't hired the kid. By the time Luke found him, he'd scraped the bottom of the barrel for cowhands. The other ranchers had beat them to the draw, snatching up the reliable ones to help with their own roundups.

The night before Luke ran into Blake, he had been involved in a poker-game-gone-wrong. The game got out of hand when the kid lost big and couldn't pay up. He'd begged Luke for a job to settle his debts, to get those unhappy poker players off his back.

Josh had felt uneasy about the boy upon meeting him, and the kid had done nothing since to dispel those feelings. He smelled like trouble, and he wasn't good at taking orders.

Blake was too young and immature for Katy. Could there be something between them? What did she see in a rebellious kid with a heap of growing up to do? The boy had a hard row to hoe ahead of him.

When Katy stepped upon the porch, Josh moved into the shadows in the kitchen. She slipped inside, quietly closing the door. Leaning back against it, her breath had come gasps. After a moment, she'd tiptoed down the hall and into her room.

Blake had frightened her, either by his threat or when he'd grabbed her arm. Rage boiled up inside Josh's chest. Not intervening had taken a lot of effort. And he would have if Katy hadn't torn herself away from the kid. He would love to teach Blake how to show respect for a lady.

Josh's jaw clenched. Wait a doggone . . . Were Blake and Katy co-conspirators? Did Blake threaten her because she tried to renege on their plan? Had they been conniving to get his ranch?

If Josh weren't so angry, he would call them both into his study and interrogate them, now. But it would be better for all concerned if he slept on it. If he could sleep.

Tomorrow, he would get answers, one way or the other.

Chapter Sixteen

❦

Carrie watched Josh fork eggs into his mouth. He was unusually quiet this morning, avoiding eye contact. Aunt Em glanced from him to Carrie. When she shrugged, Aunt Em rolled her eyes.

Carrie's eyelids threatened to drop. She'd tossed and turned most of the night. Blake was right. Payday had come sooner that she'd anticipated. It was time to tell Josh the truth. Should she pack her things first? That wouldn't take long. She'd arrived with one valise and would leave with little more. The only additions would be the dress she'd made from the material Josh bought for her and the satin hair ribbons he'd given her.

Aunt Em picked up a bowl, offered it to Josh. "More gravy?"

He flung up a hand. "No, thanks. I'm through."

Josh never turned down second helpings. Carrie reached for the bowl. "I'll have a little more gravy, and another biscuit."

Josh slid his chair back, grabbed his crutches, and rose. "I'll be in the study."

Luke met with him every morning. Today the hands would drive the herd to the stockyards where they would be loaded on cattle cars and shipped north to Abilene, Kansas.

Aunt Em's brow furrowed as she watched Josh propel himself out of the kitchen. "I wonder what's botherin' him."

Carrie sighed. "He's probably disappointed that he can't join the cattle drive."

"That could be part of it, but I think there's more."

The study door closed harder than usual. Carrie's hands shook as she raised the fork to her mouth. Had Josh seen her go back out last night? She'd thought he was in bed. Her stomach twisted into a knot. If she ate one more bite, she would regurgitate it. She rose, raked her biscuits and gravy onto the scrap plate. and stacked the other dirty plates.

Luke traipsed inside, nodded at the ladies, and walked straight into the study. Only two minutes passed before he came out and headed to the bunkhouse.

Aunt Em lifted the kettle from the stove. "I'd better quit worrying about Josh and start these dishes."

Carrie's heart skipped a beat. She felt the tension building. How long before an explosion? "I'll let the chickens out and feed them. Then I'll dry the dishes."

She sat on the sofa and began lacing her shoes. The screen door slapped to. Blake walked in. His gaze slid from Carrie to the now open door of the study where Josh sat behind his desk.

Josh growled, "Come in here and shut the door, Franklin. We need to talk."

The door closed behind them. Carrie's hands shook as she tried to lace the top eyelets of her shoes. Were they discussing her? Had Josh seen her with Blake last night?

Aunt Em clucked her tongue. "It's like bees swarming through the house this morning."

Carrie flinched. She needed to inhale and relax. While she finished tying her laces, the study door opened again. Blake walked out, his head down. He froze when Josh called out, "We will finish this conversation when you get back. No matter what time it is."

Blake tramped out the door without a glance toward Carrie.

She watched through the window until he entered the bunkhouse. She flinched when Aunt Em said, "Somethin's going on between Josh and that young man. He wasn't in the study more'n two minutes."

"The men may be about to start the cattle drive." Carrie hoped that explained her brother's short time in the study. She stood and smoothed her skirt. "I'm off to feed the chickens."

Carrie threw the latch on the chicken house door and jumped behind it to avoid a flogging. The chickens flew off the roost pole, landing in the back yard three and four at a time.

Carrie selected half a dozen ears of corn from the crib and shelled them in a pan while the impatient flock circled her, pecking at her feet. By the fifth cob, her hands were raw. Some cobs were easier to shell than others. Today the ones she'd chosen were rough. She blew on her tender hands and shelled the last one. Grabbing up handfuls of corn, she scattered it in every direction to ensure each chicken got its share.

When she'd replaced the empty pan inside the corn crib, cattle bawled and hoof beats thundered in front of the house. The cattle drive had begun. Curious to see her first one, she ran around to the side of the house to watch.

The cattle protested as they spilled through the open gate out into the yard. The cowboys surrounded the herd, each at his appointed position. Carrie stood in the shade of an elm tree, amazed at the skills of the cowboys as they moved the herd along in the right direction. Even her brother seemed to know what he was doing, although he had no experience.

Cattle as far as the eye could see bellowed and kicked up dust as the cowhands herded them down the lane. A few minutes later a cloud of dust was all that remained. The whistles and shouts from the cowboys plus the bellowing cattle had disappeared, leaving in its place an eerie quiet.

Carrie turned to walk away when voices drifted through the open window above her. The study window. She hated to eavesdrop, but considering Josh's mood at breakfast, she might benefit from learning what was bothering him.

"What are you sayin'?"

Carrie recognized Aunt Em's voice speaking to Josh.

"That whatever is going on between those two, I don't like it."

Josh's voice. Then a bang as if he'd slapped his desk. She strained to hear the rest.

Who were "those two" they were discussing? Carrie backed up against the house, below the window to hide and listen.

"Josh, don't jump to conclusions. It could be purely innocent. Things aren't always as they appear."

"How well I know it." Anger laced his voice. "Even those who appear the picture of innocence can have vile intentions."

Carrie's heart sank. Were she and Blake "those two" Josh mentioned? Or had her guilty conscience made her read too much into their exchange? She inhaled deeply. Josh and Aunt Em could be discussing a couple of temporary hands.

"Let me talk to her," Aunt Em's voice pleaded.

They are talking about me.

"Go ahead, but what good can come of it? They may be practiced con artists, out to get the ranch."

Josh's words cut her to the core. She was not a con artist, and she had no interest in the Kramer ranch. Unless the owner came with it. No chance of that now. His words had smashed that dream.

Carrie had heard enough. Tears blurred her vision as she trudged to the back door. Josh had called her a con artist. She hadn't actually stolen anyone's identity. Josh had *assumed* she was Katy Davis. She had only let him assume.

She closed her eyes and breathed, "Sorry, Lord. I should not make excuses for myself. I did wrong." In a way, she was relieved. It would soon be over, and she would no longer have to hide her identity.

Had Blake squealed on her? He'd threatened to. If it weren't for

Josh already being furious, she would march into the study and tell him the whole story, confess she was an interloper. But only by chance.

She wiped her eyes, sniffing back more tears. If she could hold her emotions in check until Blake returned, they could go to Josh and explain together.

Carrie forced herself to keep her chin up. She marched through the back door, picked up a dishtowel and a handful of silverware. As she put the utensils away, the front door slammed. She peered through the window in time to see Josh propel himself off the porch and hop to the barn. He'd become skilled with those crutches.

A few minutes later Josh drove the buckboard out of the barn and headed up the lane. Somehow he had managed to hitch the horses to the buckboard and had swung himself up onto the seat without assistance. Where was he going in such a hurry? She couldn't help wondering if his quick getaway was connected to the conversation she'd overheard.

Someone should have gone with him. Josh had no business going into town alone with a fractured foot. He could fall and make his injury worse. She exhaled. "Listen to me, acting like I care."

She did care. Why bother denying it? Carrie pressed her fist to her mouth and cried, "Oh God, I love him so much!"

JOSH SLAPPED THE REINS, urging the team to a fast trot. He had to know the truth about Katy, but he wanted to be fair and give her the benefit of the doubt. He hoped what he discovered would prove him wrong. What drove a woman like her to accept a domestic job hundreds of miles from her home? She was either running from something or someone, or her ambition drove her to set her sights on a thousand-acre ranch.

The Kramer ranch.

Somehow that didn't ring true. If her goal was the ranch, wouldn't she have used her feminine wiles to influence him? Katy had never even batted her lashes at him. He had been the instigator each time they'd kissed. If her scheme was to push him to the altar, why hadn't she put forth a little effort?

On the contrary, Katy seemed content with the domestic position. She might have wormed her way into his and Aunt Em's hearts, but it wasn't because she'd tried. Katy was just naturally sweet and loveable. She came through as honest and responsible too.

He had to find Katy's connection to Blake Franklin, whatever it was. Those two were the most improbable match imaginable. While she oozed with goodness and purity, Blake was a full-bloodied rebel.

Josh figured he'd send a telegram to the Denton sheriff and have him investigate Blake's background—if Blake really came from Denton. If that wasn't the kid's hometown, Josh would send a telegram to Hope, Arkansas, to inquire about a young lady named Katy Davis who caught a train to Abilene on the fifteenth of September.

"Whoa!" Josh drew in his horses at the telegraph office and managed to disembark with the aid of his crutches. He clopped inside and up to the window.

Sliding the note and money to the telegrapher, he asked, "How long will it take for a reply?"

The wiry little man pushed his glasses up his hawkish nose as he counted out Josh's change. "Mr. Kramer, it depends on whether the sheriff in Denton is in town. If you have other business, you could take care of it and return in thirty minutes. Maybe by then you'll have a reply."

Josh hopped back to the wagon and using his crutches, propelled himself up onto the seat. He headed the horses toward the feed mill. When the wagon was stacked with bags of feed, he drove to the mercantile to purchase the items on Aunt Em's list.

Wood's Mercantile was empty except for a pretty brunette

woman digging through bolts of fabric. Mrs. Wood set Aunt Em's items on the counter one at a time until the order was filled. "Mr. Kramer, do you want to pay for your order or put them on your tab?"

The check from the cattle drive would be a welcome relief. Josh could pay off both the mercantile and the feed mill. "Put these things on my tab. I'll pay the bill in a few days."

Josh felt a tap on his arm. The pretty brunette stood behind him, clutching a bolt of yellow floral material. "Would you happen to be Josh Kramer?"

Josh tipped his hat. "Yes, Ma'am. Have we met?" She didn't look the least bit familiar.

"No, but a young woman I became acquainted with on the train gave you a message at the depot two months ago." Color tinged her cheeks. "You see, I came from Arkansas in answer to a mail-order bride ad. Carrie and I shared a seat on the train. I asked her to deliver a message to you about Katy."

"Carrie? I don't know her, but I know a Katy. What was the message?" Josh scratched his chin. "You must have me confused with someone else."

Her brows drew together. "Then you aren't Josh Kramer, owner of the Kramer ranch?"

Mrs. Woods handed Josh the receipt. "Yes, he is Josh Kramer."

Josh nodded at the young lady. Mrs. Woods should mind her own business. He could answer for himself. The woman wasn't happy unless she could stick her nose in everybody's business.

"Carrie and I became friends on the train. She'd boarded at Denton and I—"

"Denton, Texas? Wait. You came here from Arkansas?"

"Yes. Hope, Arkansas. That's what I'm trying to tell you. Katy—"

"And this Katy . . . what is her last name, and where is she from?"

"She is from Hope, Arkansas also. We're friends. We went to school together."

Josh's mind whirled. "This girl you met on the train, did you say her name was Carrie?"

"Yes. Carrie Franklin."

Franklin! How was she related to Blake? This had to be the woman living at his ranch. This could not be coincidence. Were Carrie and Blake married? Surely Katy . . . *Carrie* had better sense! Josh's stomach churned. He swallowed the lump forming in his throat, He'd been played for a fool. "And the message Carrie was supposed to deliver was what?"

"Mr. Kramer, I'm sure she told you. You couldn't have forgotten so soon. Why, I just ran into Carrie at the post office, two or three weeks ago. She said she saw you. I assumed she told you Katy Davis had changed her mind about . . . Well, you know."

About the ad for domestic help, he assumed. "Yes, I know. Will you describe Carrie?"

"She is about my size, same age. Carrie is blonde, very pretty, with gorgeous green eyes."

It was her all right. Katy Davis was in fact Carrie Franklin. Josh would bet the bank on it. Anger burned like gall in his throat. "Yes, I remember her well." The big question was, why had she stolen another woman's identity?

"Then she did find you at the train station?"

"Oh, yes. She found me." No, he'd found her. Sitting pretty on a bench inside the depot looking lost, her hands folded in her lap. The soft, sky blue jacket she'd worn looked as if it had been made for her. That might have been the moment he'd fallen for Katy. *Carrie.*

Josh was on the defense from the beginning, the driving reason he'd treated her coldly. One look at Carrie told him she would be a threat to his sanity. His heart had not recovered from Leah's treachery.

He'd better get Carrie out of his head. This woman who had taken the place of Katy Davis was in fact a designing woman who had drawn Josh in with her innocence. His jaw clenched. To think her innocence was only a cover for what she had planned for him.

"Mr. Kramer, did I say something wrong? I'm sorry Katy backed out of the agreement. I hope you understand. She's really a nice person. Something just didn't feel right to her."

Mrs. Wood smiled at him. "Since you are incapacitated, I will carry this box to your wagon."

"Thank you." Josh flashed her a smile and turned back to the pretty brunette. "Good day, Miss—?"

"Hanks, now." She blushed. "Molly Hanks. Slim and I had just gotten married before I saw Carrie that day in town."

Josh propelled himself up into the wagon. He'd bet Molly Hanks had divulged more information than he would ever learn in a telegram. Nevertheless, he clucked to the horses and turned them toward the telegraph office.

The telegrapher rushed out to meet him, waving the telegram. "Here you go, sir. This just came in." He handed it up. Josh thanked the little man who had saved him the awkwardness of swinging down again with the aid of his crutches.

The injured foot was a nuisance. He would be happy when he could get back to ranch work. He'd lain around the house too long. Not that he didn't enjoy having Katy, or rather Carrie, nearby. She stayed within ear shot, always fluffing the sofa pillow, ensuring he was comfortable. Even her touch soothed him when she changed the dressing on his foot.

Josh skimmed the telegram. *Franklin. trouble. Has sister who vanished mid-September. Franklin left last week.*

Carrie was Blake's sister? He stuffed the reply into his shirt pocket and shook the reins to get the horses moving.

As he passed the general store, someone yelled, "Kramer!" Ben Grady ran toward him, waving one hand, carrying a sack in the other.

"Whoa!" Josh pulled on the reins.

"Do you mind if I catch a ride with you?"

What choice did he have? The good Lord said to treat enemies with kindness. "Hop up."

"Thanks. I rode in with Nancy, but she was in a hurry to get back. The ladies' sewing circle is meeting this afternoon. I told her to go ahead, that I'd catch a ride. This bag could get heavy." He set it in the wagon and climbed up beside Josh.

The wagon rolled along and Josh offered no interest in conversing. Ben finally shifted toward him. "Look, Kramer, I know I acted like a jerk toward Katy. But I did apologize to her. And she accepted it."

"Oh?" Josh had already heard the story and preferred not to hear it again.

"Yes, at the post office."

"Then she seemed satisfied with your apology?"

"It seemed that way. She accepted it graciously." Ben scratched his temple. "But something else has been on my mind since that day. I can't figure it out. Maybe you can clear it up for me."

Josh sighed. He would not give Ben the pleasure of knowing he'd piqued his curiosity. But his feigned disinterest didn't stop Ben.

"As I was leaving the post office, a cute brunette apparently recognized Katy. The strange part was I could have sworn she called her Carrie instead of Katy." Ben shrugged. "It could have been nothing more than a memory lapse."

Carrie, Katy, the names sounded similar.

Another nail in the coffin of so-called Katy Davis's innocence. Josh made no comment but changed the subject to the drought and the effects it had wrought on Taylor County ranchers and farmers.

CARRIE PEELED the last potato and dropped it in the pot. How much had Blake told Josh?

Aunt Em dried her hands on her apron. "Listen to that wind moaning through the eaves. It's a sure sign cooler weather is on the way. Let's take a break. You look like you could use one."

"Let me put these potatoes on to cook, first." Carrie filled the pot with water and set it on the stove, covering it with a lid. Aunt Em set cups on the table along with the cream pitcher and sugar bowl.

Carrie sat down with a sigh. She stirred sugar into her coffee and poured in cream. Aunt Em sat down at her usual spot at the head of the table. She sensed Josh's aunt was about to ask her personal questions. Carrie's hands felt clammy as she raised her cup to sip.

"Hon, is there anything you'd like to tell me? I'm a good listener."

She studied Aunt Em. Could she trust her? Would it help or hurt her if she confided the atrocious thing she'd done? Carrie set her cup down. "What do you want to know?"

"Did you ever meet Blake Franklin before Josh hired him to help with the roundup?"

"Yes." Carrie swallowed hard and took another sip of coffee while collecting her thoughts. Aunt Em didn't beat around the bush. What did it matter now? She had nothing to lose. Josh was already suspicious. Why not get it over with?

Compassion filled Aunt Em's eyes, making Carrie's guilt surface. Tears blurred from her vision. "I've done a terrible thing," she sobbed. "I'm sorry. I didn't mean to hurt anybody."

Aunt Em rose and wrapped her arms around Carrie. "You poor thing. It can't be that bad."

"Yes, it is. You don't understand. I'm not really Katy Davis. I've just pretended to be her."

Aunt Em pulled back and eyed her. Confusion replaced compassion on her face. "Then who are you?"

"I'm Carrie Franklin, and I'm from Denton, Texas. Not Hope, Arkansas."

"Franklin? The same as the temporary cowhand I just asked about?"

"Yes. Blake is my brother."

Aunt Em's mouth gaped open. She dropped back down in her

chair and wiped her brow. "You'd better tell me the whole story. From the beginnin'."

Carrie wiped damp tendrils off her face. "You don't know how many times I've tried to tell you and Josh the truth. But every time I thought about it, I stopped because I couldn't stand the thought of losing either of you." She sniffed back more tears. "You see, our parents were killed in an accident. Their buggy overturned five years ago. Blake was fourteen, I was seventeen. I'd promised my mama I'd look out for him if anything happened to them."

She wiped her hand across her eyes. "I didn't realize how difficult it would be to discipline him. My brother has a knack for getting in trouble. He doesn't think through his decisions before he acts on them."

Carrie laced her fingers together, laid them on the table. "But who am I to talk after what I did?"

Aunt Em patted her hands. "Tell me, how did you come to assume Katy Davis's identity?"

"Blake's drinking and gambling habits got so bad, there was no money for food. I warned him if he blew his paycheck one more time, I was leaving. I probably wouldn't have had the nerve if I hadn't had an altercation with Big Jim Counce."

"Who's Big Jim Counce?"

"The meanest man in Denton. Nobody crosses him and gets by with it. I've never been inside a saloon. But that night I was so angry at Blake. I knew he was in there gambling away his paycheck, because his horse was tied out front."

"Heavens, child! Don't tell me you went in there?"

"I started to, but I stopped in front of the swinging doors. That's when Big Jim staggered out. I could tell he was drunk by the way he stumbled. And his breath reeked of whiskey. He grabbed me and tried to kiss me. I pushed him. The next thing I knew he'd fallen off the boardwalk. I didn't know if he was dead or just unconscious. I panicked. I was afraid I'd be arrested for murder. Or if Big Jim came to, he'd come after me."

"My word! What did you do?"

"I packed my valise and bought a ticket to Abilene. The train was due to leave around four in the morning. Since Blake was at the saloon, I figured he would stay caught up in a poker game until the wee hours. I would be gone before he came home."

Aunt Em shook her head. "Why did you pick Abilene as your destination?"

"I asked the stationmaster for a ticket that would take me far away. I held back barely enough money for a meal and a night's stay in a hotel."

Carrie shook her head. "At least I thought I had enough for a night's stay, until I looked in my bag. Back to my brother. I had to talk to him to find out if I'd killed Big Jim or just injured him. Blake laid my fears to rest. He said a woman had beat up Big Jim the night I left, that a man found him lying outside the saloon with a big knot on his head. Lucky for me, he didn't recall anything about the woman." She whooshed out a breath.

"Well, at least it's over. A man who forces himself on a woman deserves what he gets."

"One reason I went to the post office was to see if my picture was on a reward poster."

Aunt Em sniggered. "Wouldn't that have been somethin'? But you could have claimed self-defense." She scooted her chair back and stood. "I'll add water to the potatoes. Then you can tell me how you came to take Katy Davis's place."

"That's exactly what I want to know." Josh stood in the doorway, one shoulder against the doorjamb, his crutches supporting him.

Carrie wiped clammy hands down the sides of her skirt. Why hadn't she heard the buckboard pull up or Josh come in? He'd returned from town earlier than she'd expected. Or maybe the wind whistling through the eaves had drowned out the sound of his crutches clunking across the porch.

He stood across the table from her, flames shooting from his eyes. "Miss Franklin, meet me in the study. First I want a few words with my aunt."

Carrie cringed like a mouse beneath the scrutiny of a hawk. How could she make him believe she had intended no malice toward him? She laid a hand on his arm. "Josh, I—"

His brow furrowed. "Not now. I'll meet you in the study."

She shivered at his icy tone.

Chapter Seventeen

Josh watched Carrie flee from the kitchen, tears streaming down her face. When she was out of sight, he turned to his aunt. "Suppose you fill me in on what's going on here."

Aunt Em raised one hand. "Calm down. Katy, I mean Carrie, was explainin' everything to me when you busted in on us."

Josh's brows arched. "Do you want to know what I discovered by sending a telegram to Denton?"

Aunt Em shook her head. "Probably not a thing more'n I found out just by askin'. Askin' don't hurt, and it might've saved you some trouble and money."

Josh thumbed over his shoulder. "That young woman has played us both for fools."

His aunt glared at him. "And how do you figure that?"

"Her real name is Carrie Franklin. She's Blake's sister."

"Yes, I know that. So, what?"

"So she's bound to be after something. Why else would she assume another woman's identity?"

Aunt Em poured him a glass of cool water. "Drink this. You've gotta be thirsty."

He turned it up, swigged it down, and plunked the glass on the table. "Has Miss Franklin told you anything else I should know?"

"Not a thing she won't tell you, if you'll ask in a civilized manner. You need to calm down before you go in there." Aunt Em pointed toward the study. "That girl's been through plenty already without you addin' to her problems."

"You're taking up for her? I can't believe it." Josh yanked off his hat and raked his fingers through his hair. "We have no idea what she and her renegade brother were plotting."

Aunt Em wiped up a water drip from the tablecloth. "Not one thing, that's what."

Josh pointed at his aunt. "You are too trusting."

She pointed back. "And you jump to conclusions before hearin' all the facts."

"She had a good reason for stealing another woman's identity and coming here?" Josh huffed. "I can't wait to hear it."

"She did. And it's not a pretty story."

"I know. The real Katy Davis changed her mind about the job." Josh's words were laced with sarcasm. "That still doesn't explain why Miss Franklin decided to take her place."

"Go in there and ask her. Nicely. We were just gettin' to the good part when you stormed in."

He ducked his chin in mock humility. "Then excuse me for walking into my own house."

Aunt Em exhaled. "Before you talk to Carrie, I have a confession of my own to make."

"And what might that be?"

"The ad you insisted I place in the paper was not for domestic help."

Josh rolled his eyes. "Oh? Then what was it for, a live-in seamstress?"

"A mail-order bride."

Josh coughed. "A mail-order bride? You expect me to believe that?" If his own aunt could deceive him, who could he trust?

"It's true. So, if you have any ideas about tossing that girl out, you can toss me out too."

Josh shook his head. "Why would you do a fool thing like placing an ad for a mail-order bride?"

"Because it hurt me to watch you fume and sulk over Leah. It's been a year now. Enough time to let go of your anger, forgive and forget about her. And it's time you quit blaming yourself for not being there when your pa died. It wasn't your fault. It just happened, and you couldn't have done a thing to stop it. The doctor's report even stated it."

Josh sighed. "You're right. Blaming myself hasn't brought Pa back. As for Leah, she doesn't even cross my mind anymore. That's over."

Aunt Em's face glowed. "I like the sound of that. What did she say in her letter?"

His lips pulled into a smirk. "You don't give up, do you?"

"Not when someone dear to me is involved."

"Back to Miss Franklin. How did she come to take the place of Katy Davis? What you said only proved my point. She came with the notion of matrimony, to get her hands on the ranch. I'd wager she and her brother are in this together. It can't be coincidence that he showed up now."

Aunt Em shook her head. "You've got Carrie figured wrong. She didn't get to the part about taking Miss Davis's place. But, I know Carrie is a sweet young lady without a devious bone in her body. She's smitten with you, and you're smitten with her. You think I haven't noticed the way you make goo-goo eyes at each other? Give her a chance to tell her side before you get all fired up and say somethin' you'll regret."

Josh wasn't sure he trusted Aunt Em's conclusions. Carrie's interest in him could be part of the plan. Cozy up to the cowboy and take him for everything, lock, stock, and barrel.

His conscience shouted, *Wrong! You are the one who cozied up.*

"I'll give her a chance." He propped his crutches under his arms and hopped toward the study. A minute later, he returned. "Carrie's not in there. Check her bedroom."

Aunt Em hurried to Carrie's bedroom, Josh on her heels. The

closed door was unusual. When she didn't answer the knock, Aunt Em opened the door to an empty room. After sliding out drawers and finding them empty and her valise missing, she drew a ragged breath. "She's gone, Josh. Go after her. She couldn't have gotten far."

Josh stepped into the room and scanned it. "Gone? Where would she go on foot?"

"Probably to Abilene, to catch the train. You've got to stop her. No tellin' who or what she might run into walkin' along that road."

"Abilene is twelve-miles. She'll never make it before dark."

"Unless she catches a ride."

With someone like Ben Grady? "Oh no." He might be angry at Miss Franklin, but the visual of Ben putting his slimy hands on her infuriated him. No woman deserved that kind of treatment.

Josh swung himself forward on his crutches. He made it off the porch and propelled himself toward the wagon. He'd be glad when his foot was completely healed. The wagon stood in the yard, the horses hitched to it.

Unhitching the horses was the last thing on his mind when he came up. At least he'd thought to pull up to the water trough to let them drink. Confronting the green-eyed beauty who had stolen his heart was the one thing that consumed him. Admitting he'd let himself be lured in by her presumed innocence fueled his anger more.

Carrie, the woman who had fooled him into believing she was Katy, had made him forget Leah. But no one could make him forget Carrie. His feelings for Leah only scratched the surface compared to his love for Carrie. If his heart survived this wrenching, how could he trust it again?

Josh wanted to believe his aunt's words. "That girl is smitten with you." She was right on one account. He was the one smitten. He wished he was more like Aunt Em, who gave everyone the benefit of the doubt and believed the best of others.

He yelled, "Giddy-up!" urging the horses to a fast trot. He headed north at the end of the lane, figuring to turn back after a couple of miles. Carrie couldn't have gotten any farther than that on foot. Only fifteen minutes earlier, he'd told her to meet him in the study.

Cupping his hands around his mouth, he yelled, "Carrie!" After several minutes, his throat hurt. She could be hiding in the woods. She couldn't have walked any farther. He swung the wagon around to backtrack, still calling her name.

Josh reached the lane leading to the ranch and drove past. Three miles later, his team showed signs of exhaustion, and still no Carrie. She must have caught a ride into Abilene, or maybe gone south to Buffalo Gap. Which way?

The horses needed a break, regardless. Josh slowed them to an easy canter. When he closed in on the Grady ranch, he was tempted to stop and ask Nancy if she knew where Carrie might have gone. After deliberating, he changed his mind. Who needed the neighbors gossiping about their family's personal business?

The men would drag in from the cattle drive later, looking for their pay. He needed to be there to settle up with them. The checks were already written and jotted down in the ledger. If Carrie had caught a ride to Abilene, she would be halfway there by now. She probably wouldn't catch a train until morning. He would ask the first cowboy who rode in if he'd seen her somewhere along the way.

Carrie's brother might have had an idea of her whereabouts. He hadn't gotten a thing out of Blake this morning regarding his meeting with her in the moonlight. The kid might be reckless, but he was staunchly loyal to his sister.

A HALF-MILE from the ranch Carrie heard hoof beats behind her. She peered through the dust at a buggy heading her way. She started to duck behind a bush when she recognized Doc Sullivan as the driver.

"Whoa!" he yelled. "Young lady, you want a lift into Buffalo

Gap? I'm headed that way." His bespectacled gaze raked her from head to toe. "Say, aren't you the young woman Emma Roberts hired to help her with housework at the Kramer ranch?"

Carrie sniffed back tears. "Yes, sir. I'm Carrie. The position didn't work out. I've accepted a job in town." She tried to sound happy, hoping her eyes didn't show red.

"Hand me your bag and climb up." From the sympathetic look he gave her, he must have noticed her distress.

"I appreciate the ride." Carrie sighed as she lifted the valise and climbed up. Her luggage had become burdensome in the short distance she'd walked.

When she was seated, the doctor asked about Josh's foot. "I've a hunch he hasn't followed my instructions. Am I correct?"

Carrie smiled. "You would be right." Josh amazed her the way he got around on crutches.

Doc shook his head. "An independent one, that Kramer boy. He came into this world red-faced and screaming at the top of his lungs. I knew then he'd be a fighter."

"You delivered him?"

"I did. He weighed a hardy eight pounds, eight ounces. His mama had a long, hard labor."

Carrie closed her eyes and visualized Josh as a baby. If she had his babies, would they look like him, have dark hair and dark eyes? She silently admonished herself for thinking such a far-fetched thought.

Doc slowed the buggy as they reached town. "Where do you want off? I'm heading south a ways."

"I'm headed to Owen's boarding house."

"Why, that's right on the way, Miss Carrie."

When they reached the white-framed house surround by a white picket fence, Doc yelled "Whoa!" and stopped the horses. The stone path leading up to the door welcomed Carrie. She climbed down from the buggy. Doc handed her the valise and she thanked him. "I appreciate the ride."

"No inconvenience at all. I enjoyed the company. You take care now." He tipped his hat and drove off.

When Mrs. Owen answered the door, she frowned. "Aren't you the young lady who inquired about the vacant room yesterday?"

"Yes, ma'am. I'm Carrie Franklin." She set her valise down to extend her hand. "I can move in today, if it's all right."

"I'm sorry, Miss Franklin. The room isn't ready. I'm having new wallpaper hung. Check back in three days. It should be ready by then."

"Thank you. I will be at the hotel." The hotel would quickly suck up her savings, but she was out of choices.

Mrs. Owen nodded, then closed the door on her. Carrie scanned her surroundings. Shadowy houses lined the road. The sun would set soon and the walk back to town was a good mile. She prayed she would be safe. Carrie picked up her bag to start walking.

Because Sonja's Boutique had closed at four-thirty, she had not arrived in time to tell her she wanted the job.

A LONE RIDER rode into the yard at dusk. Josh hopped out to the porch using his crutches. "Franklin, come to my study. I need to talk to you. Take care of your horse first."

"Sure thing, boss."

For some reason, Josh cringed every time Blake called him "Boss." He clomped to his study to wait while Blake unsaddled and watered his horse. If the kid didn't know which way Carrie had gone, Josh would head to Abilene at sunrise. Meanwhile Blake had better be ready to answer questions on how he was involved in this deception. Josh figured he held the winning hand with the information he'd garnered from the telegram and Molly Hanks.

Josh flipped through the ledger and pulled out Blake's check. As he returned the ledger to the desk drawer, the study door opened and the kid walked in.

Blake removed his hat. Dust covered him from head to toe, and he looked as if he might drop any minute. "How did the drive go?"

"We made it. Didn't lose one head. A couple of times a steer ran astray, but we drove it back in line."

He handed Blake his check. "Good." As the kid looked at it, Josh asked, "Do you know where your sister is?"

"My sister?" Blake shifted his gaze to the door behind him.

"Yes, Blake. I know Carrie is your sister. No more pretense, please. Where is she?"

"She's not in the kitchen with your aunt?"

Was the kid trying to mislead him? "No, she isn't. She packed her bag and disappeared nearly two hours ago."

"I'm not sure." He raked through his hair and dust fogged, settling on Josh's clean desk. "Wait. She said something about movin' into town and gettin' a job at a dress shop. She didn't say which shop."

"Buffalo Gap?"

"Yeah, that's where she mentioned."

"All right. Now, tell me how you happened to show up here, and why Carrie left Denton and stole another woman's identity?"

"I'm not for certain why she took the name Katy Davis, but I think it might've had somethin' to do with Big Jim Counce. Some woman clobbered the daylights out of him outside the saloon the same night Carrie left on the train. Big Jim's not one to take that lightly. Carrie probably thought he'd come for her."

"That makes no sense. Why would your sister be standing outside a saloon?"

Blake's face flushed beneath the dust. He hung his head. "She'd come for me, to drag me back home. I have a bad gamblin' habit, sir. She'd done told me she couldn't take any more. That she'd leave if I didn't quit blowin' my paycheck."

"Are you saying you and Carrie didn't have some kind of a plan when she came here?"

"Sir, I didn't even know where she'd gone. Not until I got a letter from her a couple of weeks ago. Then I figured I had nothin' to lose. So I hopped the train to Abilene and caught a ride to Buffalo Gap. It didn' take much askin' around to figure out she was here after I described her to the old lady at the mercantile."

Mrs. Woods, the busybody. That figured. The kid's words rang true. Josh's gaze raked him. "Go out and hitch up the buckboard. We are going to town. You are going to help me persuade your sister to come back."

Blake slapped his hat against his shirt. Dust fogged again. "Can I at least change clothes?"

"Yes, please change clothes, but hurry."

CARRIE GRASPED the handles on the valise that held all her worldly belongings. As she trudged toward town, the canvas bag tugged on her wrist, shooting a pain up her arm. She stopped, set it down, and rubbed her arm. After stretching her back, she picked it up with the other hand. Her stomach growled, reminding her she hadn't eaten a bite since breakfast. Doc had passed a cafe along the way. If she could recall exactly where, she'd stop in for a bite.

Dusk had settled when Carrie reached town. She scanned the signs above the businesses and spied the Gilded Bullet saloon just ahead. Lively piano music drummed in her ears while slurred voices drifted out, making her tremble. A cheerfully-lit diner squeezed between the newspaper office and the saloon, beckoned her. Its lights beamed a welcome relief to weary travelers.

Three of the six tables were taken. Two families including giggling children were seated near the window. In the corner, a young couple, obviously smitten, held hands and gazed into each other's eyes. Carrie was met by a matronly waitress who led her to a small table by the window and handed her a menu. She plopped down with a sigh and dropped her valise at her feet. The waitress smiled at her. "What can I get for you, sweetie?"

"I'll take the beef roast with mashed potatoes and carrots, with a glass of water, please."

When the waitress left, Carrie rubbed her sore wrists. Loud music and raucous laughter drifted through the open window. Her stomach clenched. If only she could find a route to the hotel without passing the Gilded Bullet saloon.

She closed her eyes. *Lord, what have I gotten myself into? Please protect me. I'm afraid.*

Carrie already missed Josh and Aunt Em. No, she would not think about what she'd lost, or she would start crying in front of these people. She had to find the strength to forget Josh and the tender moments they had shared.

Tears blurred Carrie's eyes. She sniffed them back as a plate of food was set in front of her. She picked up her fork and dived in. The beef roast could have been leather for all she could taste. Her appetite was gone, but she forced herself to eat. She couldn't afford to waste money on food and leave it untouched.

When she'd paid her bill, she stepped out onto the boardwalk and listened. The music and voices from the saloon were louder. The men inside would become rowdier as they imbibed.

Carrie hiked her shoulders to begin her trek to the hotel. She could do this. Praying no one burst through the swinging doors as she hurried by, she quickly placed one foot in front of the other.

She released a slow breath after she had passed the saloon. The hotel loomed just ahead. She could do this.

Clop-clop! Clop-clop-clop!

The noise came from behind. Heavy footsteps and the towering shadow of a man on the wall moved toward her. Closer now. He was stalking her!

Clop-clop-clop-clop! He moved faster while her heart drummed against her chest.

The shadow loomed larger. Carrie's stalker had gained ground. She moved faster while tears streamed down her face. "Lord, please help me!" She flung her valise in the alley, hiked her skirts, and raced toward the hotel, praying she wouldn't trip and fall.

"Carrie! Carrie!" *Clop-clop-clop-clop!* "Stop running. I can't catch up to you on these wretched crutches."

"Josh?" She slid to a stop and leaned back against the building, gasping for air. She began to sob.

Clop-clop-clop-clop-clop! Josh caught up to her and propped his crutches against the building. Then he reached for her. "Come here, let me hold you." Josh pulled Carrie into his arms. "You're trembling. I didn't mean to frighten you."

"I thought you were a stalker." She laid her head against his chest, reveling in the sense of security and the sound of his rapid heartbeat.

"I'm sorry. I would've yelled out your name sooner, but I didn't want the whole town running out to investigate." He kissed the top of her head and stroked her hair. "Some things a guy likes to say to a woman in private."

Carrie leaned back and looked up at him. The streetlight made his dark eyes glow. "Like what? Oh, Josh, I am sorry for what I did, letting you think I was Katy Davis. I planned to tell you the whole story this morning, but you were strangely quiet at breakfast, so I was afraid to."

"Your brother told me."

"Blake?" She had not given her brother any details. "What did he say?"

"That you'd walloped some old drunk in Denton and thought he might be coming for you. So you took the first train out."

Blake must have put two and two together, because she hadn't told him she had knocked Big Jim out. "That was part of it. The other part happened by accident. I met a lady on the train. She was a mail-order bride, headed to Baird."

"Molly. I saw her at the mercantile."

"You did?" Carrie's breath caught. "What did she say?"

"She asked about Carrie Franklin, and if she gave me the message from Katy Davis."

"Oh-h. No wonder you were upset when you came in from town."

He hugged her closer. "My pride was hurt. I thought I'd been played for a fool."

"No, Josh. I would never do that to you. Not intentionally. When you found me at the depot, I tried to explain. Honestly, I did. Molly asked me to tell you Katy had backed out. It so happened I was dressed like Katy and had the same color hair."

"I remember you tried to tell me something, but I wouldn't let you talk. I was in a hurry to get back to the ranch. And I was annoyed at my aunt. I couldn't understand why she didn't just tack up a poster in the local mercantile or the general store. Then, when you said you were not looking for a husband, it made me wonder why you had come. Unless you *were* looking for a husband."

"I said it because I meant it. Katy Davis was a mail-order bride. I was afraid you would rush me off to the justice of the peace on a whim, before we even had a chance to get acquainted. What I didn't know was—" Carrie stopped, not willing to implicate his aunt.

"That Aunt Em had tricked us both?" Josh chuckled. "She'd placed the ad for a mail-order bride and let me think it was for domestic help."

Carrie's jaw dropped. "How did you find out?"

"Aunt Em was making her confession while you were packing and leaving. She also threatened me with, 'If you have any ideas of tossin' that girl out, you can toss me out too.' You've made a loyal friend for life in my aunt."

He grinned. "I wonder if you don't rate higher than I do with Aunt Em."

"Oh, Josh. I am sorry I didn't tell you everything sooner. The longer I waited, the harder it became. I thought you would throw me out, but I didn't want to leave." She circled her arms around his waist. "I had become attached to you and your aunt. I sensed the love between you two. You became the family I'd lost. It felt good to have the load of responsibility lifted that I'd carried five years."

"Aunt Em told me how you'd lost your parents and were left to raise your rascally brother. I don't know how you did it. You must be a strong woman, Carrie Franklin."

"Not really. The only strength I have comes from the Lord. I'm afraid I've failed Him and my parents. I couldn't keep Blake out of trouble. That's why I was outside the saloon that night, to drag him back home. Then Big Jim came out and grabbed me. He tried to . . . I shoved him to get free and he fell off the boardwalk."

"And when he didn't get up, you thought you might have killed him. Well, if you had, it would've been self-defense. A man like that needs a lesson or two in how to treat a lady."

"I've worried about Big Jim ever since. That's why I had to talk to Blake last night, to find out if he ever came to."

"Your brother has a reckless streak, I'll admit. But with enough hard work, I think I can purge it from him. That kid is loyal to you, Carrie. He wouldn't tell me a thing when I asked how he knew you. He wouldn't admit you were his sister even after I had already learned it through a telegram. Not until I told him my plans."

Josh had sent a telegram to Denton and discovered she and Blake were siblings? *Oh, dear.* "What plans?"

"My plans to sweep you off your feet and to the altar, as soon as I can plant both feet on the ground."

"Are you saying . . . ? Is this a proposal?"

"Sometimes actions speak louder than words." Josh pulled Carrie closer and claimed her lips in a sweet, lingering kiss that left them both breathless."

He straightened, whooshing out a breath. "Does that answer your question?"

"Yes," she breathed. "Josh, I love you so much."

He brushed his lips against hers again. "Let's go home, my love, and tell Aunt Em."

Carrie smiled. "Home. I like the sound of the word. Aunt Em will be delirious."

Someone swung a lantern at the entrance to the alley, blinding Josh and Carrie. "Hey, what's goin' on back there?"

Carrie clapped her hands to her cheeks. "Blake, where did you come from?"

"I rode in with Mr. Kramer. I sat in the buckboard until my backside got stiff. Are you all right?"

Heat rushed to her face. She cleared her throat. "I'm fine."

Josh tugged a strand of Carrie's hair. "I figured your brother would come in handy in case I had trouble convincing you to come back." He nuzzled her ear and whispered, "Plus, it doesn't hurt to have an extra driver on the way home. I might get a little distracted."

Blake cleared his throat. "Mr. Kramer, you forgot to mention that gettin' up in a wagon by yourself ain't easy when you're hoppin' around on crutches."

Josh ignored him and kissed Carrie thoroughly. When they were both breathless, he asked, "You ready?"

Eyes still closed, Carrie lifted her chin. "Hmm?"

Blake yanked off his hat and popped it against his thigh. "Look, you lovebirds, how long are you gonna stand here gawking at each other? I've had a long, exhaustin' day. I'm starved!"

Josh chuckled, offering his arm to Carrie. "Let's pay a visit to the diner. The least I can do is fill your ornery brother's stomach."

Carrie glanced from one man to the other, linking arms with both. "I've already eaten, but a glass of lemonade sounds refreshing."

"Food at last?" Blake gazed heavenward. "Finally. The most wonderful words I've heard all day."

About the Author

Laurean Brooks lives in rural northwest Tennessee with her flea-marketing/antique-hunting husband, two labs and a cat. She writes inspirational romance with heart, humor, and unpredictable characters. Chivalrous heroes stand by to rescue their ladies from a plethora of disasters along the way. Her sassy heroines are familiar with the taste of their own shoe leather. "Foot-in-mouth" disease prevails throughout her stories.

Ms. Brooks' over-active imagination wrought trouble in fifth grade when she was assigned to write about, "The Adventures of Columbus." Laurean's version should have been titled, "The "Mis"-

adventures of Columbus." Evidently her teacher did not approve, because after Laurean read the comical story to the class, she demanded a complete rewrite.

You can learn more about Laurean by visiting her website: LaureansLore.blogspot.com

Also by Laurean Brooks

Taylor County Brides Series - Book Two

Half-Price Bride

To escape a contentious relationship, Emily Hammons answers a mail-order bride ad from a dentist in Abilene. Arriving a day late, she is shocked to find him exchanging vows with another woman.

Handsome rancher, Clint McCall came to town to fetch the doctor, but Doc is attending a wedding. As he waits outside the church, the bride tears out, slamming a pretty brunette into him. Clint tries to steady her, but loses his balance, becoming a cushion for her fall.

With an injured foot and an empty purse, Emily accepts Clint's offer to care for his ailing mother.

Clint has arguments to back his opinion of mail-order brides. His mother suffered years of abuse at the hand of an angry man when she answered an ad.

With no relatives in Abilene, why did Emily travel more than 600 miles from Memphis? Clint feels she is hiding something.

The dentist in on the hunt for his "other" bride. Will he find Emily? Will Clint's love be strong enough to endure Emily's secret, or will it destroy them?

More Historical Romance from Scrivenings Press

Books Afloat

Columbia River Undercurrents

Book One

Blaming herself for her childhood role in the Oklahoma farm truck accident that cost her grandfather's life, Anne Mettles is determined to make her life count. She wants to do it all–captain her library boat and resist Japanese attacks to keep America safe. But failing her pilot's exam requires her to bring others onboard.

Will she go it alone? Or will she team with the unlikely but (mostly) lovable characters? One is a saboteur, one an unlikely hero, and one, she discovers, is the man of her dreams.

Scrivenings
PRESS
Quench your thirst for story.
www.ScriveningsPress.com

Stay up-to-date on your favorite books and authors with our free e-newsletters.

ScriveningsPress.com